Critical Acclai
Historical Mystery Nor

"Hays turns a time-honored historical legend on its head, creating a new mystery series steeped in mythology.... The popularity of both historical mysteries and new twists on the Arthurian tales will provide a tailor-made audience for this promising new series."

—*Booklist* [on *The Killing Way*]

"Sure to appeal to fans of medieval intrigues and stirring battles."
—*Kirkus Reviews* [on *The Divine Sacrifice*]

"Hays has captured the Arthurian legend and made it his own. Many complex plot threads and believable characters make this a series to be savored by historical mystery and Arthurian fiction fans."

—*Library Journal* [starred review of
The Beloved Dead, RT Book Awards finalist]

"Utterly convincing characters and a perfect balance between action and sleuthing distinguish Hays's suspenseful fourth mystery set in King Arthur's Britain.... Hays just keeps getting better with each entry in this intriguing historical series."

—*Publishers Weekly* [starred review of *The Stolen Bride*]

Shakespeare No More

MYSTERY FICTION BY TONY HAYS

Murder on the Twelfth Night
Murder in the Latin Quarter
The Trouble with Patriots

The Killing Way
The Divine Sacrifice
The Beloved Dead
The Stolen Bride

Shakespeare No More

A JACOBEAN MYSTERY

by

TONY HAYS

MMXV
Perseverance Press · John Daniel & Company
Palo Alto · McKinleyville, California

A Perseverance Press Book
Published by John Daniel & Company
A division of Daniel & Daniel, Publishers, Inc.
Post Office Box 2790
McKinleyville, California 95519
www.danielpublishing.com/perseverance

Distributed by SCB Distributors (800) 729-6423

Book design by Eric Larson, Studio E Books, Santa Barbara
www.studio-e-books.com

10 9 8 7 6 5 4 3 2 1

LIBRARY OF CONGRESS CATALOGING-IN-PUBLICATION DATA
Hays, Tony.
Shakespeare no more : a Jacobean mystery / by Tony Hays.
pages ; cm
ISBN 978-1-56474-566-8 (softcover : acid-free paper)
1. Shakespeare, William, 1564–1616—Fiction.
2. Murder—Investigation—Fiction.
3. Great Britain—History—James I, 1603–1625—Fiction.
I. Title.
PS3558.A877S53 2016
813'.54—dc23
2014041969

To the Donegans—
Tonya, Rob, Marc, and Amber

Dramatis Personae

In Stratford

Simon Saddler, *constable of the Stratford Corporation and Shakespeare's oldest and dearest friend*
William Shakespeare, *playwright and poet*
Hamnet Saddler, *close friend of Shakespeare's, and Simon's cousin*
Anne Hathaway Shakespeare, *Shakespeare's wife*
John Hall, *physician and son-in-law to Shakespeare*
Susanna Hall, *Shakespeare's elder daughter*
Elizabeth Hall, *Shakespeare's granddaughter*
Judith Quiney, *Shakespeare's younger daughter*
Thomas Quiney, *tavernkeeper and son-in-law to Shakespeare*
Henry Smythe, *bailiff of the Stratford Corporation*
Jack Addenbrooke, *watchman*
Sir Walter Devereux, *sheriff of Warwickshire*

In Oxford

John Davenant, *innkeeper*
Jane Davenant, *his wife*
William Davenant, *their son*

At the Globe

Richard Burbage, *player*
Cuthbert Burbage, *manager*
Henry Condell, *player*
John Heminges, *player*

In London

Henry Wriothesley, *earl of Southampton*
George Wilkins, *tavern owner and would-be playwright*
Ben Jonson, *poet and playwright*
Sir Francis Bacon, *Attorney General of England*

Sir Edward Coke, *Chief Justice of the King's Bench*
Lancelot Andrewes, *bishop*
Malcolm Gray, *servant to Sir Edward Coke*
John Donne, *lawyer and priest*
Inigo Jones, *architect*
Thomas Howard, *earl of Arundel and Suffolk; Lord High Treasurer*
Frances (née) Howard, *countess of Somerset*
Robert Carr, *earl of Somerset*
James Stuart, *king of England*

Shakespeare No More

Chapter One

I AM SIMON SADDLER, WOOL MERCHANT OF STRATFORD-UPON-Avon, but more importantly, one of two constables of the Stratford Corporation. My duties include supervising the watchmen who walk the alleys and roads, hauling recusants before the bailiffs, seeking out those who fail to pay their debts, investigating thefts and enquiring into the occasional murder.

My entire life, except for three years in the Low Countries as a soldier, has been lived here within the confines of the village. I know its streets and people better than I know myself. I used to be one of the happiest men in the town.

Used to be.

But no longer.

WILL SHAKESPEARE was dead. The news ripped through Stratford like a cruel north wind, chilling the town and dampening spirits. Black wreaths appeared as if by magic on the door at New Place and the house on Henley Street. God must have thought it a sad occasion as well, for He opened His eyes and let His tears pound the land with a vengeance. Women wept in the lanes as if they had lost their husband or child. Children gathered in small groups, heads hung in sadness.

Some of the men, however, were barely concealing their pleasure. And though Will Shakespeare was my friend from childhood, I too breathed a deep sigh of relief at his passing.

Such a cacophony of emotions! We had schooled together here in Stratford, played children's games. Harassed the aldermen, Will's father included, with boyish pranks. I was by his side when he fell in love with Anne Whateley, and even when that Puritan she-devil Anne Hathaway forced him to marry her.

Perhaps that was when I should have seen the future. For it was his own fault. Pretty Anne Whateley loved him above all else, but she would not lie with him until the marriage vows had been said. So, he plied the handsome Hathaway woman with his charms and lay with her. That would have been all right, but he got her with child, and Puritan that she was, he was trapped.

And then, in reality, he abandoned us all, his wife, his children, me, all of his friends, to chase that dream of his in London. When he returned, as a successful poet and playwright, he entranced us all with his tales of the city and his poems of love and loss. All of us, even Peg, the wife of town constable Simon Saddler. Oh, yes, he entranced my Peg, all the way to his bed. And though it was but sport to him, he left my family in ruins. Yes, I smiled too at his death, because Peg had never forgotten him. And so the ghost of Will Shakespeare had made three in my marriage bed for nearly five years, long before he became a real spirit.

And that was why, the week before, I had been shocked when he called for me, when he looked up at me with blackened eyes and sallow cheeks, and said, "Simon, I think someone is trying to kill me."

I had simply pursed my lips and voiced the thought that had tempted me since the day I caught him lying with Peg. "Are you certain that it's not me?"

"No, I am not. But you are my last hope."

"Then you have no hope at all."

At that, my eternally confident friend had dropped his head to his chest, coughed with a horrendous crackling sound as if his lungs were about to spew forth, and fainted.

When his eyes slowly opened once more, panic fluttered inside me. I had never seen a person so pale and yet still breathe.

"Please, Simon," he gasped. "You have every reason to hate me, but I need you now."

"You surprise me, Will."

"How so?"

"I never thought to hear you admit that you had harmed me."

At that my old friend, his face slack, turned from me. "I have been arrogant."

"Yes, you have. And your arrogance has cost me. But hate you, Will? I loved you as a brother. Until you ruined my life."

"Please!" But the effort sent him into a paroxysm of coughing.

"Why do you think someone is killing you?"

"A fortnight ago, there was nothing wrong with me."

"But the story in the town is that you were out carousing with Ben Jonson and Michael Drayton and that you caught a fever."

Will looked at me with those wan eyes. "Simon, I no longer live in London. You know Anne. Do you think she would allow me the pleasure of drinking with Ben Jonson?"

I could not stifle the chuckle rising in my throat. Anne Shakespeare was a Puritan to the bone, and Will's retirement to Stratford had caused much calamity at New Place. Will's son-in-law, John Hall, would not even visit except to minister to Will. Hall was a good physician, the best in Stratford.

"Will, neither of us is young any longer. And let us be honest, your life in London, among the fleshpots of Bankside, would have cut any man's life span in half."

His face reddened and he slammed his hand against the coverlet on his bed. "You are not listening to me!"

My face flushed too. "Do not scream at me, Will. You are not in a position to do that. We are no longer children at school. I am a constable and you are, at best, a player on the stage, and at worst an adulterer."

"Do not forget that I could buy and sell you, Simon. I hold tithes. I am a man of influence!"

"And what have your precious tithes brought you but more debt?" Tithes were a tax owed to the Stratford Corporation by local landowners. Men of means would purchase portions of the tithes from the corporation as investments, generally for a term of thirty-one years, betting, of course, that they would increase year after year. Such had not been the case for Shakespeare, at least not so far. "But if you are correct, you won't be a man of property much longer. You will be dead."

He began that awful, hacking cough again. "I know that I wronged you—"

"You have wronged many people, but tell me, who among them would do more than wish you dead? Who would put the deed to the wish?"

Will turned away from me, coughing yet again. "I have been involved in many things in my life, Simon. Some honourable; some not so praiseworthy. The list is long."

"Bah! Even if you were being murdered, you can hardly expect anyone to seek an answer from that."

"Speak to Southampton, Heminges, and Condell."

"What of Jonson?"

Will swept the query away with a trembling hand. "Jonson has his own devils. Burbage, Burbage knows all. The enclosures. The tithes..." His voice drifted off as his eyes closed slowly.

I simply shook my head. Neither the tithes nor the enclosures had aught to do with Burbage and Jonson. Although the enclosure controversy had certainly sparked bloodshed. Just two years previously, it had been proposed by certain parties to enclose lands near Welcombe and old Stratford. When property was enclosed, rights to use of that land were restricted to the owner. It was no longer available for common pasturage. The reasons for this were many, but enclosure was one of the most hotly debated topics in those days. Some nine years past, there were riots over enclosure in Northamptonshire and Warwickshire. Indeed, the Newton Rebellion brought more than a thousand folk to riot against the notorious Tresham family, who enclosed ever more land. Nearly fifty poor souls were killed in the revolt.

The conflict was still fresh in the minds of our people, and so passionate were they on the issue that Will had kept everyone guessing about his stance; he did not want to offend either side, not the freeholders nor commons.

"How much of what you say, old friend," I mumbled to the now unconscious Shakespeare, "has root in anything but your fever?"

"He does that," a woman's voice sounded from the doorway. "He will talk sense for a bit and then lapse into some sort of delirium and spout nonsense."

Anne Shakespeare was a severe-featured woman. In her youth she had been comely, but time and her famous husband's wandering ways had cut deep lines in her face and widened her girth. She had never liked me, and I cared not for her. In my mind, it was her caustic personality and Puritan ways that had driven Will to London.

"I take it that you do not share his belief that he is being murdered?"

She drifted across the room before answering. "The only thing that has ever harmed Will Shakespeare is Will Shakespeare."

"He said that contrary to the rumours, he did not get drunk with those poets Jonson and Drayton and catch a fever."

"Well," she answered with a scowl, "that much is true. Ben Jonson is not welcome in my home. He is an immoral man and a plague on this land. Bah! If William had stayed here in Stratford and helped his father, he would not be lying on his deathbed now."

"You think he is truly dying?"

She whipped around towards me. "I think even a stupid man could just look at him and see that. Perhaps your much vaunted abilities have been overestimated."

"Mistress Shakespeare, whatever ails your husband, I can easily see that you have made life no joy for him." I was heartily tired of her insults.

"Life was not made for joyful purposes, but to test and challenge us and see if we are worthy of entering God's kingdom."

"Well, if your goal has been to eliminate joy from life, I think you have earned God's kingdom many times over."

Anne Shakespeare narrowed her eyes until they seemed but slits. "Leave my house, Simon Saddler. You are not welcome here."

"With pleasure."

I started for the door, but I could not shake the image of my old friend, haggard and pale, and I turned back.

"You have no reason to believe that someone is poisoning Will?"

"I have no reason to suffer your presence any longer! Now leave!"

And I did.

And a week later, just as he predicted, Will Shakespeare was dead.

One of the watchmen brought me the news of Will's passing. It left me strangely restless, and though I did feel relief, I was not certain if it were because he was dead or that his suffering had ended.

The dark clouds seemed like a roof over the town, holding in the news of Will's passing. I made my way through the streets that afternoon to Perrott's tavern, near the old market, and pushed past the patrons until I found my cousin, Hamnet Saddler, at a table. Hamnet and his wife, Judith, had been closer to Will than I had been. But then again, Will had never lain with Judith. Or, if he had, Hamnet did not mind. And that was of no matter now. Judith had died some two years before, leaving Hamnet alone with their fourteen children.

"Simon!" Hamnet hailed me. "Sit."

I did, and he called for a pot of strong beer for me.

"'Tis a sad day, Simon," my cousin said, taking a deep draught from his own pot.

"For you perhaps." I was not inclined to be sorrowful over Shakespeare's death.

"Simon! You were once Will's closest friend."

"Aye, and I was once a child, but no more." I left it at that.

The whole town knew of our falling out, but to Will's credit, he had never bragged about his conquest in our household, and I had no reason to share it with my cousin. But I could understand his sorrow. When Will's twins were born, he named them for Hamnet and his wife, Judith.

We busied ourselves with our beer. Across the crowded room, I saw a tall, thin man with a pinched face walk in. I considered him for a moment. Thomas Quiney, one of the banes of my existence as constable. The Quineys were a fine and respected family—aye, his father, Richard, had been one of Will's best friends—but somehow Thomas had missed out on the family's better traits. About a fortnight before, he had been charged with bastardy. And, about a fortnight before that, he had married Will Shakespeare's daughter, Judith. He was a sour-faced man who always sought some advantage, either at dice or in life in general. It was not unusual to find him drunken in the lanes of a Sunday morning.

Judith was as comely as her new husband was not. I never understood why she agreed to marry Thomas. She was not with child. And her mother abhorred Quiney. On that point, at least, Anne Shakespeare and her husband agreed. Will detested the living scarecrow, and he made no secret of it. But Judith, who had been a very pleasant child in her youth, changed after the death of her brother, Hamnet.

"There's one that would have profited from Will's death," Hamnet Saddler said, waving his pot in Quiney's general direction.

"Aye?"

"Aye," Hamnet confirmed. "But Will managed to change his will in the last days to take care of Judith but to deny Quiney. Or so I hear."

Rumours and Stratford were like twin children, forever mated, forever entwined.

"Tell me, cousin," I said. "You knew Will better in these last years than I have. Did he ever tell you that he feared for his life? That someone might intend him harm?"

Hamnet frowned. "Will said many things; he was quite dramatic."

"But did he say anything recently? In the last days or weeks?"

"No. At least not to me." Hamnet paused. "Last week a stranger arrived in town and asked his way to New Place. I did not like his looks, but he was probably just some friend of Will's from London. Why?"

I was not ready to share what Will had said to me with too many others. In all likelihood, it was just some manifestation of his illness. Oddly, I did not wish to soil his reputation by talking freely of his ramblings. "No reason, really. Here, let me stand you to another pot."

And that ended the conversation.

SLEEP DID NOT come easily that night. Though we still shared the same bed, Peg and I had been distant for some time, since I had returned one day from a journey to Coventry to find her in Will Shakespeare's arms. She suffered my tossing about, but did not venture a word. When I finally surrendered to the sleepless night, I rose and sat by the hearth, staring blankly at the fire, sipping from a tankard of small beer, trying to find some drowsiness, some relief.

No matter how hard I tried, I could not shake the image of a pale, wan Will Shakespeare and his trembling voice saying, "Someone is trying to kill me."

We had traveled so far, he and I, running and playing in the fields between Stratford and Shottery, tormenting the schoolmaster and our fathers with our pranks, stealing our first kisses from hapless maidens. But 'twas Will who succeeded in bedding a girl first. I was not as forward as he, more fearful of rejection I suppose.

But who would want to kill Will Shakespeare? He was a playwright and a player by trade. Maybe it was a Puritan? They hated the theatre with more than a passion, and, indeed, there was a growing wind of Puritanism blowing across the land. But his daughter Susanna herself was a Puritan. She had supported

Thomas Wilson, a Puritan vicar, when that troublemaker John Lane attempted to start a riot against Wilson. Lane accused Susanna of adultery with young Rafe Smith, a hatter. Susanna sued Lane for slander and won the suit.

Or maybe Will had met his end by a cuckolded husband, like myself. In my youth, I had enjoyed the stews in London alongside my friend Shakespeare. But the war in the Low Countries changed me. I saw such death and devastation....When I returned, I wanted only a home and a family and peace. To my delight no one had married Peg before my return. We wed, and we quickly produced a pair of daughters, as bright and beautiful as their mother. Fortune had smiled on me.

Or at least I thought it my good fortune until that day in my house. I shuddered at the memory, the two of them entangled in the bed, laughing with the abandon of new lovers. I had not spoken, simply turned away and rode out of town, stopping for a few nights at a tavern near Kenilworth Castle.

When I returned, I said nothing about it to Peg, nor would I speak to Will at all. I did not pretend that nothing had happened. But I did not try to sort it out either.

"WHAT TROUBLES YOU?" Peg. Slipping into the room as quietly as a mouse.

"Nothing." I was not disposed to tell her. Will had been too much a part of our lives already. I saw no reason that he should continue so through eternity.

I paused to look at my wife. "Mouse" truly described her. She was petite, with long brown tresses and huge brown eyes. I had loved her almost as soon as I saw her, on a soft summer's eve in Wilmcote. Will and I had gone up there to fetch some sheep for my father. We were only boys, but boys feeling the first stirrings of manhood. And she was in front of her parents' cottage, watching over her little brother.

We did not speak, that first time. But I could not take my eyes from her. It took more than a month for me to summon the courage to speak to her. And when I did, I feared that every sentence would prove me to be an idiot. And those fears were probably justified, at times, but Peg seemed not to care.

Curiously, Will seemed not even to realize that Peg existed, for which I was grateful. *Then*. He had a grace that escaped me. He glided. I stumbled. Words came easily to him. I was at a loss when saying "Good morning," especially to a beautiful girl.

And Peg, or Margaret, was still a beauty now. And I still loved her. But I had not found forgiveness in my heart yet. She knew it.

"Will you never speak to me again?"

"I did not know that I have stopped."

"You speak to me of our children. You speak to me of our parents' health. But you never speak to *me* anymore."

My eyes were locked onto the fire and I could not move them. "I never speak to anyone anymore. Ask Hamnet."

"I spoke to Hamnet," she said. "And he claims that you intimated that Will was murdered."

Though I would have throttled Hamnet at that moment for speaking of that to her, I was successful in not showing my wayward wife any reaction.

"Was he?"

I looked at her then, without a smile. "He's dead and you still cannot chase him from your mind."

"He is dead, and like every other citizen of Stratford, I am curious. I am curious at what you have learned that has set you on this path."

"Was it curiosity that led you to invite him into our bedchamber?"

No answer.

At first.

"No, Simon, it was your absence. I have no excuse for the sins I have committed. But you were never here. Always out at your duties. And Will would come to see you. He was lonely and bored with life outside of London. And I was bored and lonely without you." She stopped, biting her lower lip until I thought it might bleed. "It was you that drew us together. You turned back the covers and bid him enter your bed just as surely as if you had been there."

"Of course, Peg. I am the maker of all sins, the bringer of all evil."

She did not speak for a long moment. "I still love you, Simon."

And then, I did not answer.

In seconds, she had retreated, leaving me confused, angered, and in pain. For I still loved her, loved her with my very being, but I could not erase the vision of her enwrapped in my best friend's arms.

I did not sleep the rest of the night, but stared into the fire and remembered Will Shakespeare.

We met in Henley Street. I was six and he was seven. Of average height and brown hair, he was a comely youth. Though I was a year younger, I was the larger. But I did not notice such differences; all I saw was the wooden sword in his hand. I wanted it.

"Would you like to play?" I asked innocently. Bullying was not my nature, but his sword was so expertly carved, so exquisite, that I could not resist.

He leaned on the sword and looked me up and down. "You do not wish to play. You want my sword."

"I do not!" But my denial rang false, and the little brown-haired boy just smiled.

"Then why do you keep staring at it and not at me?" Even then, at that age, he had an uncanny knack for reading souls. But his question shamed me, and, in moments, we were playing some martial game. By the end of that day, we were fast friends.

The fire was dying, and I fed its hungry maw with more wood. The flames leapt red, yellow, and blue.

Then came the day that a traveling troupe of players arrived in Stratford. A young Richard Burbage was among their number, along with his father, James. The council allowed them to perform. This was surely not the first time that players had come to Stratford. As small children, we would go with our fathers and watch them act out their stories of kings and pirates and lovers torn asunder. And Will went to every performance, as did I. But something about those occasions captured him as they never did me.

The arrival of the Burbages was different. Will was eighteen, and already champing under the bit of marriage. I noticed that the expression on his face as he watched the plays had changed. Where once the look of awe and wonder had marked him, now he seemed to be studying their actions, movements, words.

One afternoon, after the play ended, Will hung about as the players put away their equipment and costumes. I was curious and stayed too. After a moment or two of hesitation, Will approached James Burbage.

"That last speech. It needs work. I-I could help with that." Will did not generally stutter, but his usual self-confidence had fled.

Burbage, a look of irritation on his face, turned. "You could, could you? Then you run along and do that and leave me to my work."

Any other man of Will's age would have been crestfallen, but my friend simply turned and retreated to the school room in the Guild Hall. I followed after him, but did not speak. He gathered some scrap paper and with a quill began writing furiously.

A half hour later, he arose, ignored me standing in the door, and returned to where the players were packing away the last of their appurtenances. He walked up behind James Burbage and tapped him on the shoulder.

Burbage, obviously tired and irritable, swung around on him. "What do you want now, boy?"

"Here is the last speech," Will replied, holding out the papers.

"Bah!" Burbage huffed, knocking them from Will's hand. "Go home and bother your elders no more."

At that, I saw the glint of moisture in the corners of Will's eyes. He turned away and did not see a young Richard Burbage come up and gather the papers from the ground. I slung my arm around his shoulder and, without a word, started walking him back toward Henley Street.

We had covered less than ten paces when we heard a cry rise behind us. Richard was shouting at his father, waving Will's speech. I watched with interest as Richard shoved the papers in James's face, saying something we could not hear.

James Burbage took the sheets and studied them carefully. Richard continued to speak. Finally, his father raised his head and turned to us. "Boy! Come here!"

I felt the hesitation in Will's shoulders; he had been embarrassed, and he was afraid of garnering more. But he straightened and, with me at his heels, marched back to the Burbages.

"What is your name, boy?"

"William Shakespeare."

He waved the speech. "This shows promise. Where did you study?"

"Here, in Stratford. I spent some time in the north as a tutor and a player."

At that, even I was surprised. I knew that Will had been a tutor, but he had never mentioned that he had been a player as well.

"Come to London, and I will find you work. It will not be much, at first, but if you can write like this, it might turn into something. Here, Richard. We yet have work to do."

The younger Burbage grinned at Will and then hustled back to his work.

And that sparked our first major argument.

Another log to feed the fire.

"You have no heart for adventure," Will accused me. He was attempting to cajole me into accompanying him to London. He had long since tired of life in Stratford, and Burbage's offer was a temptation indeed.

"You have a family to care for."

"Bah! Can you see me working for Father? London! London is where I will find my fortune, Simon! Come with me, and we will capture the city together!"

"What of your father? His health is not good. What of his business?"

Will waved my words away as if swatting a fly. "Gilbert will work with Father. He is far better suited to such a life than I."

Capturing cities. Adventure. Will's mind was ever filled with drama and dreams. "Please, Simon. You are my dearest friend."

"I wish only to marry Peg and make a life for myself here, Will."

He pushed by me, hurt by my refusal. "You will be sorry, Simon. The future will be glorious."

"Will! You are making too much of this. I will visit you in London. Often."

"It will not be the same."

I slapped him on the back. "We will make it the same."

But we did not. Within the year, I had gone to the Low Countries as a soldier with the earl of Leicester to fight the Spanish, and Will had begun his ascent to the top of the London theatre world.

DAWN STOLE through my window before I finished my musings. I felt a hand on my shoulder and turned to see my oldest daughter, Margaret, standing next to me. Named for her mother, she was sixteen that year and lovely in a way her mother never had been. Peg was a beauty, but her looks were more homespun. Margaret had the kind of beauty usually reserved for the nobility, and I had never felt quite comfortable in my daughter's presence. Her mind was turned much as was mine, more thoughtful than emotional, which might account for some of my discomfort.

My other daughter, Mary, was younger by three years. She was still in the throes of childhood and was without guile. Her beauty was more like her mother's, as was her character.

Three other children had graced our marriage, but none had survived its first year. As much as I adored my daughters, I regretted not having a son.

"Did you not sleep, Father?" Margaret asked.

"No, child. I have just been sitting here thinking."

"Of Cousin Shakespeare?"

I nodded.

"Father, is it not time for you to forgive Mother?" Margaret had been in the house that day; she had inadvertently borne witness to her mother's adultery. Little Mary knew nothing of it.

"This is not something I will discuss with you."

"You will not discuss it with Mother. You will not discuss it with me. William Shakespeare is dead, and you cannot discuss it with him. Mary does not know of it, but she senses the distance between you and Mother. She is a loving child, but that will disappear!"

I looked at her then, astonished both by the maturity in her words and the passion in her voice. My child was becoming a woman, and I had nearly missed the transition. During my hatred and anger, my daughter had grown from playing with dolls to become a beautiful woman. But I still did not intend to speak to her of this matter.

"Go, see to your sister. It is time to break our fast."

Margaret showed a last vestige of her youth then, stamping her foot against the floor and rushing off in a huff.

I rose from my chair and went to get dressed and ready for the day. But though I would not speak of Shakespeare to Margaret, I wondered if, perhaps, she were right. Perhaps now, with Will dead, I should put him and the entire matter to rest.

Chapter Two

W ITH THE GROWING CONVICTION THAT MARGARET WAS right, I straightened my doublet and slipped through the door and away from all the questions and conflicts in my house.

Morning in Stratford was always filled with a comforting blend of sounds and smells—greetings and grumblings. I could walk down Henley Street with my eyes closed and tell you which house I was passing from the smell. Goody Anne Badger made an excellent roasted joint of mutton, even if she and her husband could never eat it all, and Mistress Smith changed her rosewater every day.

When Will and I were young, Henley was more prosperous, the houses filled with some of the most influential families in the borough, like my father's and John Shakespeare's. But now most of the wealthier families had moved on, and the upper storeys of the half-timbered homes sagged from lack of upkeep. Will had inherited the two adjoining houses upon his father's death, and when his mother died several years later, he had let the larger of the two dwellings to Lewis Hiccox for an inn. And just the week before, he had moved his widowed sister, Joan, into the other. Peg had importuned me for years to move us closer to my cousin Hamnet on the High Street.

I spoke to a couple of friends as I passed the High Cross, asking the whereabouts of one or two of their kinsmen, men I had warrants on at the Guild Hall. Hamnet lived further down, near the corner with Sheep Street, where most of my competitors lived and worked. In the distance, down by the river, I could hear the pleasant bleating of sheep.

"Master Simon!" Matthew, the young man I hired to take care of my business, stayed ever agitated it seemed. "It's the broggers again," he proclaimed breathlessly as I entered the shop.

I sighed. In the wool business, it was always the broggers causing trouble. Though the practice was illegal, broggers traveled the countryside freely, buying wool from sheep farmers and selling it to cloth manufacturers. I did both legally. As a licensed wool merchant, I had my own herd of sheep, but I also bought from other shepherds.

"Which one?"

"Ned Grayson. He's mixing moss into his cloves."

Poor Ned. His wife had died the month before and left him with six children to care for. He was an ugly man and stuttered, lacking in self-confidence, so his prospects for remarriage were not good. But moss in his cloves of wool! Instead of buying a full seven pounds of wool, the weight of a clove, the cloth manufacturer would get perhaps two-thirds that much. Of course, Ned would claim it was an accident, but it wasn't. I couldn't remember the last person who tried that.

Wait.

Yes, I could.

John Shakespeare, in the wake of his financial downfall.

It happened not long after I met Will. I was no more than seven or eight years old, and I remembered my father in a rage one night. That by itself was worthy of note as he rarely ever became angry. But that night, he was furious. My mother tried to calm him, but even as young as I was, I understood that there was more to his wrath than some brogging. And I saw that my new friend's father was at the heart of the matter.

But back then, I didn't understand the pain of trust violated, the agony of friendship betrayed. I just knew that John Shakespeare had hurt my father.

"Master Simon?"

Matthew's voice shook me from my memories.

"I will see the bailiff this morning and secure a warrant," I reassured him. A few moments later, after a detailed accounting of the shop's business, I was back outside, seeing that the laws of England and the corporation were followed. But as I served papers and tracked down recusants, two voices occupied my thoughts—Margaret's plea to let go of Will Shakespeare and his betrayal finally and forever, and my oldest and dearest friend saying, "I think someone is trying to kill me."

As NIGHT began to fall about me on what had become one of the longest days of my life, I found myself walking back towards town from Holy Trinity Church. No one else was in the lane. The old college on my left was dark, and on my right the Dower House and the Reynolds farm were dimly lit. Only the singing of the robins joined me. In the solitude, I again found myself troubled by Margaret's pleas and Will's suspicions. So, rather than turn my feet towards home as I should, I found myself at Hall's Croft, the home of John and Susanna Hall, Will's daughter, and the silence was quickly shattered.

"SIMON!" John Hall raged when I related what Will had told me. "This is ridiculous!"

"Were it anyone but Will, you would not be that certain," I challenged.

"Were it anyone but Will, I would not have followed his case so closely." John was fiddling with one of his notebooks. He was forever writing in one. They chronicled each of his cases; I doubted not that Will's death was described in one.

"It is a simple question, John. Could Will have been killed by some sort of poison?"

John Hall was a handsome man, and clever, just the sort of fellow to win the heart of Susanna Shakespeare, though that had not always been clear. "Your entire question, Simon, presupposes that someone wanted Will dead. Besides you, that is," he added. As a member of Will's family, he knew of Peg, and her ill-fated dalliance. John was also one of those who found me at fault for Peg's adultery. In a town like Stratford, personal affairs all too often became town affairs. Our ties with each other were often closer than those between blood relatives. Hence our custom of calling dear friends "cousin" even if they were not, actually, kin.

"Could he?" I persisted.

Grimacing, he snatched up one of his notebooks and peered at the pages. "Yes, the symptoms are consistent with several different, known poisons." John spun around again. "But I ask you again, 'who' and 'why?'"

"Why are you fussing at Master Simon?"

The voice was unexpected but welcome. Little Elizabeth Hall, Will's granddaughter and only eight that year. Her blond hair framed her delicate features, more Hall than Shakespeare, but Will had adored her, and so did I. She stood beside her father, next to his workbench. John just shook his head at her sudden appearance.

"I am not fussing. We are discussing. Now, run along and help your mother."

She spun about and ran from the room, her hair flying behind her. "It sounded like fussing to me."

"She is her grandfather," I noted.

John, a little grey already marking his temples, shook his head. "Too much so sometimes. She has quite the saucy tongue, and Will encouraged her beyond all reason."

The doctor was considered stuffy by most in town. Will had once told me that he truly believed that Susanna's acceptance of Hall's proposal was simply a bad joke. But the two seemed happy: Hall and his serious approach to life complemented Susanna's wit, as sharp and biting as her father's. And she was quite willing to let that wit out in the light of day, something that most women just did not dare to do.

I suspected that much of the ill feeling that I sensed from everyone in this matter came from a confluence of events. Just days before, aye, even as Will lay ill, his sister Joan's husband, Will Hart, had died. Hart was a likable man, a good father and spouse.

"Could his body yet tell us anything?"

"You would violate his mortal remains to chase this fantasy of yours?" John was not my strongest admirer.

"I would do what is necessary to arrive at the truth in the matter. Will called me to his bedside a week before his death, and he claimed that he was being poisoned. We were friends once, best friends, and I owe him this much if nothing else."

"Bah! He was delirious in the final days."

"He was lucid enough to apologize for bedding Peg!"

John drew back as if struck. "What day did this happen?"

"On Thursday last."

He fumbled through his notebook until he found the page he wanted. After a few seconds, he looked at me, a far more troubled man than he had been just moments before.

"What is wrong, John?"

"'Twas on Thursday last, late in the evening, that his condition unexpectedly became very much worse. He did not regain his senses again."

I sat stunned. I had only mentioned Will's words for me to one person, Anne Shakespeare. Well, I intimated as much to Hamnet, but murder was not in him. But Anne? No. Anne was a Puritan to the marrow, and Will Shakespeare represented everything that Puritans hated, but she was no murderess. At least I hoped against hope that she wasn't.

"Simon..." John began. "Mistress Shakespeare did not kill her husband."

"I pray that you are right, but can I easily dismiss his warnings?"

"What, exactly, did he say?"

I did not respond at first, casting about in my memory for that moment. "He said that he had been in perfect health and then suddenly fell ill. And that despite everything you did to help him, he grew more and more feeble."

"Well, at least that much was true. It was a very puzzling case, Simon. But I had assumed that the stories of Ben Jonson and Michael Drayton coming to visit were true."

"Anne says they were not."

"Oh, Jonson and Drayton were here in Stratford, and I assumed Will did go drinking with them; he simply kept them away from New Place and avoided telling Anne of their visit."

My friend had a complicated social life, of that there was no doubt. Beside his frequent dalliances, since his return to Stratford some five years before, he became immersed in town affairs, involving himself in two important areas—the enclosure controversy and the tithes.

The Stratford tithes should have filled Will's purse. But those citizens required to pay ignored their responsibilities, which was nothing new, but Will was very particular when it came to legalities. He demanded that the law be followed in all cases, which was somewhat humourous as he so often lay with women other than his wife. And while that may not have been criminal, it certainly broke church law.

"Simon!"

I realized then that John was calling to me. Looking over at him, I saw that he had donned his cloak.

"Come, we must to Holy Trinity. Will's body has been laid out, but we might learn something by looking at his internal organs."

THE SPIRELESS Holy Trinity Church was barely visible in the daytime, set back against the river as it was. But at night, were it not for the two lamps at the front door, it would be impossible to discern. And yet again I was struck by the great stone college building, sitting dark and empty since Henry, the old king, reformed the church. For some reason, it sent my thoughts to Will and my eyes to John. We had not spoken since we left his house; his anger was still too palpable. But there were questions that needed asking.

"What will you look for?"

John glanced sharply at me, as if I were an idiot. "Anything that is not normal."

"Did you not assist in preparing his body?" It was the practice then to wash and clean the body, being careful to close the eyes and the mouth and straighten the limbs, remove the internal organs and pack the empty spaces with herbs and spices. The organs would be placed in another container and buried with the body. I knew that Anne, Susanna and Judith would have helped with the washing, but I assumed that Hall had taken care of the other chores.

He shook his head, though. "I was busy with other patients, and Will was dead. There was no other service that I could offer him. Anyone can remove the organs."

Despite the grimness of our task, a grin slipped across my face. John Hall had no medical degree. Indeed, his father, himself a physician, did not leave his library to John. Our John was a practical man, who eschewed alchemy and such other occult fields as "stuff and nonsense," although the study of these things was a prominent part of a medical education. For John, anything that did not directly benefit his patients had no place in the medical profession.

A young priest stood in the doorway at the church. I had seen him but did not really know him. My family and I attended church, as was expected, but I rarely paid much attention. All my prayers had done nothing to keep Peg from straying, and all of her prayers had failed to secure my forgiveness.

"Master Hall, Master Saddler, why do you come so late?"

I stayed behind John and let him fend off the inevitable questions.

"We need to examine Master Shakespeare's body."

Aye, I thought, keep it simple.

The boy, for that is what he really was, drew back as if struck. "But, master, he is already prepared for burial."

"We will do nothing to disturb those preparations. This is important or I would not ask it."

Then an older man's voice came to the boy's rescue. "These men mean Master Shakespeare no harm." The vicar. He was new, like the boy priest, and I had not yet met him. "This way, Master Hall, Constable."

I elbowed John in the side. "Do you suppose that he will avoid the fate of Master Rogers?" I whispered.

The stuffy physician allowed a little smile to mark his face. "I pray for that every night."

John Rogers, the previous vicar, had proven unable to avoid the strong beer. And he had also proven to have a quite unvicar-like attitude in general. Will and the other tithe holders had done their best to redeem him, but he had proven too much for their efforts. Two years past, he had been stripped of the vicarage, although he remained in Stratford.

We followed the new vicar down the main aisle to the chancel. Will's coffin was a plain wooden affair, not at all what I would have expected. Just beyond, in the chancel itself, a grave had already been prepared. But this honored place came not because of his writing, more as the result of it. When he bought a portion of the Stratford Corporation's tithes, the management and administration of the church came with it, and the right to be buried in the chancel.

"This is what he wanted," John said, apparently reading my mind.

"I did not know that you had studied under Simon Forman, John." I could not resist the opportunity to tease him. Forman had been some sort of occultist who had predicted his own death some years before. Will had once told me that he thought Forman one of the most despicable men in London. "And considering some of the lords at court," Will had laughed, "that is saying a great deal." Forman was infamous for using his position to bed his "clients."

The good doctor just grunted. He pulled his cloak off and laid it on the floor. The coffin lid had not been put in place, and I took the chance to gaze once more at my childhood friend, wrapped now in a simple sheet, while John spoke in hushed tones to the vicar. After a few seconds, they disappeared into the nave.

Will's illness had cost him much of the weight he had put on in his last years. He seemed younger, more like the boy I remembered so fondly than the man I had come to hate. Whatever the cause of his death, he had suffered for his sins. If his Puritan wife needed evidence, she merely had to look at the empty shell before me, lying in this box.

John, appearing suddenly at my shoulder, shoved me abruptly out of the way. He leaned over Will and studied his face closely.

Then, he swiftly pulled each of Will's hands up and held them close to his eyes.

After a few moments, he replaced the hands carefully and backed away from the coffin. "I failed him," John said, softly. "I should have seen it."

"What?" I whispered. The vicar and the young priest were approaching us up the main aisle.

"Will was right. He was being poisoned."

"VERILY?" I asked, after we had taken our leave of the church and had some privacy in the darkness.

"Without question," John confirmed. "I suspect it was arsenic. His organs looked as if acid had been poured on them. Did you not see the blackened sores on his hands? His face held some as well, though not as prominent as those on his hands."

"Do you know how it might have been administered?"

John shrugged. "Any number of ways. It could have been given to him in a broth, or as a purgative, an enema. I gave him several, hoping to flush the illness from him."

"Did you not prepare them yourself?"

"Not usually. Most often I had one of the women mix such a solution. My notes might say, but I don't always record such details, as what was administered is far more important than who administered it. The same would be even more true in terms of a soup or broth."

"You will look tomorrow and see if there is aught of value there?"

"Of course," he answered after a moment. "Simon," John said suddenly, "do not pursue this thing. Will is dead, and if this person was willing to kill him, he will think nothing of killing you."

"I appreciate your concern, John. But I am the constable of Stratford-upon-Avon, and this surely seems like a murder to me."

"You may be renowned at solving local matters, but this is beyond your abilities, Simon."

Something in the severity of his tone bothered me. "You have fought me every step of this path, John. You did not want to believe anything I said until it appeared that you had missed something in treating Will. Now that you have confirmed what Will himself said, you are eager to scare me away. You know that it falls within my duties to investigate such things. You know that I have done so successfully before. Yet you try to diminish my office in order to persuade me to turn away from this matter. Why?"

John Hall turned and took me by the shoulders. "Think, Simon! William Shakespeare was not an ordinary man. His poetry and plays have been the toast of London for more than twenty years. In his retirement, he has become the first citizen of his birthplace. God's blood, Simon! His patron was the earl of Southampton, a man Queen Elizabeth thought important enough to imprison for his part in the Essex Affair. Why, Will's own theatre company was called to task for even their small part in that doomed rebellion. He was friends with Kit Marlowe, and whisperings from here to London have spoken of Marlowe's being a spy for Burghley. Will Shakespeare held many secrets, and many and far more powerful men than you would have paid handsomely to shut his mouth forever!"

He paused, suddenly realized he held my shoulders and released them. "You are not the only man that Will wronged. Those stories are legion too. You are a good constable, Simon, and I think you do this parish a service. But the crooked turns and false exits that were Will's life could swallow you up, and I would not have that happen. Promise me that you will forget this. Go home and kiss your wife, love your children, and do not risk your life on a man already dead."

"Your warnings are not without merit, and I will be careful. But I can do nothing other than to move forward." I stopped. A cooler breeze had stirred along Mill Lane. "You should go home, John, before you catch a fever yourself."

"Simon, I mean only the best for you."

"I certainly hope so, John."

"Come with me, if you are intent on pursuing this folly. You will want to speak with Susanna, and I would have that finished before her father's funeral."

We returned to Hall's Croft. Susanna was just coming down the stairs, from putting Elizabeth to bed, I suspected. She was yet clothed in her black mourning dress, and she greeted me with a frown.

"Simon, I am not certain that I wish to see you."

"Susanna, I am sorry for your father's passing, but I think if you will listen to your husband for a moment, you will understand the reason for my visit."

At that she looked at John who nodded. It took but a moment to let Will's daughter know what we had found, and the disbelief was as clear on her face as letters on a slate.

"Are you certain?"

"As certain as I can be," John answered. "The symptoms were all there, and I failed him."

"John, you did not fail him. 'Twas I that failed him," I consoled. "He told me that he was being poisoned, not you. You had no reason to believe it was other than a fever gone bad."

Susanna crossed the room to her husband and touched him lightly on the arm. "John, would you allow me to speak to Simon alone?"

The physician jerked his head back in surprise. He looked from me to her and back again. He did not understand her request, but he could find no reason to deny it. John nodded curtly and started to climb the stairs, each riser seeming a herculean effort.

"Sit down, Simon."

She sat as well and for a moment said nothing, just stared at her hands in her lap. I could see Will in her face and her manner. "You should know that Father told me the same thing that he told you, and I ignored him just as you did. So, you should not feel remorse. He was very ill towards the end, and he did not always speak true."

I shook my head. "It is different, Susanna. He summoned me in my role as constable. I should have taken him seriously for that reason if no other."

She pursed her lips at me. "And I was his eldest child and

should have listened to him no matter what. We are both at fault, and neither of us is at fault."

"You did not mention it to John?"

"I saw no purpose. Father would speak one moment of some nonsense about love letters, and the next he would swear that someone was poisoning him. How was I to give credence to any of it?"

Susanna was right. We had all been with those stricken with a fever, who talked without reason, caught in the delirium of their illness. "He seemed lucid to me when he made these accusations." I paused. "But, as you say, he quickly lapsed into random sentences that made no real sense."

"What will you do? How will you proceed?"

I paused before answering. These were questions I had not fully resolved myself. "I will speak frankly to you, Susanna, because I know that you were your father's confidante as well as his daughter. I will first question your new brother-in-law Thomas Quiney. As I am sure you are aware, your father was able to change his will to ensure that Judith's inheritance was safe from her husband's grasping fingers."

The grimace on Susanna's face did not hide her feelings. "My sister is a fool. I yet believe that she married Quiney to strike back at my father."

"Why?"

"Understand that I love my mother with all my heart, but she is a strict Puritan. That did not mix well with the children of William Shakespeare. Puritans do not believe in frivolity, but Father taught us that life is to be enjoyed, that laughter is no sin."

"But you championed the Puritan vicar, Wilson."

Susanna nodded. "I did because he was unfairly accused. Yes, I am a Puritan, but that does not mean that I agree with everything they teach." She was her father's daughter. That was certain.

"Where, then, was the conflict?"

"Father lived in London. He refused to overrule Mother when it came to disciplining us. I understood and saved my rebellions for when Father was home. Judith was not as 'restrained' as I was. It embittered her."

Could Judith have killed her father in revenge? I kept the question to myself.

"Did he have any strange visitors during his illness? Anyone unfamiliar?"

"Not really. A man from London came twice, but I do not know his name. He was a very large man. Otherwise, it was simply John, myself, Judith, Mother, oh, and Peg and Margaret helped out a few times, when Father needed to be moved so that we might change his linens."

I nodded. This was usual. That Peg helped might seem odd to some, but Anne Shakespeare was very understanding of her husband's wandering eye. I suspect that she did not care where he found his pleasure as long as it was not in her bed.

"This large man, was it Ben Jonson? What did he look like?"

"I have never met Ben Jonson."

"But surely he visited New Place," I protested.

Susanna smiled. "Mother always locked us away when Jonson visited Father. She was afraid his sins would taint us as well.

"Beyond the man's size, he looked ordinary enough. Something like a tavernkeeper. Good clothes. Not expensive, but well made." Susanna, much like her father, had a discerning eye.

It could easily have been Jonson. "And you say he came twice?"

"Aye. Both times he left with some documents. I asked Father, but he said it was of no consequence. 'A debt paid,' he told me."

What could that have meant? From my admittedly limited acquaintance with poets, I found that they often spoke in riddles, and Will had been no different. Still, it may simply have been connected with Will's London affairs. He owned several properties there, the Blackfriars gatehouse among them. But it had been some time since I had talked to Will about such things, and he might have divested himself of some, if not all, of his London property.

Before I could think of another question, Susanna reached over and clasped my hand. "Simon, John will counsel you to leave this be. He is a good man, but overly cautious. I would have you find my father's killer. My daughter adored Father, as did I. To have him ripped away from us before his time is the definition of cruelty. I know that Father wronged you, and I know that you have borne a grudge against him ever since. But I have never done you harm, and so I ask you to do this for me if for no other reason."

Moisture grew in the corners of my eyes. "I will do this for three reasons, Susanna—for you, for the friend Will once was to me, and because it is my duty."

I left without speaking further to John.

I TURNED away from Hall's Croft then and followed Southern Lane, on my way to Bridge Street and then my house on Henley Street, just a few doors away from where Will was born.

But before I could reach my home, an idea struck me. It had been but a few minutes since I had heard the bells tolling the ninth hour. This, I knew, would be an ideal time to beard the lions, or at least one of them.

I WAS not certain where I would find my quarry but I suspected he would be at Atwood's, a tavern he himself owned; if not there then I would find him at Perrott's. Reputation was a good predictor of actions.

But there he was at my first choice, young Thomas Quiney, vintner and, in my estimation, common ruffian. In my duties as constable, I had come to know him well. He was a disgrace to a respectable family. Indeed, in the months prior to Will's death, I had dealt with him many times.

"Master Saddler," Quiney greeted me. He was a tall, thin scarecrow of a man, with greasy brown locks. I had never fathomed why he was so popular with women. Just a few weeks before, he had been charged with bastardy for impregnating Martha Wheeler. The poor woman proved to be doubly unfortunate. She died in childbirth, along with Quiney's bastard child. Or perhaps she was the fortunate one.

Only two or three other men graced Quiney's tavern. They looked as if they had crawled from the same cess pit as their host.

"What brings you here, Constable? To drag me before the Consistory Court again? I have already been excommunicated." Quiney's voice rasped roughly against my ear.

I sat at one table. "A beaker of your best cider, Thomas."

The son-in-law of Will Shakespeare retreated behind his bar and filled a beaker. He brought it back to me and sat. "I will ask you again, Master Saddler. Why are you here? Your kind usually does their drinking at Perrott's."

"I am enquiring into the murder of William Shakespeare," I said, keeping my eye on him.

He just nodded. "I heard."

"You heard that he had been murdered?"

"Think you that I do not speak to my wife's relatives? For many weeks I have been the most hated man in the Shakespeare household. But overnight you have stolen the crown from me, and I was glad to relinquish it."

"I doubt that my fall from grace has been partnered with a rise in respect for you."

Quiney chuckled, a bit nervously I thought. "Perhaps not. But when you are so universally reviled as I, any relief is a blessing. So, Simon, am I now your chief suspect?"

"You are," I confirmed with a smile.

"Well," he replied, "if I killed him, I made a mess of it. He changed his will to keep me from profiting from my marriage."

I did not like Quiney. I had never liked him. "How did you manage to convince Judith to marry you?"

Quiney grinned, revealing crooked teeth. "I taught her what a man and a woman can do for each other."

"Please, Quiney. You come from a fine family, but you yourself are disgusting. You are a rogue and a scoundrel. Judith is the daughter of Stratford's leading citizen. Where is the attraction?"

He did not answer immediately. First, he refilled his own beaker, draining it as if it were water. "You are a constable, Simon. Have you not observed that it is the children of the best families who cause the most trouble?"

I could not argue with that. Judith Shakespeare had been a problem to her parents since her twin, Hamnet, died. The boy's death was a tragic accident; he had fallen into the River Avon and drowned before anyone could reach him.

Hamnet had been very much his father's son. Bright, active, he was beloved in Stratford. And Judith had been his constant companion. Will once told me that he believed that Judith blamed herself for her twin's death. "I can see it in her eyes, Simon," he said. "And I fear she will never believe otherwise."

It was after Hamnet's death that Will began preparing for his eventual return to Stratford.

Pushing the death of young Hamnet from my mind, I answered Quiney's question. "Yes, I have noted that in the past. But Judith Shakespeare is a young woman of intelligence. You are a worthless piece of—"

I slapped away Quiney's pathetic attempt to strike me, without even rising from my seat or spilling my drink. The other patrons chuckled at his discomfiture. And embarrassed he was. "The next time, Quiney, come at me with something more than a drunken punch."

Standing, I threw a halfpenny on the table, which he snatched up. Quiney might have poisoned Will, but he had help if he did. And that realization led me down a path that I had been avoiding. Could Judith have poisoned her own father? Could a rogue as disgusting as Quiney have persuaded her to kill William Shakespeare?

ANNE SHAKESPEARE very nearly slammed the door of New Place in my face. "Are you here to cause more trouble?"

"I am here, Mistress Shakespeare, to speak with your daughter, Judith."

"You are not welcome."

"I am here on official business. It seems that your husband was murdered."

Anne Shakespeare, the lines in her face growing even more severe, narrowed her eyes. "Is that your judgement?"

"No, Mistress. It is the judgement of your son-in-law, John Hall."

For the first time in my acquaintance with her, Anne Shakespeare was without words. She stepped aside and hung her head as I entered.

Judith was in the kitchen, sitting silently at a table. She looked up at my entry and attempted a smile. Though she had given Will her share of trouble, I had never doubted that she loved him. But the sparkle in her eye could flash to anger in a moment, and she often turned the full fury on her father.

"I am sorry for your father's passing, Mistress Quiney."

"He loved you, you know," she said, turning away from me. "I understand the pain he caused you, but he did love you."

"You know of that?"

"We spoke often of you. We spoke often, once."

"But not later?"

She smiled wistfully. "No. As I grew older, the limits that Mother set upon me grated against my soul. I went to Father for relief, but he would not entertain my suit."

"He supported your mother?"

"He told me that as he lived in London, it was not his place to overrule her. That surprises you?" She read my face well, just as her father once had.

"I would think that, given Will's disposition, he would have encouraged you."

Judith shook her head. "Father felt sorry, I think, for Mother. He was not a man without feeling, Simon, though I know you might disagree." She paused. "I even begged him to take me to London with him."

"And he refused?"

"I think I would have been more burden than help. If only

Hamnet…" But her voice trailed off before she could finish the thought.

I had no need to ask further questions. This girl was no murderess. I saw quickly that while her twin lived, they had found solace in each other's company. But her spirit was much like her father's, and when Hamnet died, she was left adrift.

I would not ask her why she had married Quiney. That act of rebellion, and rebellion it was, had been directed at her mother, not Will. I feared that she faced a lonely and unhappy life, a product of her own nature and making.

I found Anne sitting before a fire in their front room. She was sewing and barely glanced up when I entered.

"Mistress Shakespeare?"

"I suppose you wish to ask me if I killed my husband?" she answered without looking at me.

"I wish to ask you several questions. Of which that is one."

She stopped her sewing and finally looked at me. "Why can you not leave well enough alone? William is dead. Let him stay in the grave where he can do no more harm."

"Harm?"

"I need hardly tell you of his proclivities, but far more than that, he has corrupted an entire generation with his plays and his poetry. We are not meant to enjoy life, but to use it to prove our worth for Heaven. Yet, his plays preach a false gospel, one that will condemn those corrupted by it to eternity in Hell. Is that harm enough for you?"

I realized that I had recoiled at her assault. "Yes, Mistress, so you have told me, but I am not here to debate religion with you, nor what influence Will might have had. I am concerned only with the manner in which he died. Susanna has already told me some of the details, but you live here. Other than this man from London, who came twice, did Will have any other visitors from outside Stratford?"

"Just one other. That brute Ben Jonson showed up on our door about a week after William fell ill. I did not wish to let him in, but he was sober and seemed very concerned."

"Did he act suspiciously?"

"Ben Jonson always acts suspiciously, but I saw nothing nefarious in his visit."

I knew Jonson, in some ways better than Will. He was capable of murder, but I saw no reason he would want Will dead. "You had no wisewomen in to see to him?"

"I had John Hall. Several women of the town helped me care for him."

Which was exactly what Susanna had told me. This line of enquiry was getting me nowhere. Anne may have hated all that Will symbolized, but she would not have killed him.

I took my leave as Anne returned to her sewing.

My STUBBORNNESS in this affair would come back to haunt me, I knew. Susanna would tell Peg. They were great friends. Or Anne or Judith might. I had not told John truly why I felt so certain about my path in this affair. It was indeed my duty as constable, and I did owe it to my old friend. But more than that, more than all of that, I wanted to find out who Will Shakespeare had been, what had made him the destructive soul that he was. I needed to know what manner of man could destroy the marriage of a dear and trusting friend without a hint of regret, unless I was to believe Judith. But what bothered me most right then had nothing to do with such deeply guarded secrets. No, what troubled my heart as I hurried along the streets was the passion with which John Hall had attempted to dissuade me from my course. For it carried less concern and more warning, and that was out of character for Shakespeare's son-in-law.

Chapter Three

YOU SHOULD AVOID ALL OF THIS, CONSTABLE SADDLER," said Henry Smythe, bailiff of Stratford. Will's own father, John, had once worn the robes of the bailiff, the town's highest officer, as had my own kinsman, another John, in the years after. But John Shakespeare, driven by the desperation of his financial failure, had broken the law, something that cautious Henry Smythe would never do.

Smythe was a fat little man, more concerned with the privileges that came with his office than the duties. But we had got along well in past years and had never truly clashed, not even when I delivered a summons to his son for failure to pay his debts.

"And why is that?" We were entering the Guild Hall.

He shrugged. "Shakespeare is dead. I never liked him all that much, and I suspect that others feel the same. Some feel that Stratford is a better place without him."

"And some do not, Master Smythe. Do not forget that he was my friend. If he met his death at another's hand, then as constable it is my duty to enquire."

"Whatever you wish, Simon," he waved me off, yawning to impress upon me his lack of interest. "I would not expect to find everyone eager to cooperate though, if I were you."

"Remember, Master Smythe, that if I find the man who did this, I will have to bring him before you as Justice of the Peace."

"Ha! You think I would be allowed to sit on such a case? No, you should speak immediately with Devereux to determine the path you will travel in this. Mind you, he will either order you to cease your enquiry or to keep it as quiet as possible. He dislikes controversy."

Sir Walter Devereux was the sheriff of Warwickshire. It had been something of a family office as his father and grandfather had both held the title in years past. I did not know Devereux well, as almost every case in Stratford was settled by Smythe serving as justice. Rare was the situation that called for the high sheriff to be disturbed.

Smythe's attitude did not surprise me. In his time on the council, he had evinced little interest in my duties, unless they touched upon him in some personal way. I had been smart enough to make certain that any cases involving aldermen were handled quickly and with due discretion.

Excusing myself, I hurried away from Smythe and swiftly went to the chamber allotted to me. Decorum had dictated that I tell him of my investigation, but beyond that I had no responsibility to him for its conduct. Indeed, at that particular moment, the fewer who knew my plans, the better.

I did not need my key, as the door stood open. But it should not have.

"Ho! Master Saddler!" came a pleasant voice from within.

"Good morn, Master Addenbrooke."

Jack Addenbrooke was one of my watchmen. Supervising the watchmen was a sometimes onerous part of my duties. All of us worked without pay, according to the records, but we all received some small compensation by way of expenses. Usually, we all had other occupations, but I was fortunate. My father had been a miserly old man and a trader in wools and other goods with more than just a bit of luck. I was the only child who survived infancy, and so I inherited all—house, money and business, which I simply hired a good man to run for me. Jack, who had been hauled into court for debt less than a decade before, had been bequeathed to me by the last constable. He was more fond of drink-

ing than watching, but no serious incidents could be ascribed to
him. Yet.

"Was all quiet last night?"

Jack, seeming as round as he was tall, with cheeks painted
a merry red by the Gascoign wine he swilled, smiled. "Verily.
Hardly anyone about the lanes."

"Good." If I were to concentrate on my new task, I did not
need problems elsewhere. I opened the parish coffer, where we kept
our valuable parchments and documents. Rummaging through
it for a summons I needed, I almost did not hear Jack's next
words.

"Except for one ruffian, hanging about outside Master Hall's
house. I ran him off forthwith."

"Who was he?" I tried to show only moderate interest; Jack
was renowned as Stratford's nosiest gossip.

"Some scoundrel from London, or at least his tongue sounded like someone from that hellhole."

"That's odd," I answered. And it was. Stratford was a rural
town, where everyone knew everyone else. Several of our sons
had made good careers in London—Richard Field, aye, even
Will's brother Gilbert, and Edmund too, Will's youngest brother. But Ned had died nearly ten years before. A messy affair involving an illegitimate child, I had been told. But few Londoners
ever came to Stratford. Remembering Hamnet's comment from
two nights before, I realised that this marked two Londoners in a
fortnight, or perhaps two visits by the same man.

"Let me know if he appears again, Jack. It may be that we can
arrange some time in the stocks for harassing our watchmen."

"Aye. I will. Off to bed now. Tonight will come quickly."
And Jack stumbled out the door, though whether he stumbled
from fatigue or wine, I did not know. Truly, at that moment, I
did not care.

Why would anyone from London be hanging about outside
John's house unless it had something to do with Will? Or was
I making assumptions? I did not know for certain. Will often
went to London in his last years, and John frequently joined him.

This stranger could easily be someone with whom Will had done business, heard of Will's death and had come to offer his condolences. Or it could be something else, equally as innocent. Or, certainly, it could be just a common cutpurse who had tired of London and opted to try the provinces.

Finally, my eyes found the summons I sought, a minor affair with a young boy who had rather disturb the public worship than join it. I trusted that Smythe would be able to find a suitable punishment for him. Stuffing it in my pocket, I reminded myself to give it to one of the other watchmen later.

How to proceed? I sat in one of the two chairs allotted to us to ponder my choices. What was it that Will had said? "Burbage knows all." Perhaps my next task should be to travel to London and speak with Richard Burbage. He was one of Will's oldest and closest friends among the players. I knew him well, first when their company was traveling the countryside as the plague decimated London, and then later in London with Will. Although there was much opposition to it, the Stratford council had paid for them to perform.

Burbage was an honest fellow, not a temperamental sot like many of Will's theatre friends. I would also have to search out Heminges and Condell, as Will had said. And Southampton. Aye, and that interview I feared above any of the others. Primarily because nobles can be as changeable in their nature as the wind. But that would be for a different day.

Lowering my head back into the chest, I sought a special bundle of summonses, those for men who no longer lived in Stratford. Tucking the packet inside my doublet, I hurried to Smythe's chamber.

His honor, the bailiff, was in.

"What is it now, Simon? I was working on something of great import."

I stifled the laugh building in my throat. Looked to me as if I had interrupted his daily nap. "Master Smythe, I have been planning for some time to go to London to seek the men for whom these summonses wait." I pulled the corner of the packet far enough from my vest so that he could see. "I will leave within the hour."

"Simon, is that wise? They will bury your friend Shakespeare this afternoon. For the constable to miss that might be seen in a poor light."

"My attendance will make no difference. Indeed, I believe that Mistress Shakespeare would prefer it. Besides, three of these summonses are ones that you issued for men in debt to you."

Smythe straightened. "Then, certainly, you must see to your duty. Should anyone enquire, I will instruct them that you are away on official business at my direction." He grabbed a sheet of paper and began scribbling something.

"Thank you, Master Smythe. God will reward you for your attention to duty."

"Here is your pass. You will need it." To travel without a pass in those days was illegal. It was one of the ways that the government tried to keep the plague in check. I took the proffered document with a smile.

With that, I excused myself and hurried home. I found Peg and the children preparing for Will's funeral.

"You must hurry!" Peg scolded me.

I just shook my head. "I depart for London within the hour."

She did not even try to hide the shock on her face. "Simon Saddler, you will put on your mourning clothes and attend your best friend's funeral."

I eyed her closely, wondering if Will had enjoyed kissing her full lips as I once had. Sadly, I could no longer look at her without seeing Will's hands on her, touching her where only I was supposed to touch. "No," I said finally. "Will Shakespeare is dead. My presence at his funeral will change nothing. Besides, Master Smythe has ordered me to London to seek out some of the men for whom I have summonses."

"Henry Smythe is a fat ogre. He has done this only because he is afraid of you."

At that I laughed. "The only thing that Henry is afraid of is that he will miss his dinner."

She opened her mouth to speak again, but I raised my finger. "No, Peg. No more argument. You and the children go to the funeral. I am off to London. I will return in a few days, when my business is complete."

"Fine! Go! But do not pretend that you do this for the council. You are doing this to snoop about in Will's past, to chase this silly idea that he was murdered." Peg stopped and turned her eyes directly upon me, throwing me a stare that reached into my heart and grasped it between icy fingers. "Such ideas are frivolous. No true believer in Christ would harbour such ideas. Be careful that you do not find answers you do not want."

"You have spent too much around Anne Shakespeare. You have become a greater Puritan than even she, and with more to repent."

Ignoring her scowl, I took my leather bag and left the house for my shop to give instructions to my man, Matthew, who cared for my wool business.

"Father?"

I looked back and saw Margaret hurry from the house. "Is it as Mother says? Are you going to London seeking Cousin Shakespeare's murderer?"

A frown grew across my face. "I have several chores in London." I chose not to answer her question, but she understood.

"If you hate Cousin Shakespeare as much as Mother says, I do not understand why you would seek out his killer." Poor child. 'Twas a strange world indeed when you were forced to look it in the face at such a young age.

"Because it is my work." It was not a satisfactory answer, and she felt that even if she could not put her feelings into words.

"I love you, Father."

"And I you, Margaret. Take care of your mother and sister. I will return in a few days."

Mounting my horse, I saw the lines of people heading to the church. It was a Thursday, a dark, bleak Thursday, not a good day for a player, but Will would have a fine audience at his last performance nonetheless.

Turning away, I kicked my horse and, with a jerk and a leap, she bore me out of Stratford and on the road to Castle Bromwich, home of Warwickshire Sheriff Sir Walter Devereux at Castle Bromwich Hall.

GOING TO see Devereux took me in the opposite direction from London, but it was a chore that had to be done. As High Sheriff of Warwickshire, any such enquiry fell under his jurisdiction. In practice, nearly all enquiries were handled by the constables and adjudicated by the bailiffs. But Smythe had been correct. An investigation into William Shakespeare's death demanded the approval of the High Sheriff prior to even beginning.

My journey took me due north of Stratford, to the west of Coventry and a few miles east of Birmingham. It was a hard day's ride of some thirty miles. I had hoped that, as I rode north, the overcast sky would clear and offer a little sun to brighten the day. But the grey clouds ran deeper and thicker the further north that I rode, so I resigned myself to dark skies and tried to avoid thinking about Will's death by studying the fields and forests.

Though I left Matthew to manage my business, I stayed informed, usually by rides like this one. The countryside between Stratford and Castle Bromwich at that time was mostly pastureland for sheep and cattle. In later years, the fields, properly manured, would be sowed in wheat and barley. And while those were valuable crops, the real money lay in sheep. The raw wool was sold to cloth manufacturers in both England and Europe. At that moment, my herd numbered some 8,000 sheep. A small village might have a combined total of 10,000 head. One wool merchant in southern Warwickshire held 14,000. One did not need an Oxford education to see their value.

I noted few enclosures, which did not surprise me; indeed, it pleased me. For two reasons. Were land owners in this region to talk of enclosing their lands, an army of farmers would instantly appear to oppose them and bloodshed would swiftly follow. The second reason was just as practical. I understood why owners would wish to do it, but given my thousands of sheep, I profited from the open grazing more than not.

My musings and observations had the desired effect, making

the ride seem far shorter than it actually was. I made good time as well, riding through the hamlets and villages of Warwickshire, stopping only when necessary to water and feed my horse. Few people were on the roads I took, choosing the lesser-traveled ones. Highwaymen stayed on the more popular routes in the nighttime hours, so I was spared their company as well.

It was still early afternoon as the tower of St. Mary and Margaret's rose in the northeast. Pausing at the crossroads, with the church to my right and Sir Walter's home to the left, I took a deep breath and turned my horse towards the high sheriff's residence.

CASTLE BROMWICH HALL was a fine brick manor house of one storey on the western edge of the village. It had been built more than sixty years before by Sir Walter's father, Sir Edward Devereux, brother of the notorious Robert Devereux, the second earl of Essex, who attempted to overthrow Queen Elizabeth and lost his head when he failed.

And while the earl's side of the family had been disgraced and stripped of lands and titles, Walter's branch had survived. Not that it mattered; I remembered that King James restored all that had been taken from Essex's line not long after coming to the throne.

Sir Walter was a good man, logical and more interested in improving his home and properties than spending time in London currying favor with the king. And he was a Member of Parliament for this district. But, despite the well-known animosity between His Majesty and Parliament, this had not really harmed Sir Walter's standing at court. Given his family background, he was a good man to have on my side.

A servant ran out and helped me dismount, then took my horse away. I was not an unfamiliar visitor at the manor. On a handful of occasions, my enquiries had required me to consult with Sir Walter. He had always treated me well; as I followed another servant to the front door, I hoped for another exhibition of his reason and goodwill.

"Constable Saddler!" Sir Walter greeted me at the front door, unusual, but our last enquiry had resolved itself in a very positive manner, increasing the sheriff's prestige. "Please, come in."

We moved quickly to his library, where he sent a maidservant for some refreshment. "You must be tired."

"I am, but duty dictated that I consult with you on an important matter."

Devereux had short, curly hair and a thin moustache and beard. His face, too, was thin and wrinkled. He favored his infamous uncle a good bit. "Another theft or killing?"

"A killing, Sir Walter. William Shakespeare, the poet, has been murdered."

Had I struck him with a plank of wood, I do not think I could have drawn a more surprised look.

"Murdered? Are you certain? You know that Shakespeare is a kinsman?"

I nodded, remembering that the Devereux and Shakespeare families were connected through the Ardens. Will's mother had been an Arden. "All too certain, Sir Walter." The maid appeared with tankards, and we both took a deep draught of what turned out to be excellent perry, pear cider, before I continued. "Shakespeare himself called for me during his final illness and suggested that he was being poisoned. I did not think much of it at the time; he was delirious with a fever. But after he died two days past, I endeavoured to find if there was any truth to his claims." I held up a hand. "Yes, Sir Walter, I know I should have done so at the time he made them, but I did not. I consulted John Hall, Shakespeare's son-in-law and a physician in Stratford."

"Aye, I know John well."

"He examined the corpse at my request and found evidence of arsenic poisoning. While studying his notes on the case, he found yet more signs that pointed to arsenic. It was his conclusion that Shakespeare was very likely murdered by poison." By putting that burden on John, I forestalled any hesitance by Sir Walter in accepting murder as the cause of Will's death.

"I see. John arrived at this conclusion."

"Aye."

Sir Walter stood and stepped slowly to a window. He stared

out over his gardens for a moment. "You know, Master Saddler, that Shakespeare had strong, influential friends at court?"

"I do. That is why I think that I should continue my enquiry in London. I have ferreted out all the information I could find in Stratford, which was not much. He had a visitor from London though, who came twice, and bore papers away each time. No one in Shakespeare's family knew who this man was, but whatever his identity, if I can find him, he could have information that would further my cause. Oh, and the poet Ben Jonson, too, came to Stratford during Shakespeare's last illness. I would hear what he can tell me. Beyond his friends at court, Shakespeare had numerous business dealings in London. It may be that one of those brought about his death."

Again, a long pause. Finally, Devereux turned and looked at me. "Your plan of action is a logical one. You may proceed, but with this caveat. Confine your enquiries into his property and business dealings. Do not involve the royal court."

"But, master, I do not know where this enquiry may take me. If you limit me—"

He held up a hand. "Simon, if your enquiry leads you to court, we will both rue the day. I believe in justice and finding the truth every bit as much as you. But I am also a practical man. And logic tells me that a murderer with ties to the royal court is someone that neither of us has the power to bring down. And I also know you well enough to know that you will go where the path leads. But I have given you my instructions."

He was right; I did not intend to obey him. So, it did not bother me to accept his terms. Sir Walter was a good man, but a cautious one. I had got what I came for, his permission to continue my enquiry in London. I truly believed that it was there that I would find my answers.

With that settled, he insisted on showing me the gardens then under construction. I feigned interest, though it was not all that difficult. The sheriff had excellent taste, and he exercised considerable restraint in the design of his gardens, at least in comparison to the nobility.

By the time we finished, it was far too late to begin the journey to London. Sir Walter directed me to an inn in the village.

THE ROAD to Oxford was muddy and crowded. Muddy from our many April rains. Crowded with a press of humanity on the move. Some pedlars, with horses loaded with goods, sacks and small caskets, carefully tied and balanced across the horses' backs, sought conversation with whoever would answer, sometimes just talking to themselves about the weather, the prices.

Most of those riding alongside me preferred silence, as did I. Outside the villages and towns, our land was vast, wide fields of wheat or rye or barley, separated by long stretches of forest, green now that spring had made its entrance.

One thing that made a ride like this pleasurable was freedom from the ever-present reek of Stratford's middens. We all had them, hidden from sight behind our houses, but not hidden from our noses.

CORNMARKET STREET in Oxford was where many of us from Stratford stayed on our journeys to and fro to London. The Crown Inn was a fine public house with some twenty rooms for guests and sufficient wine to inebriate half of Oxford. It was Will's favorite inn, and, indeed, he was the godfather of innkeeper John Davenant's son, William.

Rumour had it that young William was actually the son of our Will, but my friend told me once that he had never bedded Mistress Davenant, and he rarely failed to claim success between the sheets when deserved. Aye, he would shout it to the heavens.

I had risen early from Castle Bromwich to make up for my detour, and it was a hard, pounding ride to make Oxford by dark. I would have preferred to continue, but my horse was spent, and I rarely missed a chance to stop over at the Crown. As I dismounted from my horse, a lad of ten rushed up to take the reins. I ruffled his hair, and he grinned up at me. "Much thanks, Master Davenant." A flip of the wrist and a penny dropped in his hand.

"You are welcome, Master Saddler." He ran off with his smile still beaming.

Surely they knew of Will's death. It had been three days. Sighing, I lugged my bag into the tall, half-timbered, two-storey structure. Fatigue had the best of me. My journey had taken me through Shipston-on-Stour, Chipping Norton, down through Woodstock and Yarnton to Oxford. I had skirted the great university, irritated for some reason by its very existence. Though Will had never studied there—few of us from Stratford could afford such a luxury—I still linked it in my mind with sarcastic poets and preening writers.

"Simon!" Jane Davenant's hearty greeting echoed off the roof beams. More in the manner of an innkeeper's wife than that of the bailiff of Oxford, Jane wrapped me in her arms and held on tight.

She was a handsome woman, with a heavy bosom and red hair. I wondered for a moment whether Will had been truthful with me. He loved red-haired women. They were his special weakness.

"Jane, no traveler could ever leave the Crown feeling unwelcome."

"Come, John will stand you to an ale."

Her husband, the smiling, portly vintner, stood behind the bar. He shoved a pot of strong beer at me. "First, down that to cut the dust from you. Then, an ale."

John Davenant served fine beer, of that there was no doubt. And he was a fine winemaker as well. With the brew warming my throat and stomach, I took up the ale. The Davenants leaned in about me.

"We haven't told young Will about his godfather. We have hardly taken in the news ourselves. Tell us something of how this came about," Jane pleaded. The other patrons, perhaps a half dozen, showed little interest in our conversation.

"It came fairly swiftly, as deaths go," I explained. "He lay abed for perhaps three weeks. Most have put it down to a fever contracted after a night of drinking with Drayton and Jonson. They did come to visit him just before he fell ill."

"But you do not believe that," John said, judging from the tone of my voice and the look on my face that I was certain.

Part of my time on the road had been spent trying to decide how much I would trust to the Davenants' discretion. But they had been two of Will's closest friends, and they deserved to hear the truth. "Will feared that he was being poisoned. He called me to his bed not a week before his death and made this accusation."

I needed to be no reader of minds to see that even the idea shocked John and Jane.

"Who in the world would wish Will dead?" John said finally, shaking his head. "He was as gentle and kind a man as God ever placed among us."

The tears dampening Jane's eyes kept her from speaking as well. I could nearly see the catch in her throat. But finally, she willed it out of the way and spoke. "Even the gentle and kind can raise the ire of madmen," she answered her husband.

John Davenant swallowed hard. "Did he have any idea of who it might be?"

I shook my head. "By the time he called for me, he was barely in his right mind. Aye, he drifted off into wild rantings more than once. But he did not seem to have a particular culprit in mind, or if he did, he did not share the name with me."

"But you believed him," Jane pressed.

"His words had a ring of truth. And I believed his son-in-law, John Hall, more certainly."

"The physician?" Davenant asked.

"Aye. He found obvious signs of arsenic poisoning in Will's body."

"Verily?"

"Aye," I answered with a sigh. "It was John's findings that convinced me." I paused. Will had been circumspect with others about our schism. His general response had been, I had learned, that some business dealings had soured our friendship. I felt certain that he had not shared the truth with the Davenants. "Will and I have not been close in recent years," I admitted to them. "We fell out over some unwise investments."

"Money is an evil thing," Jane clucked, shaking her head. "How horrible. And the two of you were as thick as thieves."

"Thicker," I recalled. "Still, I think we reached an understanding at the end."

"Well, that is something to be thankful for. Simon," Jane continued, "our boy will be distraught. You know how he and Will adored each other."

I did. Sometimes, I believed that Will had transferred all of the pent-up love left over from his dead son, Hamnet, to little Will Davenant. I remembered well when the boy was born, and how delighted Will had been to be named the child's godfather. Even the mention of Hamnet Shakespeare's name was enough to thrust Will into a dark place, a darker place than man should have to see. Perhaps that was why the gossipmongers saw Will as the Davenant boy's father. He certainly sparkled when young Will was at hand. They did not know the melancholy that our Will suffered from his son's death.

"I will not mention it then," I said after a moment.

The Davenants nodded as one. "Good. We will tell him after you have gone tomorrow," Jane said. "'Twill be a blow to him."

"So, you will pursue Will's killer in London?" John asked.

"Aye, Sir Walter, high sheriff in Warwickshire, approved my enquiry. He is most anxious that I find the truth of it."

"As are we all," John agreed. "Poor little Will, he will be crushed."

"Only the first of many disappointments that life will give him," Jane agreed. "More ale, Simon?"

And we left the talk of death, sad little boys, and great poets for lighter, happier things. But our boisterous talk belied the sorrow in our hearts.

LATE IN the night, as the three of us sat around a table, our tongues too tired to talk, John stood and went to his bar. I paid little attention to what he was doing, the long day's journey weighing heavily on me.

"Here," I heard John say, setting a tankard on the table. "It will help you sleep."

I took a sip and smiled. A caudle. Hot wine thickened with an egg, an old concoction that Will and I had both shared a passion for in our younger days. But John was right, and I stumbled up to my chamber, nearly falling asleep as I walked.

"SIMON?"

"Yes?"

Jane came in, bearing a pair of blankets. "The nights still get a bit chilly," she said.

After spreading the blankets out, she sat on the edge of the bed. "I have been arguing with myself about telling you this."

I shook my head to clear it. "Tell me what?"

"I cannot be certain, but several weeks ago, John sent a package to someone in Stratford."

"So? He has many friends there; you both do."

"It contained poison. Or, at least, that's what John said. I asked him what it was, and he looked at me darkly. 'Poison,' he said. 'Poison for a rat.'"

"Perhaps that's all it was, Jane." I found it difficult to believe that the jovial John Davenant would conspire to kill anyone, especially Will.

"Simon, he has never believed that young Will was truly his son." She dropped her head, those red locks falling about her shoulders. "Oh, he has put up a fine show, telling everyone, including Will, that he did not listen to such trash. But nothing has been the same between us for these ten years past."

"I see." In truth, I knew not what to say. "Thanks for telling me of the poison. I pray it is nothing but coincidence."

Turning to collapse back on the bed, I felt her hand on my shoulder.

"You have never asked me if the rumours are true."

"I am not your husband, Jane. Nor am I a constable in Oxford. What you and Will did or did not do is not my concern. For what it is worth to you, Will denied the story."

"Perhaps you should have made it your concern." Her voice was at my ear, and her breath smelled of freshly chewed mint.

I turned to see her lips moving toward me. It took but a second for our tongues to be entwined; the soft smoothness awakened many feelings long dormant in me. She took my hand and placed it on her breast, and I could not help but gently caress it. But this was not the time for such. I broke off the kiss and snatched my hand away.

"Jane, this is not a rejection. But you should not have plied me with so much drink." 'Twas a weak argument, weakened further by the growing bulge in my breeches. But doing to John what Will had done to me sapped the lust from my heart.

She smiled, seeming to know what I was thinking. "Perhaps next time I won't." And then she was gone.

A full minute passed before I could calm my heart. Strangely I felt no guilt or remorse at the sudden kiss. Indeed, for some reason, I felt satisfaction at it. And that bothered me, deep into the night.

Chapter Four

LONDON APPEARED ON THE SOUTHERN HORIZON LIKE A smudge on a white cloth or a gathering storm. But the clouds never seemed to move, just grew larger as I approached. The closer you got, the more it looked like a giant dust cloud, hovering over the city. But that was London, blanketed by the smoke of ten thousand chimneys. It was a rare day when the citizens actually saw the sun shine.

The only town of any consequence on my second day's journey was Chepping Wycombe, a mill town about halfway between Oxford and the city. Fortunately, I had been troubled by few beggars or cutpurses on the road. I kept a strong sword on my hip and a dagger at my waist, but no one had attempted to molest me.

And now that I was come to London at last, I remembered why I had never sought my fortune there. Noise! Everywhere! You could not shut it out. Between people yammering, merchants hawking their wares, and workmen hammering on everything from tin to wooden barrels, you could scarce hear your own voice, even if you shouted. The air was filled with the stench of human waste and spoiled food. A passerby needed a helmet to safeguard his head from the barrage of wash water and garbage tossed from the tightly packed houses along the streets. Water carriers dashed through the lanes at breakneck speed. And dark, hulking shapes seemed to lurk down every byway.

Though I had entered the city's walls, I still had a good distance to travel. My path led me across the city, past great St. Paul's, on to London Bridge, down the narrow lane, between the crowded buildings, with the screeching of their housewives ringing in my ears, through the gatehouse and past the hideous skulls of those executed on pikes, and off the other side of the bridge at St. Saviour's in Southwark.

Someday, I thought, they will make this one of the largest parishes in England. It was yet a small parish then, if a large church, but situated there, at the foot of London Bridge, it was ideally situated to grow into a true minster.

I turned my horse through the churchyard. Some ten years before, I had come to St. Saviour's, at Will's request. His brother, Ned, had died. He sent a rider with instructions not to stop until he reached me in Stratford. We returned without waiting, on fresh horses. We rode around the clock; it nearly ruined our mounts and drove me to exhaustion.

Will was sitting on a bench, outside the church. It was night. He did not look up as I approached, but he knew that it was me. "I did not want him to come to London, you know," he had said.

"I know," I answered, sitting beside him. "But he would not listen to you. He would not listen to anyone. Ned saw only that you had escaped Stratford and found success here, in London. He saw your fame and wanted his own taste of it."

Will laughed, a sad little laugh. "He was quite good, you know. He would never have been an Alleyn or a Burbage, but he was a solid player. He had an uncanny ability to remember lines. Ned never had to be prompted. Ever. I was proud of him."

"How did it happen?"

My old friend stood and walked a few paces, staring across the grave markers in the churchyard. "Remember the girl he got with child a few years ago?"

I nodded. It had not been long after Ned came to London. Players were little prized by the nobility, more commodities to be bought. The Puritans scorned them. Ned did not understand how things stood. He began an affair with the younger, rebellious daughter of some royal cousin, perhaps trying to prove that he was his brother's equal. He got her with child, but the child died. It almost cost Ned dearly at the time, but Southampton, Will's patron, handled matters.

"She died in childbirth last week," Will said.

I remembered then that her father had married her off properly a pair of years after the event.

"The physician said that her death was caused by that earlier confinement. Her father set a pack of rogues on Ned; they caught him behind the Rose and beat him to death."

I put my arm about his shoulders and he cried, giant tears. It took no great insight to know that Will blamed himself for his brother's death. I stayed with him for a week, coaxing him to eat, entertaining him with tall tales. By the time I left, he looked and acted more like the Will Shakespeare that I knew.

THAT WAS then. On this journey, I passed through the churchyard and headed for the Globe.

It was a newer, more impressive Globe. Some years before, a cannon shot had set the thatch on fire, horribly damaging Will's theatre. I remember how upset he was, on returning from London where he had viewed the destruction. He was yet a shareholder in the company then, and I suspected his dismay had more to do with lost income than melancholy about the building itself.

Morning was not yet done, and I found Richard Burbage just where I expected him to be—inside the Globe, directing the morning's rehearsals.

A great deal of grey had crept into his hair and finely manicured beard since I had last seen him. He sat up in the gallery, watching the players go through their paces.

"Master Burbage!"

Richard looked up and squinted. "Simon? Simon Saddler?" He stood slowly and approached me the same. I was shocked. Richard was so frail! A stiff breeze could blow him about at will.

His hand grasped my arm so lightly that I barely felt its touch. And he was a year younger than Will, I remembered. He had long been one of my favourites among Will's friends in the players' company. When I had been younger, I would often come to the city and the three of us would drink and carouse.

"Oh, it's good to see you here, Simon. I've only just heard of Will's death. Here, pray sit."

I joined him in the gallery.

"Cuthbert!" he called to his brother. "Show them their marks once again!"

He turned back to me and smiled. "These young players, Simon, they take so long to learn things. Tell me, has Will been properly buried? Did he suffer much at the end?"

"Yes, Richard. He was buried two days past. In the last week or so, he was unconscious most of the time, so he realized little that was going on about him. But, how are you? You look as if you had been ill."

He waved me off with a hand. "I am fine, just a cough. I probably need to be bled, but I hate surgeons with a passion. Aye, a passion I used to reserve only for Henslowe, but he is no longer available for my hatred."

Philip Henslowe had been the business manager of the Rose, the theatre most often in competition with the Globe and the Blackfriars. But Henslowe had died a few months before. The faces of Will's London world were disappearing.

"Well," Richard continued, "enough of that. What brings you to the city, Simon? It has been years since I have seen you."

Burbage knows all, Will had told me. So I resolved to speak frankly.

"Will thought he was being murdered, Richard. He thought he was poisoned."

The blood drained from Burbage's face. "No, it is not possible. Everyone loved Will."

He spoke the words, but no certainty lay behind them.

"Richard. I need to know. I am constable of Stratford and

this is an official enquiry. One of the last things that Will said to me was that 'Burbage knows all.'"

At that Richard chuckled weakly. "Would that I did. And that I say to you honestly. Will Shakespeare had many secrets, Simon. Yes, I was privy to some, but certainly not all."

"Like what, Richard? Please, for Will's sake, give me something other than generalities."

Burbage pursed his lips, apparently thinking of what he could say and could not. "You know, of course, of his friendship with Southampton?"

"Of course."

"Lord Southampton did not simply give his patronage away. Will was required to serve at his lordship's bidding. Nothing comes without a price, Simon. Not even an earl's patronage."

"And that price?"

"Tasks. Chores. Errands."

"Of what sort?"

"I do not know, and Will did not say. The nobility involve themselves in things that we commoners are not privy to, nor should we want to be. A discreet messenger is often worth his weight in gold. I suspect that it was in that role that Southampton employed Will most often. But I have no certain knowledge of that." He paused. "You remember that Southampton was imprisoned, aye even sentenced to death, for his part in the Essex Affair. I do not doubt that Southampton involved Will in that. You know that we nearly lost our players' license over that affair. Master Tilney was under great pressure to close us down."

The earl of Essex, the queen's favourite and some said her lover, had attempted to overthrow the queen fifteen years before. The Globe company had been induced to resurrect Will's play *Richard II*, which included a scene where the king stepped down from the throne. How much Will had to do with all of that, I had never known. Essex was beheaded, and Southampton was imprisoned in the Tower for some three years.

Master Tilney, of whom Richard spoke, was Edmund Tilney, Master of the Revels. It was his job to oversee many things, but his biggest headache was most assuredly watching over the players and their theatres. Some claimed that he was more Puritan than not, but I had heard Will speak well of him enough to know that he was a friend of the player.

"So," I speculated, "it might be that Will knew things of that affair that could still harm Southampton."

Burbage shook his head. "That is not for me to say, Simon. But you asked, and it was worthy of note. Will had many friends, from every corner of London. When James came to the throne, and Southampton returned to court, the king's patronage also came with a price. In all truth, though, such chores amounted to nothing more sinister than being ready to perform whenever and wherever the king said. Other whisperings marked the city though.

"Will often absented himself with little or no notice. Whether this was at His Majesty's request, or Southampton's, or some business of his own, I do not know." Now that Richard was speaking, it seemed he had much to say. From the pulsing of his veins beneath the wrinkled skin in his throat, I could see that these answers resurrected unwelcome memories.

"You did not like this."

Richard smiled at me sadly. "You can see that in my face? 'Tis no wonder that you are good at your task. After the Essex Affair, we were frightened, all of us. Augustine was called before the commission to explain our actions."

I nodded. Augustine Phillips was one of the shareholders in the Globe, and, when necessary, served as the theatre troupe's spokesman. "I never asked Will, but I always assumed it was his doing, at the behest of Southampton."

Burbage shook his head. "No, it was Southampton himself who met with the six of us, including Will and Cuthbert. He reminded us of favours done in the past, and he called his request to put on *Richard II* simply 'a small thing.' Of course, Essex was not mentioned. We saw no harm in it, and agreed. But Will seemed uneasy, and we all suspected that he knew more of it than he admitted. At any rate, we kept him as far away from the commission as we could. Augustine answered their questions, without mentioning that Southampton had been involved."

Some might think it oddly indiscreet for Richard to speak so openly of these things, but they had happened some fifteen years before. The climate was much different under James, especially for players.

"Who else will you speak with?"

I thought for a moment. "Southampton, if I can. Jonson. Drayton must wait until I return to Warwickshire."

"Go and see George Wilkins, if you can find him. He sometimes wrote plays for us. Will collaborated on one or two." Richard paused. "Well, in truth Will took plays that were barely worthy of the name and made something of them. Wilkins has harboured a grudge against Will for many years. And he is of the lowest sort, consort of thieves and murderers. He might not have killed Will, but he spends his days in that sort of company."

That Burbage, a player, spoke so of one like Wilkins would have been laughable in Stratford. The town was much inclined towards the Puritans, and I long suspected that Puritans would find more need for murderers than players. Puritans had no need for anything that gave one pleasure.

"Tread carefully, Simon," Burbage warned. "I loved Will as a brother, but he was forever a difficult man to understand. He always left me with the feeling that he knew more than he would tell, and perhaps he did, perhaps he did not. With Will, you could never be certain. A never-ending stream of odd creatures was constantly seeking him at the rear of the Globe."

Richard stopped again and chuckled. "Do you know the story of when he first came to London?"

"No," I answered. "By the time that I returned from the Low Countries, he was already well established here."

We were at the Theatre then, he said, *beyond Bishopsgate in Shoreditch.*

I saw him first, looking more like a young scarecrow than a promising poet. He stood outside the Theatre, his hat in his hands.

"Master Burbage," he said. "Perhaps you remember me, from Stratford-upon-Avon."

"Ah! The young poet. So you have come to the city? Follow me and we will speak with my father."

I was surprised that he had come so far on a half-hearted offer from months past. But there was something in his eyes, something that seemed to reach out and absorb everything around him. His earnest nature made me smile.

Father was busy as always, shouting at the apprentices, shouting at Cuthbert. It seemed that Father was eternally shouting at someone.

"What is it, Richard? The costumes have not been repaired. Will Kemp is drunk again. We have a performance this afternoon. I do not have time for interruptions."

"Father, this is the Shakespeare boy from Stratford. You remember him. He rewrote that speech."

Father glanced quickly, rudely at Will. "Oh yes, the writer. Well, I haven't time or room for him."

"But, Master Burbage, you said—" Will began to protest.

"I know, I know," Father answered with a wave of his hand. "Very well. Richard, we need someone to tend the horses during performances. Show him his duties."

"Tending horses!" Will exclaimed.

"That is the best I can offer you," Father said. "Perhaps later we can talk about other things."

To his credit, Will did not protest. Within a fortnight, he had organized a pack of urchins to handle his duties. After that, you could find him amongst the groundlings, watching every performance from the crowded floor where the cracking of discarded nutshells underfoot sometimes overwhelmed the voices of the actors. In less than a year, he had written a play that my father loved. Then he no longer had charge of the horses.

BURBAGE NODDED. "Go and see that Silver Street family," he said after a moment of silence. "That Mountjoy affair. Will had to be deposed. I never heard how it was resolved, but someone was sure to be unhappy."

"Unhappy enough to murder Will for revenge?"

Again, Richard shrugged. "Perhaps. That suit was brought about the time that Will moved back to Stratford, and we did not see him much at the Globe."

And it was filed about the time that Will destroyed my marriage by bedding my wife. Although I did not tell Burbage this, I felt certain he knew. Nothing good could come from traveling that ground again.

"Old man Mountjoy is alive, but I think his wife is dead. Stephen Belott, the son-in-law, still trades in hats on Silver Street."

I rose. "Give my best to Cuthbert, Richard."

"You will not stay and let us stand you to a beaker?"

"Perhaps I will come by later. I intend to put up at the Cross Keys." The old inn was on Gracechurch Street near Corn Hill. The companies had often used its courtyard to perform their plays.

I turned to leave this place that was so much a part of Will's life, so much the reason that he was who he was.

"You will miss him, you know." Burbage's voice drifted over my shoulder. "I know something of your feud with Will, and I do not fault you for feeling as you do. You must remember that we players are paid for pretending to be someone else, from the groundlings who paid their penny to those in the gallery who paid two. And when you spend your life in such a pursuit, it frees you to do things that you yourself would not do. But that is a poor excuse for such behaviour, such betrayal. I am but a player, a good one, granted. But there are many players. There was ever only one Will Shakespeare. And we are better men for having known him."

I did not turn during his soliloquy. Straightening my shoulders, I slipped out of the gallery and left Will's wooden "O," his theatre, behind me.

"Aye, we have room." The innkeeper at the Cross Keys was a surly old man. He seemed not to have changed one whit since I last stayed under his roof, with one exception. His unshaven face had once been half-covered in thick black hair. Now, every single strand was pure white.

He threw me a key and pointed me across the cobbled inn-yard. But he turned back. "Don't I know ye?"

"From a long time ago. I am of Stratford-upon-Avon, and I once stayed here often."

He nodded. "I remember ye now. Friend of the player Shake-speare. Someone asked after you this morn. And this forenoon a messenger brought this."

Snatching a scrap of paper, folded over with a red wax seal affixed, he handed it to me. "You must be an important man to receive notes from a noble."

I glanced at the seal.

Southampton.

"You would do well to mind your own business."

His laugh emerged as a grunt. "You would do well to re-member that you're in London now. Everyone seeks a profit, and knowledge is the most commonly traded."

Without opening the note, I took my bag and headed to-wards my room. How did Southampton know I would be here? I had only just told Burbage an hour before, hardly time to alert Southampton and for him to dispatch a message here. And what of this other man seeking me, or was he simply Southampton's messenger?

And if Southampton were already aware of my task, then oth-ers would be also. Shaking my head to clear it as I mounted the steps to the first gallery, I dropped my bag and went for my dag-ger.

A light was shining in my chamber.

For a second, I considered fleeing; but if one man was in my chamber, another would likely be waiting outside the inn.

With my dagger in hand, I eased open the door.

"By God's grace, Simon! Would you come in and shut the door? The wind is getting chilly."

I near fainted from relief. Ben Jonson.

"Ben! You nearly caused me to have an apoplexy! How did you get here before me?"

Jonson, the redheaded giant, cut a slice of apple with his dagger and popped it into his mouth. "I was at the Rose and stopped by the Globe. Burbage told me you were in town and what brought you. I decided that you might need my help."

"But how did you know what chamber—"

Before I could finish my sentence, Ben interrupted me with a laugh from deep in his belly. "Well, of course I paid old Hal to put you in this chamber, Simon. I am hardly one of these mystics, and while I do believe that the stars move our lives, I could not tell you how."

"Old Hal could have told me you were waiting."

"Then, where would the surprise be?"

Ben Jonson was both Will Shakespeare's boon companion and chief rival, all at the same time. Their differences on poetry and playwriting could fill a book, and they loved nothing better than drinking late into the night arguing about those differences. At the heart of it, though, they admired and respected each other.

Setting my tired leather bag on the bed, I plopped down beside it. "Why should I need your help, Master Jonson?"

"Because you are asking questions that should not be asked. And if no one has tried to kill you yet, do not be concerned. They will. And soon. And when that time comes, you will need me."

Ben had a mighty reputation as a brawler, and the temper fueled by that red hair was just as legendary. I had seen both in action personally.

"I can take care of myself, Ben. But, since you are here, what do you know of Will's claim that he was poisoned?"

"He told me the same thing the last time I visited him in Stratford. And then a post rider brought the news yesterday that Will was dead and brought also the rumour that you thought it was murder. I knew that it would bring you here, but I thought you would arrive sooner."

"I went to Castle Bromwich to obtain permission from Sir Walter Devereux to conduct this enquiry."

Ben nodded. "Prudent."

"Do you believe Will's accusations?"

That red head and red beard bobbed up and down. "I do."

I did not say anything for a long moment. Ben Jonson knew London far better than I. And after speaking with Burbage, I was convinced that the answer to Will's death lay here. Jane Davenant's concerns were mostly likely a subterfuge to try and bed me. Though why she would want to, I had no idea.

"Then you should see this." My decision made, I withdrew the message from Southampton from my shirt. Ben's eyebrows rose sharply.

"He wasted no time."

"'To Master Simon Saddler. The earl of Southampton requires you to call upon him at Holborn on the morrow at the noon hour.'"

"Wriothesley has always been a man of few words," Ben quipped.

"I have only been in London a half day, and I told only Burbage that I would be staying here. Yet Southampton was able to have a message waiting for me when I arrived."

Jonson shrugged. "He probably had messages delivered to all of the most promising inns. That he knew you were coming, that begs a different answer." He paused. "What is the name of the bailiff in Stratford—Strong, Stout..."

"Smythe."

"Aye, he has business interests here. He may have seen a future profit in letting Southampton know what you were about."

It made a certain sense. "Ben, did you and Drayton really come to Stratford some weeks ago?"

He nodded. "Aye, but Will drank little. I have heard that rumour that he caught a fever from drinking with us, but Will feared Mistress Shakespeare's temper."

"Do you think she could have poisoned him?"

"Anne? Anne Hathaway would take more pleasure in beating him to death with a stick at the market cross in Stratford. She would not hide it. Will's death could have been natural. But he seemed in fine health when Drayton and I were with him. He spoke of plans to come up here to London and spend a few days away from Anne. He even talked of giving the Globe a new play. I think the country squire's life was wearing on him, Simon. Will appeared, I don't know, restless. He spoke almost without cease about his plans, even of building a bigger theatre than the Globe."

This was certainly not the Will I had seen more than a week before his death. A thought occurred.

"Did Will mention Burbage in connection to this new venture?"

"No."

"Would such a theatre hurt the Globe's receipts?"

Ben shook his head at me sadly. "Simon, Simon, you can find a reason for hundreds of people to want Will Shakespeare dead, just as you could find a hundred who wish me dead. Should you not seek other answers? Consider this: perhaps he was killed not because of something he had done or was doing, but because of something he had known."

"Answer the question, Ben. Would his plan have damaged the Globe's profits?"

"Aye, it would. But that would hardly matter to Will."

"Was he not a shareholder?"

Jonson shook his red head. "Not any longer. Three years past, when the cannon set the Globe on fire, Will sold his shares in the theatre. He had overextended himself and did not wish to go into debt to pay his portion of the rebuilding costs. It made good sense at the time."

"But he was partners with Heminges, Condell, Burbage, all the others, for so long. Why would he want to compete with them?"

"He tried to buy his shares back when his fortunes improved, but no one wished to sell." Ben stopped and ran a hand through his hair. "Few loves exist, Simon, like that of a playwright for theatres. Yes, for Will and me, our true passion has always been poetry, and we have written plays for the coins they make us, but something happens to a man when he sees a world he has created brought to life on the stage. It is as close to being a god as a man can get."

"'Tis arrogance to even believe that, let alone give the words voice."

His eyes narrowed at me. "There is nothing of the poet in you. My meaning is that when you have been part of that world, when you have seen worlds that you created come to life, all you wish to do is return to it. So, yes, his plans could have cost his old friends some money, but they would understand his motives all too well, and they would not begrudge him."

I saw the logic in his answer. I posed another question. "What do you think of the rumour that Will got Jane Davenant with child?"

That belly-deep laugh exploded from Ben. "Again, the questions." He threw up his hands in mock surrender. "Fine, certainly it is possible. We had both tasted her pleasures. She was one of the main reasons to stop at the Crown, at least for us. Jane always seemed to enjoy the company of players and poets more than that of other men."

He said it with such candour that it was difficult not to believe him.

"I knew Will Shakespeare all of his life, but I never once knew him to deny lying with a woman if he had. When rumours first surfaced that young Will Davenant was his child, he immediately told me that such was a lie, that he had never bedded Mistress Davenant. Why would he protect her?"

And before Ben could get a word out of his opening mouth, I answered myself.

"'Twas not Jane Davenant he was protecting. 'Twas the child."

"Aye. In truth, no one knows who is the father of Davenant's child, but it could have been Will. And he did not wish the mother's sins visited on the boy."

"He told you this?"

The redhead laughed again. "Remember, I was part of that select fraternity, Master Saddler. I, too, had shared Mistress Davenant."

"He doted on the boy, you know."

"Aye, he did."

I did not share my belief that Will used the boy as a substitute of sorts for his own dead son. It had no bearing on this enquiry.

"Go, Ben. I am exhausted and need my rest. Join me tomorrow if you wish. Southampton will be my first task."

The giant stood. "I have taken the chamber next to this one. You underestimate the dangers of your path, Simon. If Will was truly murdered, do you not think that that same person would not hesitate to destroy you?"

"So far," I answered, "the major difficulty that I have encountered is people who talk in riddles."

He just laughed and slipped from the room.

Alone, I considered the implications of Ben Jonson's interest in this affair. Oddly, I had first met him apart from Will. We both served under Sir Francis Vere in the Low Countries and knew each other there as only brothers-in-arms can. Since then, we had met several times over the years. When I was much younger, I often visited Will in London, as time and my fortunes allowed. Ben was frequently a drinking companion. But I could not say that I became any closer to Ben than others we caroused with. We never spoke of our common history.

Will often referred to Jonson as his greatest rival. Could that rivalry have driven Jonson to poisoning his friend? And could fear of discovery have driven him to call up an ages-old friendship to steer me from him? After all, he had visited Will at the onset of his illness and then again during it. Could he have been delivering the poison?

My head ached from such thoughts. And I finally drifted off to a sleep filled with yet more.

IN MY dreams, I was suffocating, fighting for breath, and Peg and Will stood laughing at me as I died. I opened my eyes and they disappeared.

But I was still suffocating.

A pillow or something like it was clamped over my face. A great weight pressed against my chest.

I twisted from side to side.

I kicked.

My arms flailed.

And then...

It was gone.

The weight left my chest.

I opened my mouth and swallowed a huge gulp of air.

Standing over me was Ben Jonson, holding a wiggling, jerking man by the scruff of his neck.

Coughing and hacking, I scrambled to my feet, and I crushed my fist into his face, breaking at least two of his teeth. He began spluttering and spitting blood and teeth across the room as Ben looked at me in wonder.

Ben threw him to the floor, and he cowered against the bed. "Who sent you?"

The man was young, perhaps twenty years. But his life had been hard. He drank heavily, the red-tipped nose and red-rimmed eyes telling the story all too well. Under the grimy rags that were his clothes, it seemed he had not bathed in his entire life.

Jonson's hand flashed, and the intruder went sprawling across the chamber. "Who sent you?"

"I do not know. 'Twas a man in St. Paul's churchyard, wearing a cloak with a hood. He offered me a crown to kill this one."

I was somehow insulted by being called "this one."

"Show me the crown."

The scoundrel produced the silver coin from his filthy breeches.

"Not much reward for killing a man."

"I have done it for less." The man had little remorse, if any. "What will you do with me now?"

I glanced at Ben. My first impulse was to turn him over to the local constable. But with a crown in his pocket, he could bribe his way out of the clink. After all, he had not actually killed me. "Go, and keep your blood money."

Stumbling to his feet, he bounced off of one wall and out the door.

"How do I know that you did not pay him to attack me so that you could prove yourself as a guardian?"

Ben chuckled. "Are you mad? Do you think that I have that sort of money to waste on something like that? Sit, Simon."

I did.

"I loved Will Shakespeare as much as you once did. Was there jealousy between us? Certainly. Show me two poets who do not envy each other. He was the measure by which I judged myself, though I would never have told him that. But I do not know who might have tried to steal him from our midst. All I do know is that it was not I."

The red flush had drained from my face, and my heart had returned to a normal pace. "When you last saw Will, did he say aught about Thomas Quiney, young Judith's husband?"

"Only that for a farthing he would kill the boy."

"He rewrote his will, you know, to guard against Quiney seeing any benefit from it. The thought crossed my mind that perhaps Quiney was behind his poisoning."

Ben shrugged. "Perhaps. But he struck me as more schemer than doer. No doubt he would think of it. And no doubt he would spend great spells of time planning it. I suspect that his attempts at execution would end in failure."

Such had been my assessment as well. Something Ben had said earlier came back to me.

"You said that Will's financial situation had improved. How? His investment in the tithes had brought him virtually nothing. He had some quarters of malt, but even if he sold them, they would not bring him nearly enough to even dream of building a new theatre." Quarters of malt, sixty-four gallons' worth each, were almost as good as hard money.

"I do not know, Simon. He simply told Drayton and me that he had made some wise investments and his coffers were now overflowing."

This news cast the whole affair in another light. Investments generally did not pay off so quickly. Could Will have taken part in something for which he was paid a great deal? His plays had certainly made him much money over time, but this sounded more immediate than that. And if that was behind his death, what could it have been? Murder was no stranger in our world, but there was almost always a reason. The death solved some problem for the murderer.

But if Will had already performed this task, and had received payment, what would his death solve? The answer was self-evident. He was killed to keep him from saying anything of the affair. Will was not indiscreet. So whatever knowledge he possessed must have been about something of the greatest severity.

I stopped thinking long enough to glance up and see Ben smiling above me. "And why are you laughing at me?"

"You should see yourself, Simon. Your face is a masque of total concentration, more so than I have ever seen on another human."

"Ben," I said, ignoring his comment, "if Will's improved fortunes touched on matters grave enough to demand his death, and beyond that to demand my death for even enquiring into it, than it must be very important indeed."

"Simon, if these matters are that grave, they could encompass only one thing—treason."

Chapter Five

"B E CAREFUL OF YOUR MANNERS," BEN JONSON WARNED ME as we turned off the Holborn Road onto a narrower lane, and Southampton House came into sight. "Rarely a night passes that Wriothesley doesn't have some important guest, and he is particular that the niceties are strictly followed. It is said that James favours him so much because he is an excellent host for those visitors the king finds tedious."

I had no problem in seeing why. It was a magnificent brick structure with matching gable windows on either end, and an impressive tower over the gatehouse. From this angle, I could see that it was rectangular, but I suspected that there was at least one wing extending from the back; Southampton would have to provide royal apartments for the king and queen. A royal snub might be difficult to ignore, but if this were the alternative accommodation, I would not be displeased. It floated like an island in the sea of fields north of Lincoln's Inn, and I suspected that Southampton's gardens were sumptuous. Indeed, the massive estate was the superior of some royal palaces that I had seen, both in England *and* Europe.

A row of wooden buildings sat opposite the gatehouse, shops along the ground floor with the upper floors, I presumed, for the families. A glance around showed few other residences, so I had to guess that the shops primarily served the earl's house, which meant that Jonson's comment was probably right. I also seemed to recall Will telling me that Southampton had hosted a performance by the Globe's players for Queen Anne, not long after she and James moved to London. High-ranking guests and entertainment for the royals could provide a handsome income for nearby businesses.

At least the road was free of the pedlars and strumpets and garbage that marked the rest of the city.

Ben and I presented ourselves at the gate, and Southampton's man bade us follow him through and into the garden. I had underestimated the gardens; Sir Walter could take lessons from the gardener.

He took us through the massive front doors into an entryway. A spiraling staircase climbed to the left where a black-and-white tomcat sat peacefully on the bottom step. He considered us, twitched his whiskers once or twice, and lazily padded across the hall, disappearing into the bowels of the house.

"His name is Ezra," a voice said from above. Henry Wriothesley, the third earl of Southampton, was a tall, spare man. His face narrowed to a point at his chin. On this day, he was dressed in black with a wide white collar and cuffs. His dark hair, which he always wore hanging down over his shoulders, was streaked with grey now. He was only forty-three that year, but he little resembled the youth, the young earl who became Will's patron. Though I had seen him before, I had never met him.

"Come. We will talk in my study."

We followed him through the great rooms of the house, an army of liveried servants seeming to appear at every turn, some dressed in clothing unlike Southampton's people. I heard some Spanish floating in the corridors. Finally we reached a chamber paneled in carved dark wood. The earl sat at the side of a small writing desk. "Please be seated."

One always waited until an earl invited one to sit before doing so. I could almost see my old tablet from school and hear the master teaching us protocol.

"Master Jonson, I have added my voice to the chorus

petitioning His Majesty for your pension. I suspect that it will be settled on you soon."

Ben preened. "I am, as ever, in your debt, your lordship."

Southampton cocked his head. "With the death of my friend Shakespeare, you are unquestionably the best among your fellows. Still, it is a rare gift from a king to a poet, but perhaps it will become a tradition." He stopped and turned to me. "You are Saddler, the Stratford constable?"

"I am, my lord."

"Tell me of this fancy of yours that Shakespeare was murdered."

I was not quite tongue-tied, but I was absolutely out of my ken. My encounters with the nobility had been rather few and uneventful. I did not fear Southampton as a man, but rather I feared the power that he wielded.

"My lord, Master Shakespeare sent for me about one week before he succumbed. He insisted that he had been hale and then suddenly he took ill. No matter what his physician did, his condition worsened."

"I see," Southampton said, nodding sagely. "Did he suggest who might be behind such a horrendous act?"

I held my tongue a moment. How much to tell him? The truth. "He was not certain, but he suggested several people who might prove helpful. Your name, my lord, was among those."

Southampton nodded. "So, you would have found your way to my door even if I had not summoned you?"

My turn to nod. "Yes, my lord."

"This seems a great deal of trouble to go to on the word of a man delirious with fever. Of course, all of those who knew Shakespeare well knew that you were an especial friend of his. I applaud the constancy of your devotion, and your dedication to your oath as constable, but he is dead. Nothing you do now will serve to change that. And, indeed, you could unleash hidden affairs that could besmirch your friend's name for all eternity. All on the word of a good man caught in the thrall of a fever."

"Not quite all, my lord. Master Hall, Will's physician and son-in-law, has confirmed that the signs of poison are evident both on his body and in Hall's record of his decline."

"I see," Southampton said softly, dropping his chin into his hand and stroking the beard there slowly. "So this is not just some irrational attempt to keep your friend alive in your mind a bit longer."

Something about his words made me think that he was repeating the claim of another. "My Lord Southampton, my enquiry has been authorized by Sir Walter Devereux, High Sheriff of Warwickshire. No one who was Will's friend doubts that your patronage was the most important influence on his success. But I have a duty, both to my oath and to my late friend, to find who killed him. Please do not take my stubbornness on this point as a sign of disrespect."

Southampton smiled and shook his head sadly. "You will not be dissuaded?"

"No, my lord. With regrets, I will not."

"Ben, can you not persuade our friend here of the folly of his quest?"

Jonson did not immediately respond, which told me that he was weighing his words as carefully as when crafting a poem. "My lord, if the sheriff sees enough merit in this to charge him to investigate, it is not my place to dissuade him. Just last night a hired killer tried to end Simon's life. Today, a peer of the realm tries, politely, to warn him against pursuing this. Like you, my lord, I questioned the need for this, but I am now beginning to see some value to his enquiry."

Southampton threw his head back in a genuine laugh. "Oh, Master Jonson, you tease me, you do. I am not warning Master Saddler. I am advising him, as a mutual friend of the departed Shakespeare. Let me be blunt.

"Over the course of his life in London, William Shakespeare was involved in a number of affairs of no little significance. In virtually every situation, he emerged untainted by these matters. But if Master Saddler is going to be rummaging around in Will's life, he might not like what he finds, and what he finds might besmirch the good name of one of the most talented poets of his generation."

"May I speak freely, my lord?" I seethed at how easily South-ampton could accept his friend's murder, yet have no need to bring the doer to justice. Will Shakespeare deserved better than that.

The earl nodded his assent. "Within reason."

"I find it difficult to understand why a man of your position and rank would concern himself with the reputation of a dead playwright. Half of the time, their plays are banned within the city. The plague closes their doors frequently. Within our life-times, their work was not even considered serious enough for mention. You can see why I question your motives." I did not truly believe my own words, but I was trying to provoke some reaction in Southampton.

And it succeeded.

Southampton's face grew cold and even darker. He stood and motioned for one of the servants. "Know this, Constable, your enquiry could reveal matters that threaten powerful men. They will not allow that. And one hired killer will turn into dozens."

The interview was at an end.

"I WILL say this for you, Simon," Ben Jonson began as we found ourselves turned unceremoniously out into the lane. "You are, in your own way, as fascinating as Will. Come, let us go to the Mermaid. I'll stand you to a mug of ale and we can consider these matters."

And I had violated the restrictions that Devereux had placed on my enquiry. I was certain that I would hear about that later. The midday was approaching, and my stomach growled, so I let Ben lead the way back towards the city. Though we were a short distance from the old city walls, once we were back on the main road, we found it busy with merchants hawking their wares. The stench of horse dung lay heavy in the air, held down by the smoke from ten thousand chimneys.

"Tell me, Ben. You are from Westminster?"

"I am."

"Though not within the walls, it is certainly part of London. How can you stand living here? The noise. The foul stench. You never see the sun. How?"

"I have traveled with the theatre companies when the plague closes them down in the city. I visited Will a time or two in Stratford. How do you stand so much silence? And do you not grow weary of the colour green?"

I held up a hand in surrender. "As you like. You surprised me, Ben."

"How so?"

"With Southampton. I thought you would be more accommodating because of his rank, and because he is championing the petition for your pension from the king."

"I loved Will, Simon. Oh, we argued, debated, fought like wild men. Will Shakespeare had less art in his soul than..." He stopped and smiled. "I sometimes am led down a narrow alley when I should stay in the wider street. But I know this: Will only wanted to be as good a poet as he could be. If he was involved in such things as Southampton alluded to, he did so only because of one of two traits—his zest for living or his belief that it would aid in his goal. A man cannot live his life as a pawn, shoved around a board by the nobles. And if you do not take a stand for a friend, then where will you make your stand? In this, I believe, you and I are of like minds."

My respect for Ben Jonson grew immeasurably at that moment. Oh, he was fond of praising himself above all others. And he certainly believed that he was the most talented man in British history. But a man with that sort of view of himself is, most often, not the strongest friend to others, unless he can be that friend at no cost to himself.

"Ben, you should go back home and compose a poem. If Southampton is right, by this time tomorrow, I will either be dead or in the Marshalsea Prison. You would profit no one by accompanying me on either journey."

The big redhead laughed heartily. "I have been in prison before, and I have faced death many times. Once, in the Low Countries, I fought an enemy in single combat and killed him, stripped him of his weapons. No, I think your odds of success are far greater if I accompany you."

"And what of your wife?"

Jonson rolled his eyes. "Though I do love her, she is a shrew. She would complain if I go. She would complain if I do not. So, why not do what you want since you are damned no matter which path you choose?"

That was logic with which I could not argue. And though I would never admit it to Ben, I did feel a certain comfort and easing of tension with his presence.

Ben launched then into a tirade about each of his rival poets and why their work was not worthy to wipe his bottom. It distracted me from thoughts of nobles and assassins until we reached the Mermaid Tavern just beyond St. Paul's.

His hand on my shoulder stopped me just as I made ready to enter.

"Simon, you should focus on finding the source of Will's newfound wealth. Do not be seduced by stories of Essex and that sorry affair. Elizabeth has lain rotting in Westminster for thirteen years. Yesterday's scandal is today's boast among the nobles. For a man to resort to hired assassins, the threat of exposure must be real; the danger to his person must be immediate."

I nodded. Ben's words were well chosen and as true as a well-aimed arrow.

"Be careful with any man we meet in here. Almost all knew Will, but not all liked him. And some of them earn their shillings by being informants for men like Southampton."

With that, he pushed open the door and entered.

A big, bluff man behind the bar waddled out and hastened up to me. "Simon Saddler! I thought never to see you in my tavern again." He wrapped his arms around me and hugged me so tight I thought my stomach would emerge from my throat. Will Johnson, the owner of the Mermaid, was one of Shakespeare's oldest and dearest friends. I had heard it said that the tavern-keeper befriended the young poet when he first came to the city, indeed that it was Johnson who kept him from starving during that difficult first year.

"Master Johnson!" Ben roared. "Two pots of your best ale for my friend and me!"

"Right away!"

Once armed with our ale, Ben navigated our way between tables until we came to one in the back, already occupied by a pair of men, one a priest.

"Is this the Reverend Donne that I see?" Ben bellowed.

The priest smiled gauntly. John Donne, a lawyer by trade and now a priest in the Church of England, was also a poet of some talent. I had never met him, but Will had spoken of him many times.

Donne had led a rather chequered life, for a lawyer. He ran afoul of the law early on when he married a girl without her father's permission. For that he spent time in prison. The last few years had not been kind to him, and he had been forced to live in the country in rather meagre accommodations. But then, suddenly last year, he had decided to study for the ministry.

The second man was a heavyset fellow with long, unruly brown hair and beard and piercing black eyes. I did not know him, but it was obvious that Ben did.

"Master Jones," he said. "Rumour has it that you have received the commission for the Queen's House at Greenwich."

So this was the architect, Inigo Jones, who was making a name for himself. Somewhere I had heard that he had spent much of his time traveling with nobles to Italy, most recently with Thomas Howard, the earl of Arundel. But now, with a royal commission, his future was made. If, that is, he pleased the king.

"Aye," he said pleasantly, his voice belying his age. His cheeks were a merry red, indicating that he had been celebrating his good fortune. "Who is this with you, Ben?"

Jonson clapped me on the back. "This is Master Simon

Saddler, of Stratford-upon-Avon, a lifelong friend of the late Will Shakespeare."

Donne, the priest, stood and took my hand in both of his. "William Shakespeare was a good and gentle soul, and we mourn his loss with you. God will provide a special place in Heaven for him."

Will Shakespeare was an adulterer and the only place for him would be in Hell. But I did not say that. I simply said, "Thank you." And we sat down.

"What brings you to London so soon after Will's passing?" Inigo Jones asked. "Disposing of his property here?"

I was uncertain how to answer the inquiry. No doubt my true purpose would be talked of all over the city by nightfall, but I thought that confusing the issue might be of some service. "No, no. I am here on business for the Stratford Corporation. I bring summonses for certain residents of London who have fallen into debt to citizens of Stratford."

Jonson cut his eyes over to me quickly, wondering, I knew, why I hedged on the truth.

Jones puffed out his lower lip. "Indeed. Well, you may have trouble sorting out all the debtors here."

"Times are indeed hard," Donne agreed. "Do you know the provisions of Shakespeare's will? I would be interested to know the disposition of his Blackfriars property."

I shrugged. "I do not know. Will was very ill in his last days; delirium held him in its sway and little he said made sense. His will had not yet been read when I left." That seemed the safest course, but I noticed that Ben looked again at me askance. Most probably he wondered why I was being so circumspect.

"When will you begin work, Inigo, at the Queen's House?" Ben finished his pot in one long draught, motioning to Will Johnson for another almost in the same motion.

"Later in the year. I am still sorting out the design."

"What was your interest in Will's Blackfriars property, Master Donne?" I was curious. From what I had been told, John Donne had suffered great financial losses over the last few years. Richard

Quiney, a kinsman of Shakespeare's new son-in-law but more importantly an old and firm friend, had mentioned in passing just recently something about Donne's reversals.

Blackfriars had once been a wealthy priory, Dominican if I recalled correctly. Elizabeth's father, Henry VIII, had it shut down. But before that, it had seen the trial to decide Henry and Katherine of Aragon's divorce. In more recent and happier times, one hoped, Shakespeare and other investors had opened a theatre there, and Will had purchased the gatehouse. It was there that Will stayed when he came to town.

"I have been seeking a home in the city; we were forced to move to Pyrford for a time."

"Forgive my curiosity, Master Donne, but you seem a bit aged to take the holy orders."

Donne cleared his throat, looking decidedly uncomfortable. "You are a very direct man, Master Saddler. I had hoped for a place of preferment among the diplomats, but His Majesty did not see fit to grant my wish, rather he prevailed upon me to enter the priesthood."

I nodded, suddenly regretting my own forwardness.

"Well," Ben interjected, rescuing me. "That you are seeking to buy property in Blackfriars forthwith would seem to indicate that your prior troubles are behind you. Perhaps if you had not been so intent on doubling London's population, your finances would not have been so stretched."

We all chuckled at that, even Donne. It was well known that Anne Donne had delivered a child every year since their marriage. They had nearly a dozen now. When Donne became dean of St. Paul's, some wag quipped that he would hardly have time for the job so busy would he be at getting more children. But at the time of which I write, that was still several years in the future.

"As I said, I do not know the specifics of any bequests, but I should think that the Blackfriars property will go to his daughter, Susanna. His wife has little interest in the city. And as it is one of the more valuable bits that he owned, he would want to keep it as far away from his new son-in-law, Thomas Quiney, as he could."

"This Quiney is something less than honest?" Jones inquired.

"Shortly before Will's death, Thomas was brought before the council to answer a charge of bastardy. Aye, and it was nearly on the eve of his marriage to Judith Shakespeare."

"Poor Will," Ben said sadly. "He wanted so much to have respectability. The last time I saw him, when Drayton and I went to Stratford, he was puzzled as to why Judith would marry such a scoundrel. Will decided finally that he must have wronged her in some horrible way for her to visit such scum on his family."

Now it was my turn to look askance at Jonson. Why would he care for these people to know that he had visited Will during his final illness? For I was fairly certain that the large visitor from London to New Place while Will lay ill had been Ben Jonson.

Something Hamnet had said to me returned. "Did Will seem frightened of Quiney?"

Jonson did not answer immediately. He cocked his head. "I would not say that Will was frightened for himself, but he seemed worried for Judith."

Children were famous for acting against the best interests of their parents. All knew this. Donne's face held a particularly severe look, thinking, probably, of how many problems his large brood would cause him.

Before the conversation could begin anew, two warders from the Tower entered the tavern. Pausing in the doorway for their eyes to grow accustomed to the dim light, they seemed to be scanning the patrons. Until...until their eyes lit upon our table.

"Reverend Donne?" one of the warders asked firmly, if politely.

The alarm growing behind John Donne's eyes was all too evident. "Aye. You have business with me?"

"Do not be concerned. Sir Francis Bacon, the Crown's Attorney General, and the Lord Chief Justice, Edward Coke, wish you to come before them and give evidence in their enquiry into the death of Sir Thomas Overbury."

Pointed looks were exchanged among all who sat about our table. Such a "wish" was more command than invitation, and we all knew it. But I, for one, could not see how John Donne could shed any light on the courtier's death, said to be caused by poison as he was imprisoned in the Tower. I thought I recalled that an earlier investigation had produced nothing new. Yet, here was another one, with Bacon and Coke.

Coke! The Lord Chief Justice of England. No judicial authority stood higher. I needed no Oxford education or reading by a Simon Forman to know that the decisions handed down by Coke would impact British jurisprudence for generations yet to come.

Donne went with the warders, casting a brief but telling look at the rest of us.

"Do not look so gloomy, Simon," Ben chided me. "Times are different now. A summons to the Tower no longer means that we will never see our friend again, not as it once did."

"What is this Overbury matter, Ben?" Inigo added. "I have been abroad."

My redheaded friend's face took on a sour look. "I know little enough. Thomas Overbury had been very close to Robert Carr, earl of Somerset, a favourite of the King's. Sir Thomas became incensed at the idea of Carr marrying Lady Frances Howard, and he made quite the fuss over it, privately and publicly. And I know that the king offered Overbury an ambassadorship, to get him out of the way, which he declined. That made James angry, and he confined Overbury to the Tower, from which he did not emerge. Later, someone suggested that he had been poisoned."

"And they are just now enquiring into the manner of his death, three years later?"

"The manner of his death is known. Poison. But who ordered it and who actually carried it out, that is at issue. Suspicion has fallen on Somerset and his countess. They are now in the Tower. I believe a trial is planned anon." The casual way Ben related this seemed practiced, and that bothered me.

"Still, three years is a long time," Inigo commented.

"It is," agreed Ben, shouting to Will Johnson for yet more ale. "Tell me, Master Jones. What took you away from our shores?"

The architect smiled and accepted the pot. "I was in Italy

with Lord Thomas Howard. In truth it was his enthusiasm for my work that earned my preferment from the queen. He has been a good patron, the kind a craftsman needs to succeed."

While Ben must have found this very interesting—he leant over the table and seemed to hang on every word—I thought it rather tedious, until the redhead kicked me under the table. I made to leave a couple of times, but Ben found some reason to delay our departure, usually a question designed to encourage Inigo to boast of his work. Finally, with my head swimming from ale, the architect announced that his labours called him and he left.

"Why was I subjected to hearing him praise his own work? I have enquiries to make."

"First, he is the most interesting architect in our lands today. Second, did you not understand who his patron is?"

"Lord Thomas Howard, the earl of Arundel. What of it?"

Ben shook his head. "You have lived too long in the country. The Howards are the main suspects in the Overbury Affair. For Inigo to pretend ignorance of it is laughable. He has just returned from traveling with Arundel. He surely heard about it every day."

I grimaced. Such knowledge was why I so badly needed a partner in my inquiries. The Howards were as plentiful as mosquitoes along the Thames. Indeed, Arundel was himself the grandson of yet another Lord Thomas Howard; this one was also the earl of Suffolk and the Lord Treasurer. While news of Overbury's death and the rumours of its cause had drifted up to Stratford, the details remained vague. But what could this have to do with Will's death? I said as much.

"I do not know," Ben admitted. "But it was about the time of Will's financial reverses that Overbury's problems started. And shortly after his death, Will had suddenly become prosperous once more. I need no university education to question the timing. More importantly, why did Inigo Jones lie?"

He had made some logical points, but I was not certain that they could be connected in a line to Will's death.

"Why would they wish to question John Donne?" I asked.

"One of Overbury's objections to the marriage was that Lady Frances was already married to Lord Essex. After Overbury died, the king arranged for Frances's previous marriage to be annulled and she was married to Carr. Donne, as I recall, wrote a poem on the occasion."

"So they would wish to know how much he might have known of Overbury's death. Much like Augustine Phillips was forced to give testimony after the Essex Affair."

Ben nodded. Then, strangely, his face turned grim. "What confuses me is why Southampton was so eager to warn you away. He is no ally of the Howards. Aye, he is jealous of their influence. Suffolk is his sworn enemy." Thomas Howard, first earl of Suffolk, was also Frances's father.

"Though," Ben continued, "I suspect that Suffolk's days of power are drawing to a close."

"Why?"

Ben shrugged. "This Overbury Affair for one thing, and rumours are afloat that Suffolk has badly misbehaved with the treasury, though I know no particulars. You know of the king's problems with Parliament."

"Everybody knows of that," I grunted.

"Whispers in Parliament suggest that Suffolk's misdeeds are in furtherance of the king's lavish spending. If that is true, it would provide an excellent reason for the king to ally himself with the Howards."

"But if Southampton is an enemy of the Howards, I would think that he would rejoice at my investigation?"

My friend shrugged. "I do not know. Perhaps he sees their star declining and wishes to curry favor. Perhaps his concern has nothing to do with the Overbury death. Or…"

"Or what?"

Hesitantly, he continued. "Or the rumours have some truth, that James was involved in killing Overbury. Southampton will do whatever he needs to do to protect King James. 'Twas the king who rescued Southampton from the Tower."

The import of what Ben Jonson had just said struck me with the force of a gale. "Powerful men," Southampton had warned.

No man in England was more important than the king, nor more powerful. "And Southampton would permanently secure his own preferment by protecting the king.

"Still," I went on, "the question that goes unanswered is what Will could have known that would have required his death. I confess that I do not see it. In the Essex Affair, there was rebellion afoot. Queen Elizabeth herself was in danger. The stakes were far higher." Elizabeth's favorite, Robert Devereux, the earl of Essex, had led a coup against her in 1601. Will, Burbage and the other shareholders in the Globe were pressured into a performance of *Richard II*, the conspirators hoping that the scene in which Richard steps down from the throne would help spark the crowd to join the coup. It did not.

"For a king, what is dearer? His life or his crown?"

Jonson was right, perhaps.

"The only way to find that out is to pursue the matter," I concluded.

"You realise, Simon, that you tempt the fates. And all for a man that you have come to hate."

His message was one that I had been thinking for some hours now. "It is not the man that I hated, but what he did."

"Is not that one and the same?"

"No," I argued, "I do not think it is. You do not spend a life loving a good friend and then decide that you hate him. It is the act of that friend that you object to, not the man himself. And I owe the friend that he was to learn the truth of his death."

I had started this quest trying to discover what sort of man my friend Will Shakespeare was. Now, a different sort of fire burned in my soul, the fire of a man outraged. Will Shakespeare's last days had been filled with pain and misery. Nothing he had done, even to me, begged that sort of death, and if it were truly caused by some role he played in Overbury's death, then he had died for nothing, for the nobles' pleasure.

"What will you do now?"

As he asked the question, I did not know the answer. But as he finished, the answer came to me unbidden.

"I shall speak to Bacon and Coke. Of all men, they should know of Will's involvement, if any."

"And you think that they will speak to you, the Attorney General and the Lord Chief Justice? You, an ordinary constable?"

"Yes, they will. Southampton will grease my path."

Chapter Six

THE DAYS HAD NOT YET GROWN LONG, AND I CHANGED FROM the Cross Keys to the George Inn in Southwark. I ignored the old innkeeper when he asked if I were returning to Stratford so soon.

The George is an ancient inn, well constructed for the traveler. The galleries surrounding the yard could only be accessed by interior stairways. Once I was situated at the George, Ben left to let his wife know that he yet lived, lest she begin to sell his belongings. Anne Jonson was a delightful woman who had no fear of her giant husband. And she took every opportunity to let him know that.

I told no one but Jonson where I was going to stay. If I were attacked at the George, it would be because I was being followed. And if that were the case, I could not rely on Ben forever. Indeed, if that were the case, I might have few breaths left to take.

WITHOUT JONSON at my side, I passed back over London Bridge, ducking occasionally to avoid the trash and waste water being flung from the upper floors of the houses. When I returned to Stratford, I would demand to be bathed in hot, clean water to scrub the stench of London from my pores.

I did not need Ben Jonson for this trip. I was going to Will's old lodgings on Silver Street, where he had let a room from Christopher Mountjoy, a tyrer, a maker of women's headdresses.

This was the matter that Burbage had mentioned. I knew little but that it had involved a betrothal and, some four years before, Will had been forced to return to London to give a deposition. Apparently he had earlier been pressed into service to arrange a marriage between Mountjoy's apprentice, a Stephen Belott, and Mountjoy's daughter. The apprentice was French as well. I did not like the French.

"So, the player is dead. Good riddance. *Au revoir* to him," old Mountjoy said in a crackling voice weighted heavily in his native accent.

The old man certainly was ill-disposed towards Will. But he hardly seemed capable of arranging his death. Aye, he seemed barely capable of avoiding his own.

"He was poisoned, Master Mountjoy."

The tyrer glanced at me and then hobbled across the shop to smack the hand of a young apprentice. "And you think I had some hand in that? Then you too are an *idiot*. You should visit my son-in-law, Belott. Shakespeare's deposition did his cause far more harm than mine."

His reply took me aback. "Then why do you hate him so much as to wish him dead?"

I thought for a second he would attack, so sharply did he turn his eyes on me. But then he shrugged. "What does it matter now? They are both dead."

"Who? Who else is dead?"

"My wife, you stupid man. The player was bedding her. 'Twas she that involved him in the betrothal. I saw little of him except when his rent was due. Until the day I found him bouncing in my bed with my wife. That was why I turned him out. First, it was that Forman *idiot* and then the player. *Mon Dieu!* She must have serviced half of Saint Olave's-at-Cripplegate!"

I would have paid good money to have spoken to Madame Mountjoy, but that was not to be.

For a moment, I felt as one with the old man. And I felt another thing.

He had no hand in killing Shakespeare. Mountjoy was just a

bitter man whose life had not gone to suit him, and, I suspected, Shakespeare's cuckolding him had simply added insult to the injury of his life.

I turned and left, even as old Mountjoy berated a poor apprentice, who had probably done nothing wrong but remind Mountjoy of another apprentice who had wronged him long ago.

Stephen Belott, Mountjoy's erstwhile apprentice, operated a tyrer's shop in St. Giles-without-Cripplegate, a ten-minute walk from his father-in-law's house. Mountjoy had been but a miserable old man. Belott had been far more successful, at least in his trade. I saw that immediately from the trim and neat appearance of Belott's shop front. This would demand a different approach.

I squared my shoulders and again entered the world of tyrers.

Tables ran around the room, filled with bobbin boxes, twisting wheels, spools of different gauges of wires. Tyrers used a stiff, coarse wire to form the frame for their complicated headdresses. That both Mountjoy and Belott were French was not surprising; it was a trade epitomized by French fashion.

Apprentices dashed about, some working the twisting wheels, some cutting and forming wire, some working with the precious silver and gold thread. The only sign of discord was a broken window.

"Who are you? What do you want?" A tall, middle-aged man advanced on me from the back of the shop. His accent told me that this was Master Belott.

"I am Constable Simon Saddler—" I began, but Belott waved me off.

"You are here to investigate my broken window. Well, you and I, *monsieur*, we both know who did it. I complain to the Privy Council about the horrible prices charged by those with the monopoly on gold and silver thread; their knaves come and break my windows. I complain about that and you arrive. And nothing is done. Why should I waste time with you?"

"I am not here about your broken window, Master Belott."

He stopped waving his hands. "Then why are you bothering me?"

"William Shakespeare was murdered in Stratford-upon-Avon. I am charged with investigating that murder. I know of his involvement in your lawsuit against your father-in-law."

Belott, a man with a perpetually sour face, grimaced even further. "My sympathies to his family. But what has that to do with me?"

"I seek his killer. And I understand that his deposition in your lawsuit did not advance your cause."

"His deposition was unimportant. I won my case."

"But you do not deny that it worked against you?"

"I do not deny that he failed to remember many details; who could have after so long a time? But he swore that there were such promises made. Others swore as to their content. Why should I wish to kill him?"

"Perhaps he took advantage of your wife as well as your mother-in-law." I swear that I do not know whence the words sprang. No one I had talked to had even hinted that Will had bedded the younger Mountjoy woman.

But rather than becoming enraged, rather than thrash me as he should have, Stephen Belott just laughed at me. "Perhaps he did. I have no idea. He swived every other woman in Saint Giles-without-Cripplegate and Saint Olave's."

"She was your wife! Care you nothing for the marriage vows?" I was the one incensed. Incensed beyond all reason.

Belott's smile cracked his sour face. "You are too old a man to be such a fool. The marriage was about the partnership with old Mountjoy and the dowry. I will not deny that I have enjoyed my rights as her husband, but I am sure that many others have enjoyed her as well. Her mother was the same way."

The French! I would never understand them.

Frustrated yet again, I turned to leave, but Belott's voice called me back.

"You would be better served to see old George Wilkins."

I turned. The name was familiar; someone had mentioned it in recent days. "Who is Wilkins?"

"He is a tavern owner. Marie and I stayed with him for six or eight months when Mountjoy refused to honour his promises."

"What has he to do with Shakespeare?"

"They were colleagues, it seemed. In playwriting or whore-mongering, I do not know which."

Then, I remembered. Something Burbage had said about Wilkins and Shakespeare working on a play together. And about Wilkins being a scurvy type.

"Where may I find him?"

"His tavern now is at the corner of Turnmill and Cow Cross streets, in Clerkenwell. I wish you good fortune, for if you go into that district, you will need it."

With those eerie words ringing in my ears, I started out immediately for the most notorious district of London.

'TWAS BUT a short walk, yet Clerkenwell was an eternity removed from St. Giles-without-Cripplegate. The signs of its decline were everywhere: broken windows, unrepaired latches, darkened houses, attesting to their vacancy. No shops greeted me along the narrow streets, only pubs and stews. Cutpurses lurked on every corner. If I escaped here with my life intact I would count myself lucky.

Wilkins's tavern was in a profitable location, at a busy corner. I entered the room, just now beginning to fill as night closed in around the city.

Finding an empty table was not yet difficult, and I slid into a seat. I cast about the dimly lit room but all that I saw were strumpets plying their trade and beaten-down men looking for a bit of pleasure. In one corner a man sat smoking some of that tobacco from the New World in a clay pipe. Instinct told me that he had stolen it from one of his betters.

A woman, more a girl actually, with heavy cosmetics, approached my table and leaned over. "What would you like?" Her hand squeezed my groin as if giving me a sample of the menu. I pushed it away, though I felt that familiar stirring.

"George Wilkins," I answered.

Her lips, painted a bright red, curled into a frown. "He can't do for you what I can."

"Perhaps not, but I wish to speak with him."

"Cor, you're from outside the city!" She draped her arm around my neck.

"You would wish me to think that you have never met anyone from the countryside? Please, my lady. Do not offend me. And," I continued, reaching up and grasping the back of her neck in my hand, "return my purse or I will break your neck."

With a clink, it fell on the table. "Now, go and fetch George."

She shook my hand from her neck and flounced off through a door in the back.

George Wilkins was truly of the lowest sort. A strange dark brown streak marked the left shoulder of his old doublet. That was where he wiped his dagger, and the brown stain was a mix, no doubt, of food and blood, some of it human. His black hair was greying, and a number of scars marked his wrinkled face. In one ear was a large, dangling earring.

"You seek me?" The voice matched his face, deep and gravelly.

"If you be George Wilkins."

He cast about, marking the patrons with his eyes, and then settled into the chair opposite.

"Aye. I am Wilkins. Who be ye?"

"Simon Saddler of Stratford-upon-Avon."

His thick eyebrows jerked skyward. "And your business?"

"The player Shakespeare is dead."

Wilkins shrugged. "I have heard. Good news travels quickly."

"Indeed? You consider it good news?"

"Shakespeare was a thief, and I am being kind. But if you are from Stratford, surely you must know this."

I chuckled. That someone of Wilkins's ilk would call Will a thief defied belief. "He was murdered. I was told that you are the sort of man capable of such."

And then it was Wilkins's turn to laugh, revealing blackened teeth. "You are direct. I like that. So you think I killed Shakespeare?"

"I think that you may well have had reason. Now that I have spoken with you, I see that I was correct. What was it that he stole from you?"

"My words, Master Saddler. It was I who truly wrote many of his greatest plays."

At that, I knew that Wilkins was as great a liar as he was a rogue. But that did not mean that he did not kill my friend. "In truth? You wrote *Lear* and *Macbeth*? How astonishing!"

Wilkins looked a little uncomfortable. "Perhaps not every word, but they would not have been half so great without my contribution. Upon that, you can rely. We wrote *Pericles* together. He often came to me for help."

"Forgive me, Master Wilkins, but are you not a victualler?"

"So what if I am? Your Master Shakespeare held gentlemen's horses when he first came to the city."

"Quite right. Allow me to be blunt, Master Wilkins. William Shakespeare was poisoned, and I believe that you could have had a hand in this. A man of your parts was seen recently in the lanes of Stratford."

"And you have an eyewitness that says it was me?"

"No," I admitted. "But that does not mean it was not you."

"It does not, as you say. Your Shakespeare angered many men, and women. Not just me. If you intend to question them all, you will be spending more than a few days in the city. I would plan on a few years."

"That is not the Shakespeare that I knew," I said in my friend's defense.

"Then you did not know the Shakespeare of London. He was conniving and crooked. Those who would kill him are legion."

"So you would have me believe. But I tend to think that you are just trying to obscure your own guilt."

Wilkins's eyes flashed. "You are a fool. Do you think that I will confess simply because you came here and asked? Take my advice, return to Stratford and trouble me no longer. I have nothing to say to you."

"And you are a pimp. And I do not need your leave to pursue my enquiry."

Wilkins jerked to his feet. "Perhaps not, but you may need my leave to stay alive. Get out!"

Two of his ruffians moved in from opposite corners. But

Wilkins waved them off with both hands. "Master Saddler knows the way out."

That this villain may have had a hand in ending Will's life sent a white heat searing through me.

With his hands outstretched, I took a gamble and kicked him in the groin, hard and square, taking two steps back quickly while a groaning Wilkins, his eyes bulging, collapsed to the floor.

The ruffians descended on me.

Almost.

They stopped short when a dagger magically appeared in my hand. I had been palming it in the last few minutes of talking to Wilkins, trying to decide whether to kill him on the spot or not. He would not be missed, and any high-born friends he had would be scrambling to deny him.

I backed out of the tavern slowly, with the other customers choosing to stay out of the fracas.

Once outside, I trotted a block away and stopped to catch my breath, keeping one eye on the tavern door. The day had ended some time before, and Clerkenwell was even more sinister at night.

I tensed, as the door swung open and a figure emerged.

Even in the darkness, I could see the swaying shadows of a kirtle. It was one of Wilkins's women, the one who had acosted me.

She glanced up and down the street, uncertain, but then turned in my direction.

Just as she was about to run past me, I reached out from the shadows and snagged her hand.

"You seek me, mistress?"

"Master," she said, her breathing jagged. "You take chances." In the dim light spilling from a nearby house, I saw that she had her own dagger at the ready. "You are a friend of Will Shakespeare's?"

"I am."

"And he is dead?"

"He is."

"Last month, a nobleman came to see George. They went to one of the rooms upstairs and George allowed no one else. But I took them a jug of strong beer, and I heard them discussing Shakespeare. Something about papers and that it might be too late. The next day, George left and was gone for six days. Last week, the noble came again. George left on the morrow and just returned yesterday."

"Why are you telling me this?"

Even in the darkness, I could see the twinkle in her eyes, or at least I thought I could. "The noble was Southampton. He comes here often. And they were discussing Shakespeare, and now he is dead. I needed little more."

I looked at her in earnest now. Beneath the horrid cosmetics, she was a pretty girl. Young. Too young for a life like this. "Whence came you?"

"You mean, how did I end up with Wilkins?" She paused, and for a second I feared that I had hurt her feelings. "My parents died when I was twelve. I was sent to live with an uncle, and before I had been in his house a fortnight, he began coming to my room and touching me. I did not know what to do, and he said that it was natural. His wife caught him one night; she beat me and said I had tempted him. He kept coming back, and she caught us again, and this time beat me harder. I ran away. Eventually, I found myself here. Is that what you wished to know?" Her tone was one of challenge.

"If you would like to leave this life, come to me in Stratford. I can find you work there in a decent home, if that would suit you."

She turned from me. "I am no longer fit for such work."

"You are fit for whatever you wish to do. My offer stands open. And thank you for your help." I looked at her carefully, seeing at last the girl beneath the paint. I pulled a crown from my pouch and pressed it firmly into her palm. An hour of pleasure in a stew could be had for twopence; the sum I had given her represented perhaps six months of what Wilkins would let her keep of that twopence.

Her eyes grew wide as she realized what her hand held. She stumbled backwards a step and then scampered back up the street and slipped into the tavern.

I leaned against the wall and thought about what she had told me. Could Southampton have conspired to kill Will? Why? In what damnable enterprise had he involved himself?

While I racked my brain, searching for an answer, I saw the door of the tavern open again. This time it was Wilkins himself who slipped out. I resolved to follow him. Undoubtedly, he was going to get counsel from his patron. Probably Southampton. And that might give me some leverage when I next faced the earl.

'Twas but a short walk to Southampton House, and that is exactly where Wilkins went. The guards at the gate did not even blink when the tavern owner brazenly walked straight through. Obviously, he was a frequent visitor.

And then a second man followed quickly on his heels.

My heart skipped a beat.

Ben Jonson.

I would have given half my wealth to know what those three were discussing. But I could see no way to eavesdrop. I did not know in which chamber they were meeting, and I was certain that if I tried to brazen my way in that I would find myself in a damp, dark gaol cell somewhere.

Suddenly, I was very tired. This day had been far too long already. There was little else that I could do. Even the walk back across the city to London Bridge and thence to the George seemed too tiresome a journey.

I found a simple tavern near Gray's Inn and let a chamber for the night. One of Will's muses touched me there. I took the chamber in the name of George Wilkins.

Chapter Seven

MY SECOND NIGHT IN LONDON PASSED MORE PEACEFULLY than the first. I did not find Ben Jonson waiting for me in my chamber. No assailant breached my door. But dreams of Will Shakespeare entwined with my Peg breached my sleep.

I rose early the next morning. Ben and I had made plans to meet at midday for a meal at the Mermaid. That was a meeting I longed for. By that time, I hoped to have seen Southampton again. The events of the previous evening had not changed my plans. Indeed, Southampton would find it very difficult to deny me my request. Bacon and Coke would give me what I needed because they had needs as well.

As I passed through the public room, I heard two men talking loudly about a fire. The very word struck fear in people. An unchecked fire could level the entire city.

"A fire?" Curiosity got the better of me.

One man looked up. "Aye, at the George in Southwark."

Though I tried to pretend nonchalance, my eyes could not help but grow wide.

"Do you know it?" he asked.

"Aye. When did it start?"

"After the midnight, in the southern wing. They caught it quickly though. It was confined to but a pair of chambers. Still, it killed one poor fellow."

"Who?"

"What did they say his name was?" the first man asked his fellow.

"Saddler, I think. From somewhere in the north."

A chill cut me to the bone. I knew then what course of action Southampton, Jonson and Wilkins had decided upon. The bothersome constable from Stratford needed to die. I wondered idly who the dead man was, but I had little time to spend on things I could do nothing about.

I nodded to the two men and emerged from the inn out into the same grey haze that always covered London. Though my feet moved me at a slow gait, my mind was busy, racing through all the possibilities before me.

It seemed clear now that Southampton, Wilkins and Jonson had conspired to kill Shakespeare, to keep him from revealing whatever he had known about the Overbury Affair. Jonson had probably administered the poison on his most recent trip to visit Will. Wilkins must have been the stranger from the city lurking about Stratford. They thought that they had resolved the matter permanently until I appeared, asking questions about Will's death, learning more, probably, than they wanted me to. So then I, too, had to be eliminated.

Whatever Will had done, it must have been critical to the success of the plot. Perhaps he had helped deliver poison to the Tower. Perhaps he had carried instructions to the warders.

A cold fury built within me. They had used Will and then killed him as they would any sort of creature crossing their path that annoyed them. William Shakespeare deserved better from this world he had entered, or any other world for that matter.

Poor Will! Had he known what he was involving himself in? Had his need for money been that great? I would have given him what he needed....

No, I would not have.

I would have turned him away.

And that realisation saddened me.

What had happened to us?

Then a reality struck home. I was dead. Or at least Jonson, Southampton and Wilkins thought so. I could use this with Southampton to bend him to my will. The nobles had others do their dirty work. If I appeared, alive, at his home, then he would panic. But he would not strike at me there. He would send messengers to his other conspirators, ordering them to finish the job. But if I judged him correctly, he would do whatever I asked of him, partly from shock and partly from a need to appear agreeable as if nothing were out of the ordinary.

These were the things that occupied me as I walked back to Holborn and Southampton House. Beneath the earl's anger and outrage was desperation. And desperation was a powerful motivator. Yes, he would not only see me, he would hurry to my aid. Dead men who are not dead do well as motivators.

And, as I had predicted to myself, I was rushed to Southampton's study where he sat, once more, at the small desk. Gone was the anger in his voice and manner, replaced with a naked expression of surprise, and a bit of fear, or so I thought. Hoping to build on that, I chose my words carefully.

"My lord, I have carefully considered your advice."

"I am pleased," he said, and struggled to seem to mean it. "I grew a bit frustrated yesterday. Please be assured that I mean only the best for you. I understand that you have your duty to perform, and I applaud you for your devotion to it. Would that more of our public officials cared so deeply."

"My lord, I have become aware of the present enquiry into the death of Sir Thomas Overbury."

Wait. Did I catch a flicker of panic in Southampton's eyes? Yes, and it was more than a flicker.

"Indeed," the earl said with a nod. "Bacon and Coke are conducting the investigation. It is a most serious matter."

"I have been led to believe that if Will's death is connected to London it is concerning that matter that would seem the most likely reason."

This time there was no missing the narrowing of Southampton's eyes. He was wary, and he did not respond.

"If your lordship would do me the favor of arranging an interview with Sir Francis and Sir Edward, I believe that I can satisfy my own enquiry, at least as to any London genesis for Will's death, and return to Stratford on the morrow."

He was not sure of his course. "You are here quite early this morning, Master Saddler," Southampton said, as his eyes gave him away. He did not know how to answer my request, and I could nearly see the thoughts flitting through his brain. To accede to my request could cause more problems than it solved. But it could also remove what he felt was an obvious threat, though I still could not fathom what secrets Will held that demanded his death. And, it was a simple enough request that to deny it would probably make me even more suspicious. Aye, I could see him considering that as well.

Telling him the truth of the evening before did not harm me. "I found myself quite near here late last night and I took a room at an inn nearby."

After a moment, the narrow slits that were his eyes softened and relaxed. He had decided. With a flourish, he snatched a quill and piece of parchment.

"I see your logic, and I think that these men will be as pleased as I at your diligence." The hard edge in his voice belied the amity of his words. He was not certain that this was the best move, but neither could he see a way out of it. Bacon and Coke were well known for the independence of their thinking. And Southampton did not know whether Will's name had arisen in their enquiry. I heard that in every word he spoke. "Perhaps," I could almost hear him say to Wilkins and Jonson, "this constable who is so damnably hard to kill can be used to further our goals."

He finished his note, folded it and with a practiced series of moves, dripped hot wax on and impressed his signet ring into it. Lifting it up and blowing to cool the wax, Southampton held it out to me with just a minute shudder of hesitation.

"Master Saddler, you are about to enter a world apart from that to which you are accustomed. Simple constables from Warwickshire seldom have cause to come before the likes of Francis

Bacon and Edward Coke. That you so readily seek such a meeting says much for your courage. I am certain that a man such as you sees hope in their reputations as honest, just men. Remember this: all reputation is just someone's opinion. And any opinion, anywhere, has little resemblance to the truth.

"I will offer you this: after our encounter yesterday, I was reminded of an incident at court several years ago, right after His Majesty released me from the Tower. You know that your countryman had something of a hand in His Majesty's new Bible?"

"I was not aware."

"His Majesty was not pleased with some of the work that was done. He trusted Shakespeare to set it right, but that was not widely known. I have heard that some of the official translators, most especially Thomas Harrison at Trinity, took great offence at Shakespeare's revisions."

This was something new. But I could not imagine religious scholars being driven to murder over such a matter. Then again, I knew little about such people. The laws and their fines dictated that we attend church, but if the truth be told, I had little interest in religion and less in the afterlife.

"What had he done to raise the ire of Harrison?"

Southampton waved the question away. "I did not care enough to find out, nor do I truly understand those people that do. I simply know that His Majesty was forced to call Harrison to court to calm him. See Lancelot Andrewes," he advised. "He might know what the furor was about. But I distinctly remember hearing Harrison calling for Shakespeare's death as a blasphemer."

WITH THAT, I was ushered out of Southampton House and back onto the road. Southampton had told me that I would find Bacon at Gray's Inn, back towards Newgate.

Ahead, in the crowded lane, I saw a cart approaching, carrying four women, their heads shaved: harlots, being punished for their trade. Most likely, they had given some courtier the Great Pox. Aye, Will once told me that many noblemen owned stews, places where whores plied their trade. Sometimes I wished that I had used such women. Perhaps it would have made Peg's betrayal hurt a little less. Perhaps not.

It took me but a short while to reach Gray's Inn along High Holborn. Walking alongside a low brick wall, I recalled something that Southampton had mentioned about the inn. It had been Bacon who built the wall, back when he was treasurer of the society. A member of the inn himself, Southampton said that of all the Inns of Court Gray's Inn was the oldest. Such claims, as far as I knew, could never be proven. At any rate, as I drew near the gate, I thought about what I had learned so far.

The confluence of Overbury's sudden death by poison, Will's unexpected windfall, and then Will's death, apparently by poison, spoke more loudly to me than anything. Add to that his unknown visitor from London, and I felt that this was the most fertile field in which I could plough. But the next step, once taken, could not be undone. These men were serious. They did not countenance fools.

Why was I there? Was I truly doing my duty as a constable? Or had Will simply caught me up in the masque that was his life? I did not know. All that I knew was that I had come too far to stop.

Moments later, after having given the note to Bacon's secretary, I found myself ushered into his presence.

SIR FRANCIS BACON was a clever man. Every bit the refined gentleman, rumour had it that he was the son of Queen Elizabeth and Robert Dudley. But, like the rumours of young Will Davenant's parentage, there was no way to prove it. Still, reports of ill health had marked him all of his life.

On this day, his cheeks seemed appropriately rosy as he sat studying some papers. He did not acknowledge my presence at first, but after a moment, he looked up and appraised me coolly.

"Have we met..." he glanced down at the note "...Master Saddler?"

"No, sir. We have not. I am a constable in Stratford-upon-Avon, enquiring into the death of the poet William Shakespeare."

Bacon blinked at me. "Why? I understand that he died of a fever some days ago."

"A week before his death, he called me to his bed and claimed that he was being poisoned."

At that, Bacon perked up. "Indeed?" He looked again at the note. "Saddler? Didn't a man by that name die in a fire at the George in Southwark last eve?"

I raised my eyebrows. "In truth? I was not aware." I pushed forward my response. "I did not give Shakespeare's claims much weight at the time, but a postmortem examination by his son-in-law John Hall, the physician, showed obvious signs of arsenic poisoning."

"Sit, Master Saddler," he indicated a chair with his quill. "This is troubling news. I was well acquainted with Shakespeare. Aye, I considered him a good friend. I thank you for bringing this to me, but why here? This is certainly a Stratford affair."

"I have learned that about the time of Sir Thomas Over-bury's death, Will came into a great deal of money. Then all was quiet until you and Sir Edward began your inquiry."

Bacon's expression grew stern. "Do you know why this en-quiry has been brought, so long after Overbury's death?"

"Not precisely, my lord. I assumed new evidence must have appeared."

"Rumours, Master Saddler. Rumours that the king himself had a hand in Overbury's death. He was forced to begin an en-quiry to quell them." He paused. "You seem intelligent. Perhaps you can be of service to Sir Edward and me."

My face flushed. Country constables did not get called to the service of men such as Bacon and Coke. "In what manner?"

"We are gentlemen, Saddler. We cannot simply speak with commons. They are ever on their guard. But a man of their own rank might coax important admissions from them."

A trickle of sweat grew under my collar. "Sir Francis, I am simply here to see if Shakespeare's death bears any connexion to his dealings here in London."

"You yourself drew the connexion in the timing, Constable Saddler. I see no reason for you to balk at pursuing that line."

"Would I be your and Sir Edward's servant in this?" In other words, would I have their authority?

"Without doubt, though," Bacon cleared his throat, "we would reveal such only in the case of absolute necessity."

And should I prove an embarrassment, they could just as easily disclaim any knowledge of me. 'Twas not a condition to be wished for. I should have listened to Hall, Smythe, and Southampton. But it was too late now.

"Sir Francis, you should be aware that two attempts have already been made upon my person."

He shrugged. "Then you should prepare for others." Someone stirred at the door and I turned to see Sir Edward Coke, the Lord Chief Justice of England, enter. I hurried to my feet, but Coke took no notice of me.

"Francis, we will be late for our hearing," his gravelly voice grumbled.

"This man is Constable Simon Saddler of Stratford-upon-Avon. He believes that the recent death of the poet Shakespeare by poison is related to our case."

Coke, the foremost jurist in all of England, raised his thick eyebrows. "Indeed? I did not know that he had died. How do you know that he was poisoned? And how could a simple player touch upon this matter?"

The jurist's disdain for me was unquestioned. He barely took notice of me.

"Edward, I believe he could serve a purpose for us. We need someone to draw answers from the commons. He seems a likely sort for such a chore. We have but a month before the trial, and he may be our best, last chance."

Blood rushed into my face. I did not like being spoken of in such a manner. "I will accede to your request, gentlemen, but only because it seems the surest way to discover who killed Will Shakespeare."

I was not quite taking my life in my hands with my tone, but I was not far away.

Bacon and Coke drew back in both surprise and outrage. For a minute, I expected Bacon, especially, to have me arrested.

But then Coke exploded in laughter, respect creeping across his face.

"By all the saints, Francis! I think we have found an honest man!"

"An insolent one, for certain," grumbled Bacon. "Still, he will serve us well, I think."

"If I am truly an honest man," I said, "then I will serve the truth well."

"Just see that you perform your chores."

"And what would they be, Sir Francis?"

"I assume you read?" Bacon asked.

"Aye."

He scribbled something on a bit of paper. "Find these men, buy them drinks, get them to talk."

"About what?"

Bacon looked to Coke who spoke. "We know that Sir Thomas was poisoned. We need to know who administered it. These men are warders at the Tower. They should know, but they have lied to us for fear of execution. You are of about their age and station. They may open up to you."

"So you wish me to be a spy?"

"Call it what you will," Bacon snapped. "Just do it."

"But what of my own investigation?"

Coke coughed. "If you help us, you may find the answers you desire. To this date, Shakespeare's name has not arisen. But what you say bears further investigation." He paused. "You say Shakespeare himself alerted you?"

"Aye."

"Did he say how the poison was being administered? Do you know if he was purged?"

"He did not say. But his son-in-law, John Hall, saw to his treatment and would know. Hall keeps detailed notes of all of his cases."

Coke and Bacon exchanged pointed glances, and I wondered at what they portended. "I have heard of this," Bacon said. I was not surprised; Bacon had wide-ranging interests. "And you think that Hall kept notes on Shakespeare?"

"I know that he did; I saw them myself—"

"But you did not enquire further of him," Coke interrupted.

"No. Quite honestly, my lord, I did not believe Shakespeare enough then to ask for more details. I believed it to be the ramblings of his dying mind."

Bacon shook his head. "Even the mind of a dying Will Shakespeare was far more nimble than that of a country constable. He traveled with me abroad once as my secretary, you know, when the plague had closed the theatres."

I nodded. "He told me of it. Will's mind was ever eager for such experiences."

"And too often they reappeared in his plays," Bacon grumbled.

"You will have deduced, Master Saddler," Coke interrupted, "that the earl of Somerset and his wife, the countess, will be tried next month at Westminster Hall for their part in Overbury's death. The case against them is far from compelling, and we have little time to make it so. A man named Weston has already been convicted and executed for serving Overbury poisoned food, but he did not act alone. Someone was directing his actions."

"And why would the earl and countess have any interest in this?"

"They wished to marry then. But Overbury was close to Somerset and objected. With Sir Thomas out of the way the wedding could proceed."

My ignorance of the nobility must have been frustrating to Coke and Bacon. "How did King James become the target of rumour?"

Again, Bacon and Coke exchanged knowing glances. "The king favoured the marriage, reluctantly, but Overbury was powerful. And, quite honestly, His Majesty did not care for the man."

"But surely these rumours could be dismissed as nonsense."

"These are uncertain times," Coke said. "Even frivolous rumours cannot be left unanswered. Let me explain to you how important this matter is to His Majesty. He said to me in no uncertain terms, 'Spare neither sex, nor honour, nor degree, place nor persons till you come to the root.'"

That was plain enough. "And you believe that one of the men on this list can offer evidence that will implicate Somerset and his wife to the exclusion of the king?"

Bacon nodded enthusiastically. "Exactly, Master Saddler."

I rose. "How may I reach you when I have something to report?"

Both men shrugged. "Simply call on us here. We are jurists; you are a constable," Coke answered. "It might be helpful to both our causes if you couched your questions in terms of your enquiry into Shakespeare's death."

"I doubt that warders of the Tower will have information relative to his poisoning, but I take your meaning."

Bacon stood then and clapped me on the back. "Your success will not be forgotten and, with good fortune, you will resolve both your problem and ours."

As I turned and left the chamber, Coke's voice echoed behind me. "Watch behind you, Master Saddler. The next time it may not be an arsonist trying to burn you in your bed."

MINUTES LATER I was back in the road outside of Gray's Inn, fighting the crowds and considering my unsettling interview with Bacon and Coke.

I had come to London to try to discover who killed William Shakespeare, yet now I was manipulated into being an agent for the Lord Chief Justice of England and his jurist partner in a different murder that seemed tangled in the garments of the king. What had I done? And why had I so readily done it?

I had gone to see them to gain information from them. Now, it seemed that they had turned the tables on me. That they knew much was obvious. Little, it seemed, escaped them.

I did not think that I had been intimidated by the pair, but perhaps that was just my own *amour-propre* seeking salvation. Perhaps I was more provincial than I thought.

An hour later, at the Mermaid, Ben Jonson said, "Of course you are a provincial."

Chapter Eight

"HOW COULD YOU THINK OTHERWISE?" JONSON WAS truly amused. I ignored him and took up my beaker. On my way to the Mermaid, I decided that it was wiser to keep Jonson close about me. I did not fear him physically, but the more often he was in my company, the less time he would have to plot my demise. But he was a complicated man, and when I appeared, as if risen from the grave, he showed no sign of surprise.

"He is right," Richard Burbage added. Richard had come across from Southwark on one of the myriad of wherries plying the river. He seemed stronger today.

"And you pair would be as out of place in Stratford as I am in London," I said finally.

"Not exactly," Jonson said. "We frequently travel in the country when the plague strikes the city. We are not so unused to country customs."

"There is a difference, Ben Jonson, between living in a place and visiting there. Much is forgiven visitors that is not tolerated in residents. But that is not important."

"No," Burbage agreed. "What is important is why you agreed to involve yourself in this madness." To punctuate his mood, Richard slammed his tyg, a many-handled drinking mug, on the table. I never really understood the vessel; a tankard only needs one handle. "Do you not realize that involving himself with these same people may have led to Will's death? Yet, here you are, diving in head first. No good will come of this!"

Ben Jonson's response was to rip the list of names that Bacon had given me from my hands. He motioned to a ne'er-do-well sitting at a nearby table. Ben read him the list and whispered something in his ear.

"He will return soon with the whereabouts of these men, but I know one of them. He is a good man but afraid of his own shadow. Words will not come easy for him."

I glared at Ben. His arrogance was hard to take in more than small bites. And I was not certain that I wanted him present when I attempted to question these men. After the events of the previous evening, his deep interest in this matter could scarcely be written off to grief over Shakespeare. At least I found that hard to believe. And if I were to truly pursue this matter, I would not stop with just the list that Bacon and Coke provided.

As if reading my mind, Ben abruptly rose. "I have duties to perform, Simon. I will find you later."

I was left with the dour and morose Richard Burbage. Suddenly, even as I turned back to him, I felt a hand on my arm.

"Be careful of Jonson," Richard warned. "When Somerset and the Howard girl were married, 'twas Ben that wrote the masque. If Will had some hand in the death of Overbury, Ben profited from it. And so did Donne, who wrote a sonnet on the occasion."

"By all that's holy, Richard! Is there no one in London that does not have a stake in this matter?" I paused for a moment, wondering how much I should trust Burbage. Telling him of what I had learned the night before seemed foolhardy. Better to test his thoughts. "Do you really think that Ben could be some agent in all of this? I will admit that the thought had crossed my mind."

The old actor chuckled. "Then you are not without hope. Did Will tell you much of how affairs stood with the old queen?"

I shook my head. "We were more interested in drinking and carousing among the stews."

"Life was difficult for players and the companies. Half the time we were considered a plague on the land. Elizabeth herself was rather amused by us, I think. But the Puritans worried her like a fever. Sir Edmund Tilney, Master of the Revels, did what he could for us, but Elizabeth was loath to alienate any faction, especially one as powerful and numerous as the Puritans."

"Your point?"

"A new wind blew across the country when James took the throne. Suddenly, we were no longer the Lord Chamberlain's Men but the King's Men. And we were made a part of the king's household, given the right to wear scarlet. We marched in his coronation parade. Our performances at court more than doubled. And we reveled in it. But it came with a price.

"A king's patronage is a dog that must be constantly fed or it will bite most savagely. And though this is the only king of my experience, I believe that this is more true of James than any other. And those who have tasted the king's favour are sometimes asked to do things in return. So it was with Will; so it is with Jonson. You know that the king is considering a pension for him."

"Southampton mentioned it."

"Then there is little else I can tell you. Ben Jonson enjoys privilege as much or more than others. Sometimes, I am certain, the tasks he performs rub against him roughly, but he closes his eyes and swallows whatever bitter potion has been served him."

I made to protest; this was very nearly treasonous talk. But Burbage raised a hand to stop me.

"I have been at court. You have not. I have seen the excesses. Do you not know who Somerset is?"

"A noble, and a powerful one at that. What else is there to know?"

"Robert Carr was James's favourite for many years. But I tell you, Simon, no wife has had a more affectionate husband than James was to Carr." Burbage shuddered. "I tell you, I have not seen such displays in all of my life, not in public."

"Are you suggesting…"

Burbage nodded. "Before you protest, I know that it is

illegal, but it is also not unusual. Many courtiers are known to engage in sodomy. Bacon among them. They are discreet. And while I cannot swear that James has known Carr in such a way, it would not surprise me. And now to my point: James would have stopped at nothing to please Carr. And Overbury was in the Tower to begin with because he refused the offer of an ambassadorial post by the king. Some said that James only proffered it because he knew that Sir Thomas would reject it, thus giving the king a reason to imprison him. James is said to have been horribly jealous of Overbury."

"Were Overbury and Somerset..." I paused, searching for the words.

But Burbage understood and shrugged. "Perhaps; only they know for certain, and Overbury is beyond bearing witness. But Overbury did oppose Somerset's wedding, and everyone of influence wished Overbury out of the way. He was a most dislikable man."

"Both Coke and Bacon said plainly that it was rumours of the king's involvement in Overbury's death that caused them to investigate the matter further," I said. "Coke said that the king instructed them not to allow any barriers in their quest."

"What else would he say? If he were involved, he would hardly confess it to the men he appointed to find justice."

Burbage smiled wearily. "James has another favourite now. He will not hesitate to throw Carr to the wolves to keep suspicion in the Overbury matter from falling on the crown. But he must tread carefully. Were Carr to attempt to confuse the issue by bearing witness against King James, it could be very embarrassing."

"I am not a total innocent, Richard. I know that intrigue is an everyday part of life at court. But this is surely a most sordid tale."

"Ha!" Burbage scoffed. "It is not even the most notorious! Strip off your naïveté, Simon. Discard the cloak of your blindness. Even great men, especially great men, are rarely unblemished." For a moment, I caught a glimpse of the man who first played Will's greatest characters—Lear, Macbeth, Hamlet.

"So what do you advise?"

"Run, Simon. Run back to Stratford. Say a prayer for me at Will's grave and live out the rest of your life in peace."

"And what of Will's murder? What of justice?"

"Whatever happened to Will, he brought it on himself. Close the door on that chamber of your life."

WHY I would not take Burbage's sage advice, I could not say. But the next hour found me abroad in the city, walking and musing. The ever-present cloud that hung over the buildings dampened my mood deeply, but I headed across the bridge and into Southwark. While I brooded, I thought of Southampton's advice about the cleric Lancelot Andrewes. Burbage had told me that he lived in Southwark, in the Liberty of the Clink. I did not know exactly where he lived, but a pair of well-placed queries brought me to his door.

It was a modest house, less ostentatious than those of similar prelates in the Church. I knocked on the door, and a white-haired old servant bade me enter.

"The bishop is just arising from his noon-day nap, Master Saddler. He will be down in a moment."

Lancelot Andrewes was one of the most well-respected clerics in all of England. In the business of the king's new Bible, he had led the first Westminster company of translators and, many said, was the presumptive leader of all translators.

I hardly had time to consider my surroundings before the bishop bustled into the room.

"Master Saddler! I have long wished to meet you!"

And this took me aback.

"You have?"

"Oh yes," he confirmed, ushering me to a seat. "Your friend, Will Shakespeare, spoke often of you."

"Forgive me, Bishop, but Will was hardly a religious man."

"True, true. But he was my neighbour here in the Liberty for a time. We spoke daily."

"Then you had a hand in his appointment by the king to work on the new Bible?"

Andrewes nodded. "I did. But it cost me much trouble."

"Harrison?"

The old bishop nodded again. "William had a prankster's nature. He took some liberties in his work on the Psalms, liberties that Thomas Harrison objected to most vehemently."

"What sort of liberties?"

Lancelot Andrewes smiled, revealing blackened teeth. "William was not among those translators named by the King. But after he was asked to help, he wished to leave his mark, so he manipulated Psalm Forty-six to hide his name within it. Harrison discovered it and came to me in a rage."

"A rage, Bishop? I would not think that prelates of the Church would react so violently."

"Then you are most certainly a recusant, Master Saddler, for clerics are passionate about their beliefs." His chuckle stole the venom from his accusation. "Thomas came here from Christ Church, denouncing all players but most especially Master Shakespeare." Andrewes paused, chuckling behind his hand. "I remember it so well. He marched in, shouting and waving some papers. I thought he would die from a seizure, so upset he was.

"I swore to him that I would speak to Shakespeare and set about correcting the text, but I thought it was a harmless jest."

"Did you speak to Will? Did you erase his transgression?"

"Of course I spoke to him, but I changed nothing. I simply told Thomas that the pages had already been typeset and could not be altered. But, I told William of Thomas's anger, and that I thought it best for him to keep his distance. William was even then readying his affairs to return to Stratford, so that cost him little more than annoyance."

"Would you consider Harrison capable of murder?"

Andrewes chuckled again. "Thomas is a courageous man, a champion of Christ and the Church. He would kill in their defense, but as a warrior, not as an assassin."

I liked Lancelot Andrewes, and I trusted his word. After a few more pleasantries, I thanked him for his help and returned again to the cacophony of noises and odours that was London.

UNSURE OF what to do next, I turned towards the Tower, hoping that just looking at its massive walls would somehow provide me with answers. The answers certainly lay within.

"Look what we have here, Arthur."

I could not mistake the voice. The rough tone spoke of years of drink. I turned, and the ragged, dirty clothes, smelling of sour wine told the story better than words. Chance had thrown common criminals in my path, a path I now realized had led me down a narrow side lane. In my reverie, my legs had carried my body where I could be easily dispatched.

Three men faced me. They had obviously selected me because my clothes indicated both that I was from outside the city and that I had more than two coins to rub together.

I did not have a sword with me, only my simple dagger. It would not be the first time that I faced such odds, but it had been a long time since those days. Little use would be served by shouting for help; above us I could see a window or two open with the citizens hanging out, watching to see me killed or beaten.

So, I slipped my dagger from my belt and beckoned my attackers forward with the tip. If they thought me an easy target, I would disabuse them of that notion at once. A bit of bravado might cut the odds.

And it did.

By one.

The older of the three dropped his dagger. "It ain't worth getting killed over," he groused before turning and running.

The other two, younger men, just grinned with rotten teeth and moved forward, one flashing his own dagger and the other a cudgel.

I reappraised them. They were hardly yet men. And they saw before them a man in his late middle years, not a grave threat.

They thought.

Dagger moved in quickly, trying to draw my attention away so that Cudgel would have a clear shot.

I stooped and snatched up a handful of mud, flinging it in Dagger's face and sidestepping quickly.

Dagger clawed at his eyes to clean the muck, and Cudgel's blow slipped past my head, close enough that I could feel its breath.

Seizing the moment, I stepped into Cudgel, sinking my dagger beneath his ribs as deep as I could. The surprise in his eyes was short-lived as they quickly grew blank and waxy.

But even as I breathed a sigh of relief, I felt Dagger's point sink into my arm. Without thinking I brought my knee hard into his groin, sending him reeling into the road.

I considered dispatching him then and there, but I decided not. Dagger, seeing the reprieve in my eyes, regained his feet and scampered away, still half-bent over from my last blow.

Since a fine stream of blood was already soiling my sleeve, I wiped Cudgel's blood on it. Blood pitted a knife blade badly if left.

Behind me, I heard a loud clapping of hands, not from many but from a single soul.

"Well done, Master Saddler! Well done!"

Ben Jonson.

I turned and the redheaded giant was smiling broadly. "You are a bit late for the brawl, Ben," I quipped. "Or were you watching to see if your agents would succeed in killing me?"

Jonson put on his most wounded expression. "Simon, what would it profit me to have you dispatched?"

My turn to smile. "Why, Ben, I suppose that it would pay about as much as you made writing the masque for Somerset's wedding to Frances Howard."

The teasing, mocking expression on Ben's face disappeared as quickly as it appeared. "Do you truly think me an agent?" He stepped forward as he spoke, to emphasize the difference in our sizes.

"What am I to think? You appear as if by magic at the Cross Keys, even as I was beginning my quest. You are about to be awarded a pension by King James, who, it seems, has a personal interest in the coming trial of the earl and countess. And now you are here, when I told no one my plans, and you arrive just in time to see me attacked by three men. Again, Ben, what am I to think?" Then was not the time to reveal all that I knew.

Jonson laughed. "Yes, I am hoping for a pension from the king. Yes, I was paid to write a masque for Somerset's wedding, just as Donne wrote a sonnet on the occasion. Burbage will tell you that I saw him at the Globe the day you arrived. And he told me of your purpose and that you were staying at the Cross Keys. As to my sudden appearance here, I stopped to find you at the Mermaid, but you had left. Thinking you might have gone to the Globe with Burbage, I was walking along East Cheap to the bridge when I happened upon two lads shouting about a fight. Much to my amazement, it proved to be you."

"Amazing coincidence." My sarcasm was heavy and unavoidable, but it was yet too early to let him know what I knew about his nocturnal adventures. He lied, too, as that route would not cross my path.

"You have not lost your edge, old friend. You fought as well today as all those years ago in the Low Countries." He paused. "Will never knew that you and I knew each other in those days, did he?"

I shrugged. "I never found reason to tell him."

"We know each other in ways that other men do not. No man knows himself until he faces mortal combat. We have. We have fought the enemy side by side. That creates a bond, Simon, that the bribes of even a king cannot breach."

I narrowed my eyes at him. "That is a pretty speech, Ben. But gold is like a flood that can breach the strongest dam."

Jonson's eyebrows flew up. "You have something of the poet in you, I see. Rest easy that I am not acting in the service of anyone but myself, and that I wish for you only success."

His words seemed so warm and assuring, but knowing what I knew, they rang all the more hollow. I could not trust Ben Jonson. Of that, I was certain.

"I am going to the Tower. Join me."

"And what shall you do at the Tower, pray?"

"I intend to speak with Somerset and his wife." I had not had the slightest inclination to do this before I was assaulted, but now it seemed the proper thing to do, if Jonson went with me.

And Jonson frowned at the idea. "Think you that you will even gain entry?"

"Aye, I believe I will. I will simply use the names of Bacon and Coke. And if that does not work, I will have the warders send a messenger on a fast horse to Gray's Inn. Upon that messenger's return, I doubt that we will be kept waiting."

I had succeeded in surprising Ben. Whatever his true interest in this affair, he had little choice now but to join me and see what havoc that I wreaked. "But know this: twice now I have been set upon by ruffians. You have been present both times. Coincidences like that do not escape me.

"And last night someone tried to burn me in my bed at the George. By sheer good fortune, I was elsewhere."

At that, Ben's head snapped back as if struck. He had not been so shocked at my resurrection from the dead when he first saw me at the Mermaid. And the thought struck me that Ben Jonson knew who the poor unfortunate was that had burned in my place. That was a fleeting thought at best, and I could place no weight on it.

"There are things you do not know," he began cryptically.

"Then why do you not educate me?"

"Enough of this, Simon. If you are intent on going to the Tower, then let us be off. Wasting time here dueling with words profits no one."

I did not press the issue. Since learning of the fire, my goal had been twofold—pursue my enquiry and unsettle my enemies. I felt confident that I had met with success on both fronts.

"You may delay me all you like," I told the warder at the main gate of the Tower. "I will stand here until this time three days from now. Send a rider to Bacon and Coke at Gray's Inn. They will verify that I am in their service on this matter. Of course, you will incur their wrath and your days in authority here may well be at an end."

After another bout of head-scratching, the warder let us pass.

Jonson eyed me closely. "I thought they preferred that you not announce your connection with them."

"I encountered a situation in which I disagreed with them. And since I am the one with his neck on the axeman's block, I will set the rules." My stomach fluttered though, at flouting Bacon and Coke's instructions. Until I knew for certain where Ben Jonson stood in this matter, I would show only strength before him. And I had decided, for better or worse, to go to the heart of the matter.

THEY WERE in the Bloody Tower. Somerset himself was in the chambers previously provided to Sir Walter Raleigh. The countess was in adjoining rooms. The lieutenant of the guard had scurried up and taken over our escort.

"What will you ask them?" Jonson said under his breath as we climbed the narrow, winding staircase.

"For the truth, Ben. What else?"

"Please, masters," the lieutenant said. "Wait here while I speak to the earl."

So we stood in the hallway, avoiding each other's gaze and waiting for the prisoners to grant us entry.

"Masters?" The lieutenant motioned from the doorway.

The earl of Somerset, Robert Carr, was a small, dainty man of cultured good looks, not unlike Bacon. Indeed, some would call him "pretty," but not handsome. Despite his reduced circumstances, he found himself able to paint a smile onto his features.

"I am honoured at your visit, Master Jonson. And this must be Master Saddler, the constable from Stratford who is stirring up such a fuss. Indeed, I was told just this morning that you were dead. Yet here you are, alive and well and an agent of Sir Francis and Sir Edward."

That he knew so well who I was took me aback for a moment. "You honour me, my lord. 'Tis seldom that a simple man from the countryside is known by one of your stature. My death was merely a case of mistaken identity. That you should know of my visit with your judges says a good deal about your network of agents throughout the city."

Carr smiled an endearing smile, and I could readily see why he was so popular at court. "For a man who has only been in London two nights, you have quickly become the talk of the city. I have had three or four reports of your activities so far, beside that of your death, that is."

His candour was disarming. It was quite simply difficult to dislike him.

"I will be blunt, my lord. I am seeking an answer to who poisoned William Shakespeare. That it has brought me to you is more coincidence than design."

Somerset laughed. "Why, Master Saddler, it seems that I am the favorite suspect in every poisoning in England at the moment. But, I assure you, I have been locked up here for months, and I have been nowhere near Stratford-upon-Avon. So, while I welcome your visit, I think that it will not bear fruit for you."

"That may be true, my lord, on both counts, but you are not without resources here. An agent of yours, perhaps?"

At that, Somerset ceased laughing, and his voice took on almost a giggle, a nervous one at that. "What would it profit me to have Shakespeare killed? I barely knew the man. Whilst his poetry was certainly a thing of beauty, I knew him more as an errand boy. Why, I know Jonson here much better."

"And Ben Jonson visited Stratford and Shakespeare just before he fell ill from this poisoning." I had not planned to state my suspicions so plainly, but Somerset's reply had opened a door and beckoned me enter. "Understand me, my lord. I do not care who killed Thomas Overbury. His passing bothers me not a whit. My quest centers on William Shakespeare, but if I must unravel one killing to solve the other, then so be it."

"You go too far, Simon," I heard Jonson say behind me.

I spun to look at him; his features were contorted in anger. "Aye, so do you, Ben. You may think you are royalty, but I hazard nothing by striking you."

"Enough of this!" Somerset shouted, the confidence suddenly returned to his voice. "Master Saddler, I know nothing of how Overbury died nor anything of how Master Shakespeare died. When this silly trial opens in two weeks' time, I will be proclaiming my innocence for all who can hear. Go back to your masters, Bacon and Coke, and tell them that! I know things that they would not wish revealed."

"As you like, my lord. But we shall be talking to the countess before we depart."

Somerset's face turned a bright crimson. "You will not! She is my wife and I forbid it."

"My lord, you are a prisoner," I reminded him, "and in no position to forbid anything." At that, I called for the warder.

Once in the corridor, Jonson, who had been silent, looked at me with something approaching respect.

"You are an unusual man, Simon. You have just made a powerful enemy. If you are still alive by week's end, you might have great things before you."

"I care nothing for that. I want only to find who killed Will. Somerset knows more than he is saying. You know more than you are saying. But I will not be blockaded in my efforts."

"Perhaps not, if you live long enough. I will tell you this: about the time that Will had his reversal of fortunes, I happened upon him writing something in the tiring house at the Globe. I asked him if it were a new play, but he became very agitated and covered it so that I might not see it."

"Was that customary?"

Jonson shrugged. "Not in my experience. Will and I wrote plays differently, so we rarely kept ideas or plays in progress from each other. Besides, collaboration is a part of our world. Some would argue that it is collaboration that makes so many great plays. I would not argue that, however. But all of that is unimportant. Will was not working on a play, and this was just before or just after he removed to Stratford."

No true surprise there. Ben had never been one for sharing applause. Before I could pursue that, the warder returned with permission to see my next target.

Frances, countess of Somerset, was a truly a beauty. She was every bit as pretty as her husband. "You are this constable of whom my lord speaks so often lately?"

"I am a constable, my lady, of Stratford-upon-Avon, here enquiring into—"

"Yes, yes. You are asking about the death of the poet Shakespeare," she interrupted me impatiently. This was a woman who brooked no delays. "'Tis pity he is dead, but hardly a reason to place your own life in jeopardy."

Her words bespoke a familiarity that surprised me. "You knew Shakespeare?"

She smiled, her eyes twinkling mischievously. "What woman at court did not know him, intimately?"

"Noblewomen?"

The countess laughed loudly this time. "Think you that we are made differently than common women? We simply have more advantages. Shakespeare seduced us all with his poetry and his skill."

Her candour was more than amazing; it was scandalous.

"I shock you? Why? I am already imprisoned on a charge of murder. Why should I seek to hide lesser sins? I fear you disappoint me, Master Saddler."

"William Shakespeare was murdered by the same method that you and your husband used to kill Sir Thomas Overbury. I believe that this was done to keep him from revealing your complicity in Overbury's murder." I intended to show her that candour was not hers alone.

The countess, her bodice tightly pushing up her bosom until it seemed about to explode from its confines, narrowed her piercing eyes at me. "And how would your poet know of my complicity in anything?"

At that, it was my turn to laugh. "Why, my lady, you have already admitted to lying with him. Many are the confidences revealed between the sheets."

She dropped her head and shook it. "Master Saddler, we did little talking."

I needed no mirror to know that my face was a bright, shining red. "Perhaps not. But Master Shakespeare came into a great sum of money about the time that Overbury died. Do you know aught of that?"

And now the crimson spreading in her face showed that I had hit my target.

"I was not concerned with his money, only his virility."

"Such is a facile answer."

"'Tis the only one that you will receive." She paused and turned. "I have tired of this. Go and trouble me no more."

"This did not seem so much a trouble," I said.

She looked back at me. "Master Saddler, allow me to offer some advice. If you continue to walk the path you are on, you will soon be buried next to it. I do not know who killed Shakespeare. And I do not want to know. That knowledge would put me in worse danger than I already am."

Worse than standing accused of murder? That seemed hardly likely. But I realized that I would get nothing more from her. At least on that day. For a wonder Ben Jonson had not uttered a single word. That deserved some consideration as well. It had almost seemed as if he were afraid of the countess. While she was definitely a woman of substance, and I recognized that in her world she was a woman of great beauty, beneath the ceruse and vermilion lay an ugliness that broke the beauty into hard edges. She was not for me.

Ben kept his silence as we departed the Bloody Tower and then the castle itself. But once out of the gates, he turned to me. "Simon, you came here, I thought, to find if Will's death had its genesis in London. Yet now you are bashing about through the homes of nobles, involving yourself in affairs that seem to have no connection to Will. And you are doing so angrily, as if all of these people bear some guilt."

"They do. You all do. He came to London a good lad, bright, in love with words. He returned a wastrel, corrupted by the stews and fleshpots of London, a stranger to the very morals he carried with him to the city. As children we enjoyed tweaking the noses of the nobles. As a man, Will danced to whatever tune they played. Tell me, Ben Jonson, why should I not be angry?"

"This is but so much sophistry, Simon," Ben argued. I caught a hint, but just a hint, of panic in his voice. "You have a better chance of finding Will's killer in Stratford than here."

"I have repeated this too many times already, but let me paint the portrait for you again. Will is overextended about the time or just prior to Overbury's death. Suddenly, Will has plenty of money, more than enough to recoup his fortunes. And Overbury dies. You yourself witnessed him working on something that he was hiding most earnestly. Now, as Somerset and his wife are to be tried for Overbury's murder, Will is himself murdered by the same method. It strikes me as someone ridding themselves of witnesses."

Slowly, grudgingly, Ben nodded. "To prevent you from again accusing me of hiding things, I will tell you this: I did not like Overbury. Indeed, I despised him. He was a sodomite and an overbearing dolt who pretended to be a poet. And I did not care who knew. Somerset would instinctively have turned to me for help in ridding himself of the buffoon, not Will."

Just as Southampton had when he decided that I needed to be eliminated, I thought but did not say.

But if Ben were correct, then there was truly a flaw in my logic. Simply because Ben Jonson said it, did not make it true. Time and time again in our acquaintance, Ben had lied to better his position or others' perception of him. In most men, this would be cause to dislike him, but Ben was not most men. And his braggadocio was accepted. Yet that still did not make it true.

"Assuming that you are correct, there must have been other related secrets that Will was privy to."

"Now you are reaching, Simon. Were it not for John Hall confirming that Will had been poisoned, I would think you had imagined all of this." He paused. "You and I fought battles together, side by side, so I say this in the spirit of brothers in arms. Are you certain that you are not seeking someone besides Will to blame for cuckolding you?"

The fury in me threatened to explode.

I drew back my fist and faced Jonson.

To my surprise, he stumbled backwards.

"How do you know about that?"

The big redhead blinked. "He told me when I last saw him. Simon, I believe that he regretted that more than anything in his life. You were more brothers than friends. It was an act done in haste, without proper thought. And he hated himself for having done it."

"Easy to say after you have tasted the nectar."

"Enough, Simon!"

I looked to the sky, covered though it was by the perpetual grey fog of smoke. The afternoon was all but gone. I had done enough for this day. "I am going to the George, Ben, to see if they have another chamber for me. To eat, to drink, and to sleep. Join me if you will and let us not speak of Somerset or Overbury or Will. I am heartily tired of nobles and their follies. Let us talk of the Low Countries and the friends we left there."

But that was not to be.

Chapter Nine

WHILE I WAS NOT SURPRISED TO SEE RICHARD QUINEY at the George upon our arrival, I was surprised at his purpose.

"Simon, thank God that I found you!" Quiney was sitting at a table in the tavern at the George. He often came to London on council business, but though we knew each other well, we were not close.

"Richard? You are seeking me?" I made my way to his table and sat, followed suit by Jonson.

"Aye, a most horrible thing has happened in Stratford. I rode straight here, stopping only to change horses in Oxford." And indeed, he looked haggard. His hair was in disarray and his clothes marked with dirt and soil from the road.

"What, Richard? What has happened?"

"John Hall has been set upon by rogues and nearly killed!"

Ben and I exchanged quick, anxious glances.

"How? When?"

Quiney drank a dram of cider from his beaker before continuing. "Yesterday morning, he had gone out for an early walk. He had hardly left when two men attacked him and then broke into his house."

"John, is he all right?"

Quiney emptied his beaker and waved for another before nodding. "Aye, but he will take some time before he will be well

enough to be about. He begged me to come here and tell you."
Quiney leaned across the table and spoke in a whisper. "They
took John's notebook, Simon. The one that recorded his treatment of Will."

"What of Susanna and Elizabeth?" My mind was reeling.

"They hid in another part of the house. Apparently, the
scoundrels knew exactly what they wanted and knew where to
find it. But they warned John."

"About what?"

"Simon, they told him that more people would be hurt if you
did not stop asking questions."

I burned inside. Shifting to look at Ben, I asked him, "What
think you of that, Ben?"

"I think," the redheaded giant said, "that you have unleashed
forces that you can no longer control. Perhaps there is something
to your theories after all."

"Why, thank you, Ben. It only took my friend being half
beaten to death for you to agree with me." My sarcasm lay heavy.

"What will you do? Henry Smythe thinks you should abandon this quest and return to Stratford. He believes your skills
would be better used finding these scoundrels who attacked
John," Richard continued.

"Then I should remain here, for I suspect that those men are
within the city walls as we speak. Besides, I am now in the service
of Bacon and Coke. Until I have followed that road as far as it
goes, I will not be ready to return. They could only have wanted
the notebook on the chance that it contained information critical
to knowing who killed Will. Now, they have it. I doubt that they
will see much profit in returning to Stratford."

"That is a mighty risk," Richard warned me. "They could set
upon your own wife and children."

He was right. But I was more convinced than ever before
that Will's death was decided in London. Whatever he had done,
whatever role he had played in the Overbury Affair, it was scandalous enough that not only had he been killed to hide it, but
whoever was behind that was not afraid to kill again.

"What choice do I have?" I asked of no one in particular. "Thrice already I have been set upon. To safeguard my family and friends, I must discover the truth in this matter."

"If you live long enough," Jonson reminded me.

"If I do not, God will protect my family."

"While you protect...what? The memory of a dead man? Will that earn you stars in your crown in Heaven?" Ben Jonson hammered at me relentlessly. "Will that fill your children's bellies while you float among the clouds with the angels? And your wife's? A pity that those children will never really know their father, will not have the benefit of his guidance as they grow into adulthood."

I lurched from my seat, sending the table sailing across the room. Ben gained his feet, but I was already upon him. Before I knew that I had acted, I felt my fist explode so very satisfactorily against Ben's nose.

Blood spurted in great gobbets, and so surprised was Ben by my assault that he went flying backwards under my blow.

Quiney, eyes so wide that they scarce stayed in his head, stumbled back against the wall, scattering patrons and furniture alike.

I looked through blurry eyes at Jonson, laid against a brick wall. "Take your sarcasm to Hell with you, Ben Jonson. I will follow this trail no matter where it leads and should you interfere with me again I will impale you on the walls of the Tower itself."

But Jonson, collecting himself, stared at me.

"What do you see, Jonson?"

"A dead man."

"Why? Because you, Southampton and George Wilkins decided it must be so?"

And with that I had truly surprised Ben Jonson.

"How...? You do not understand."

"That is my problem," I retorted. "Now, go! Tell your masters that they have unleashed a hellhound that will not be sated until his family is safe." Pausing, my eyes bored into him. "If you have the courage."

Jonson regained his feet and turned to go. "You will wish, someday soon, that you had not tossed me to the wind."

"Ben Jonson, you are the devil's tool in this affair. And I will suffer not your presence any longer."

"Was that wise?" Richard Quiney asked.

I shook my head. Even wise things had proven unwise in this affair. "Time will tell. Go, Richard. Get yourself a chamber and take some rest. You need it. I must think."

Quiney stumbled to his feet, but whether his stagger was from exhaustion or fear of my reckless ways, I did not know. He nodded quickly and went in search of the innkeeper.

As I brooded over my drink, an older man approached from the depths of the tavern. "Ye must be the lad from Stratford," he began.

I tensed. In my recent experience, anyone could be out to kill me.

He glanced at the retreating figure of Ben Jonson. "I am one of those you seek. Osward is my name."

I motioned to a bench.

"'Tis not the first time that I have seen Ben Jonson set on his arse."

Something about the man was vaguely familiar, and I ventured a guess. "The Low Countries?"

"Aye," he nodded. "I saw you at Antwerp, though Ben Jonson was not your quarry that day. I will tell you what you wish to hear. Any man at Antwerp has earned my attention. And, any man that could lay Ben Jonson low, the blowhard, earns my respect."

I could not help but laugh. "Ben serves a purpose," I answered. "I simply cannot think of one right now."

"I will tell you the truth of it...."

I held one hand up. "I am in the service of Bacon and Coke," I warned him, but he waved me off.

"I did nothing criminal," he continued. "Others did their masters' bidding."

I liked the man's manner. He spoke honest and true. This

man had seen much in his life, and he was unimpressed by the trappings of royalty.

"You are not worried that Bacon and Coke might imprison you?"

"Bacon and Coke? Ha! You think I fear them? For one thing, I can be out of England in hours. For another, they sit upon the jakes just as everyone else. They are nothing special."

I drew back. His words were very dangerous. To speak thus of the king's officers was to speak of the king. But I felt a certain satisfaction in hearing them. In truth, they were my words, too.

"So, tell me, know you anything of the Overbury matter?"

"As his warder, I know that certain gentlemen of the king prepared potions for Overbury that contained poison. But I know when those did not have the desired effect that Lady Somerset ordered a special purgative. Shortly thereafter, Sir Thomas departed this life. Just as well."

"Why?"

"Poor Overbury was in agony. Had he lived he would have never been the same. Such is how the nobles treat each other. Would that I never count myself among their number. Not that I could."

"Aye. Such is how I see it. Are you sure of Overbury?"

"They poured the arsenic up his arse," Osward said. "I saw it myself. As if to purge him."

"You speak openly for a murder witness."

He smiled in a way that I hoped never to smile. "I have a cancer. Nothing the king can do would do aught but ease my suffering." With a quick snap he emptied his mug, and I saw the lines in his face. I signaled for another round.

"Saw you the poet Shakespeare there?"

"No, if he had some involvement 'twas not at the end. 'Twas not but one of my fellows and the countess. His Ladyship," the warder snorted, "was not even there."

"You risk much."

"All think it. I say it. Robert Carr may be an earl, but he

should at least append 'His Ladyship' to his name. I have known many men who prefer sodomy to true sex. Indeed I have tried it. But, I am not one of those who would prefer it to the other. How a man finds his pleasure is nothing to me. But James courted the prim little earl as he would a woman. Sent him flowers and sweets and notes."

"The king risks much." I said that, but I really did not mean it. A king may do as he wishes. Sodomy was illegal, but so was adultery and if everyone guilty of that were imprisoned there would be few left to pursue the business of the nation. What I meant was that this man risked much. He was a man in pain though, a dying man, and I felt he had much to confess. If that were true, I would be his confessor.

"The king risks nothing," my visitor said. "Unless some of his notes were to fall into the hands of his enemies."

"He writes to Carr even after the earl was sent to the Tower?" I was truly incredulous.

Osward shrugged. "Not notes of love now. He is more than a little worried about what Carr will say or do at trial to save his own neck."

Something in all of this bothered me. "You seem to know much for a warder."

He responded with a hacking cough. "You seem to think that royals are discreet. The old queen, yes. She knew how to keep her business private. But James is not Elizabeth."

"And now he has done much he wishes were hidden."

He nodded. "I carried messages from the king to Carr."

"Why you?"

"The king often uses yeomen warders for such chores. I have proven useful on several occasions, and he grew accustomed to asking for me. He is very generous, and I do not mind the extra work."

James's generosity was the stuff of legends. I had heard Henry Smythe complain more than once that the king was giving away the kingdom. I said as much to the warder.

"Everyone at court knows it. Take this pension he is settling on Jonson. What service to the crown has Jonson performed to justify such a gift?"

I did not answer. I could not think of any such service, and Jonson did not stand high in my esteem at that moment. But Will would have favoured the pension, anything to raise the people's view of poets.

"How long have you been a warder?"

"Fifteen years."

"So you served Elizabeth as well."

"For two years," he said. "At first, the king was a pleasant change, younger, more open. But then the excesses were too much even for us old soldiers."

"Master Warder, I came to London seeking to find who murdered William Shakespeare."

The warder drew back. "William the Conqueror was murdered?"

"William the Conqueror?"

He waved me off. "'Tis but an old jest. In truth, Shakespeare was killed?"

"Poisoned, as Overbury. I believe that he played some role in all of this and that is why he was murdered, to keep him from revealing what he knew."

He frowned, deepening the lines in his face. "If what you are saying is true, then only Carr and the Howards could be responsible, or..." He did not need to continue; we both knew who he meant.

A slow burning began in my stomach. I was not the innocent that Ben Jonson thought me, but I had hoped for better from our leaders. We had many ills across our lands. The Puritans continued to push for reforms. There was growing unrest sweeping the country, unrest with the nobility and their excesses. My warder friend was not alone in his views.

The realisation of just how high guilt might lie in Will's death should have caused me to despair, but it did not. Indeed it focused my mind.

"You say that the king sent notes to Carr? Notes of love?"

"Aye."

"Are you still able to work?"

"For now. I work in the Tower most days. On occasion, I am sent to Greenwich Palace to serve the king. But each day becomes more difficult."

"You have been most helpful."

He smiled through the pain that must have been racking his body. "Aye, I owe you that."

"For what?"

"For knocking Ben Jonson on his arse."

And with that, he was gone, leaving me sitting and contemplating all that had occurred.

"Master Saddler?"

I looked up to see the innkeeper standing above me. He seemed flustered.

"I was about to seek you. Have you another chamber?"

He nodded hurriedly. "We do not know what happened to cause the fire. You have our deepest apologies."

I reached up and patted his arm. "Does anyone have any idea who the dead man is? I found myself on the other side of the city late last night and took a room at an inn there," I quickly explained.

"Thank God that you did. No. No one knew him. Though one of the other guests said that he had looked like a typical cutpurse. At first we thought it must be you."

"What else were you to think? No matter. It was probably, as you said, just some cutpurse. Indeed, it was probably he who accidentally set the fire."

"I am so very grateful, master, that you are understanding of this. No servant of Sir Edward and Sir Francis should be treated in this way."

And that sent my head reeling. "How do you know that I am acquainted with Bacon and Coke?"

"London has many people, Master Saddler. And each one has a mouth. And those mouths are seldom shut for very long."

I chuckled grimly. That was something I was learning quickly.

"If you could provide me with a chamber that is, if you take my meaning, out of the general flow."

The innkeeper beamed. "I have just the one for you. And a trustworthy man to watch your door."

"That is very generous of you."

"We like to take especial care of our more distinguished guests. Besides, Sir Edward sent a messenger with funds both to cover your stay and to hire a man."

"Then would you give him these instructions? Admit no one without my personal leave, no matter who they are or what they say."

The innkeeper, a burly man with huge arms and hands, nodded. "After last night's events, I would insist on that." He turned and began to leave, then reversed himself. "I have been told that you were a friend of the player, William Shakespeare."

I nodded.

"All at the George mourn his passing. He was a good friend to us."

"I will tell his family."

And then he was gone.

And suddenly Ben Jonson was looming over my table again, a sheepish look on his face.

"I would speak with you. There are things you should know."

Beyond him, I saw the innkeeper narrow his eyes and motion at someone behind the bar. A giant of a man, easily taller than Jonson, emerged. The innkeeper whispered in his ear, and the giant took up a seat in the corner, close to my table.

"Of course, Ben. Sit."

Being no fool, Jonson surveyed the room quickly and took note of my watcher. He grunted but sat down.

I waited for him to begin. No longer was I looking at an old friend. Now, I saw him only as an enemy.

"Yes, I was called to Southampton's house last night. I knew not what he wanted nor that Wilkins would be there. Wilkins is nothing but a thief and a villain. Shakespeare used him as he used many people, to learn about other walks of life."

"Why did you heed Southampton's summons?"

"Curiosity, if no other reason. While I have done some chores for Southampton since Will left the city, I have not been especially close to him. That he should call for me in the midst of all of this tumult bespoke volumes. I thought I might learn something valuable to you."

He glanced up and saw the look in my eye. "Think what you will. I sought only to advance your cause."

"And what exactly did you learn?"

"That Southampton and Wilkins have no real idea who killed Shakespeare, but they fear that certain people of their acquaintance may have done just that."

"I will ask you but once, Ben. Do you swear that they gave no hint of their own complicity?"

Jonson's eyes met mine once again, and they did not waver; they did not flinch. "They admitted to nothing in my presence, but they are frightened. I doubt not that Wilkins had your friend Hall beaten. They sought to obtain his notes on Will's last illness, in hopes that they might gain some preferment."

"Preferment?" I said. "But any preferment worthy of Southampton's notice would come from—" And then I stopped. "No," I said, shaking my head. "Is it possible that the king would have had Will murdered?"

"I cannot speak firmly of anyone's guilt or innocence, but their natural instinct is to do what they think the king would want them to do."

"Hence the attack on Hall and the theft of his notes."

Jonson nodded. "They had feared that the notes would reveal something identifiable about the murderer."

"Then why call you?" My instinct told me that Jonson was called because he was a co-conspirator. "Did they need a masque written about the affair?"

Ben Jonson had no such ready quip for me. "As soon as Southampton learnt you were coming to the city he had me keep an eye on you. I will admit that. Southampton believed that I was in for a penny or a pound.

"But hear this, Simon. I walked out when Wilkins suggested killing you. You both frightened and hurt him. He worried Southampton like a fever. I left, but I suspected that Southampton would accede to Wilkins's plans, so I waited outside. I followed Wilkins when he emerged."

"Who died in my chamber?"

For once, Jonson would not meet my eyes. "You do not want to know, and in truth it does not matter."

"You expect me to see you as my saviour, not my assassin?"

"I expect you to see what is, not what you might wish it to be. I had hoped that you would use the news of your 'death' to return to Stratford. But, no, not Simon Saddler. You seem intent on joining your friend Shakespeare in death. And, immediately, you confront Southampton, who had conspired in your attempted murder just the night before. You are either a madman or a fool. In either case, God provides protection for such as you."

"And Sir Edward Coke," I said, jerking my head towards the man in the corner, watching us intently. "So, you will see that I have no need for you."

"You have more need for me now than ever before, Simon. I fear that naught but my reputation at court will save you from sitting in Overbury's seat in the Tower. And there is an excellent chance that even I cannot save you."

I drained my beaker. "Ben, you do know that you are not the king of England? I say that because at times you sound like you think you are. But what you truly are is the most conceited braggart that I have ever known. Now, cease trying to frighten me and answer a question. Do you know what service Will did that made him a target?"

The blank look in his eyes gave me my answer.

"I do." Or at least I thought I did. And that was closer to the truth than Ben Jonson had come.

"What?"

"You have yet to give me one good reason why I should tell you. In truth, Ben, you are still my strongest suspect for the murder of Will Shakespeare. And, for that, give me one good reason why you should not be?" I raised my hand as he began to protest.

"I am not saying that you did it unbidden. But no sane man could possible absolve you of this. Three times, I have been set upon. And three times you have been present."

"You are a madman!" Jonson shouted.

"Because I will not accept your word without any support? Because you ask me to ignore the facts?"

"Can I be of service?" a voice said. I looked up and it was Sir Edward's man, a behemoth larger than even Jonson, who stood in disgust.

"Do not worry about me. Regardless of what he thinks, I am no threat to him." And with that, the redhead stormed off again.

"What is your name?" I asked.

He waved me off. "It doesn't matter, master."

"Perhaps not, but I would like to know it."

"Malcolm, master. Malcolm Gray. I hail from Glastonbury."

"Sit, Malcolm Gray. How came you to the service of Sir Edward?" I asked as he lowered himself into a chair, ill at ease and seeming to be unsure of to what use to put his hands.

"I fell in with a bad crowd when I first came to the city. I found myself in Sir Edward's court, accused of a murder I did not commit. I was much younger, and easily frightened. My old dad always taught me to be respectful, and so I was. Compared to what he usually gets, Sir Edward was impressed. He found the prosecutor's case lacking, and he set me free. Afterwards, he brought me to his chambers. Asked questions of my home. Finally, he told me that he could use a man like me, if I could hold my tongue and stay out of trouble. I decided 'twas better to serve the law than to break it."

"What orders did he give you in regard to me?"

Malcolm shrugged. "That I should do what I could to keep any harm from coming to you."

"That was gracious of Sir Edward."

My newfound protector shrugged. "Little of what Sir Edward does is gracious. He has need of you. If that ceases to be the case, he will not hesitate to assign me another chore."

At that I chuckled. "You are frank. I appreciate that in a man."

Malcolm smiled, revealing a full set of teeth, odd in a man of his station. "I am a simple man, Master Saddler. I have no ambition to be more than I am, and I have discovered that it is those with ambition who lie the most."

Once I heard it spoken, I realized that Malcolm was correct. "I am tired. I am going to my chamber. Try and see that no one disturbs me."

My newly minted bodyguard stretched. "I can guarantee that, master."

ONCE SAFELY tucked away in my chamber, I lay back on the bed and considered all that had happened in my three days in the city.

I came for two reasons—to find who might have killed Will Shakespeare and, in all honesty, to find how my boyhood friend had grown so different over the years. I had found at least partial answers to both. That Will's financial fortunes had fallen and risen in concert with the Overbury Affair was now obvious. I believed that I now knew the how and the why.

How could anyone maintain any decency in such a world of deceit and ambition and debauchery? We were not perfect in Stratford, but we did not behave thus. We were a simple, God-fearing people. But perhaps that had not been enough for Will. Perhaps the world had never been enough for such as he.

I remembered as a lad, Will would spend much of his time writing posies for a penny or two. Old John Shakespeare would simply shake his head. He never knew what to make of his son. No matter how often he laid the strap to him, he just could not make Will put aside his tablet or books and work in the glove shop. And even when John did succeed temporarily in getting Will to help, customers became offended by his constant quips; Puritans have little use for humor.

He read, everything. Will looked forward to the coming of a new schoolmaster as a normal boy would wish for Christmas to come sooner. Whenever a new master took residence, Will would finagle a way to borrow his books, even old Alexander Aspinall, whom Will Shakespeare drove to lunacy. Master Aspinall brought quite a large library with him when he took up his post.

At first, Aspinall, a sad figure of a man, past the normal marrying age, walked about Stratford glumly. He rebuffed each of Will's efforts to borrow volumes from his collection. Then, one day, Will and I were lolling about the Guild Hall. I was avoiding work; Will was avoiding the newly acquired Mistress Shakespeare.

Will had looked down the street and chucked me in the shoulder. "Look."

And there came Aspinall, clattering across the cobbles, a pair of gloves in his hand. He was a tall man, but with a decided hunch. Will often joked that he was so thin, a stiff wind would blow him hither and thither. And this day he was mumbling to himself and tripping on the occasional cobble. Will nudged me.

"Master Aspinall," I called to him. "Are you well?"

Aspinall straightened, at least as much as he could. "Oh, Master Saddler, Master Shakespeare, I am faced with a conundrum." He fingered the finely tanned gloves as though they were a priceless treasure.

"I see you have been shopping at my father's," Will said coolly.

"What? Oh, yes, Master Shakespeare." His mind was obviously elsewhere.

"Master Aspinall, tell us your problem," I began. "Perhaps we can help. Stratford needs a schoolmaster untouched by troubles."

He grimaced. He groaned. He rolled his head back and forth. "Oh, young masters. If you could but help me, I would forever be in your debt." Aspinall paused. "I have made the acquaintance of a lady at Shottery. She is quite pretty, and," he paused again, "I am quite smitten."

"That is wonderful!" I said encouragingly. "Then what's the problem?"

"I wish to give her these gloves, but I wish to give also a message that relates my intent."

At that, Will perked up. "A message," he began, "that speaks to her without boldly stating the nature of your purpose?"

Aspinall's eyes opened wide at that. "Yes! Yes! Exactly! I know little of words of love. Latin, yes. Greek, yes. But love?"

I knew, without being told, that an appropriate message was already in Will's mind.

"I could, perhaps, offer something that might serve," Will began.

Aspinall rushed forward and gripped his hands like a man in a fever. "Oh, Master Will, if you could, I would...would...you could borrow any of my volumes you wished. I swear it!"

"Simon," Will called to me. "Get a scrap of paper from the Guild Hall. Let us see if we can help Master Aspinall win his lady love."

A few moments later, a simple three lines, and Alexander Aspinall was a happy man. And Will Shakespeare had a plenitude of new books to read.

As I lay in my bed, it was difficult for me to reconcile the boy to the man. But even as my eyes grew heavy, I could not brush away the memory of that long-ago day, and I fell asleep, reciting silently, "The gift is small / The intent is all / Alexander Aspinall" knowing, somehow, that it was important.

I had found the key to Will's death.

Chapter Ten

D ID YOU SLEEP WELL, MASTER?" MY NEWFOUND BODY-
guard asked as I left my chamber the next morning.
"In truth, not much at all." And I had not. I awoke
about three hours into the night and lay thinking, evaluating what
I had learned, judging what I knew. Certain, as the sky began to
brighten, that I had arrived at the truth of it. "Tell me, Master
Malcolm. If I were to ask you to accompany me on a chore that
might not, strictly speaking, be within the law, would you?"

The giant's eyebrows came close together. "Would it put me
at cross purposes to Sir Edward?"

"Not exactly. And it would, I think, make his job a little easier."

He smiled. "Then I will gladly agree. Where are we going?"

"First, the Tower."

"Then?"

"I do not know."

WITH MALCOLM at my side, my entry into the Tower was assured. And when I requested to see the countess of Somerset,
eyebrows were raised, but the warder led us to the countess's
rooms without comment.

I ducked my head and entered, with Malcolm fast on my
heels.

"Master Saddler, I do not remember sending for you." Even

as petite as she was, she filled any room she entered. It was easy to see how Robert Carr had fallen in love with her.

"I invited myself."

"You are a presumptuous man."

I smiled and sat down unbidden, knowing what her reaction would be.

But I was wrong.

Rather than chastise me for sitting in her presence without her leave, she laughed. "I knew you were an unusual man the first time I met you. What errand brings you to me on this day? Has anyone else attempted to murder you?"

She seemed very interested in that.

"Sad that they failed yet again, my lady?"

"No, I find men who so quickly attract so many powerful enemies fascinating. They seldom live long, but they make for delightful theatre while they last."

"Well, I trust I will offer you such entertainment before my life takes wing."

"And what have you come for today?" she said, circling her chamber. "And why did you bring Coke's man? Alone, we might have had an interesting morning. But alas, I do not share my treasures with groups."

"I came to ask you a few questions, nothing more strenuous than that, I am afraid, my lady."

But I would be less than truthful if I did not admit that her easy talk of lovemaking stirred something in me. It was simple to see how she had successfully captivated so many men.

She sat then, leaning forward and exposing her bosom that much more. "Ask your questions."

"Did your husband's friendship with the king make you uncomfortable?"

I had chosen my words carefully, and she did not miss that.

"Why should I be uncomfortable? That is something to be wished for, not criticised."

"Even the special relationship between them?" Beside me, Malcolm grunted. I was nearing treason.

At that, the countess did begin to look restless, indecisive. "Some questions are better left unasked, Master Saddler."

"Surely, a lady of your...sophistication would not mind such things."

"Surely, a lady of my...sophistication would not discuss such things."

"Perhaps not. But your husband intends to discuss these matters, at length, before the court." I had no idea that Somerset would do this, but given his general disposition and the situation, it was conceivable that he might. "He believes that if he embarrasses James deeply enough that James will pardon the both of you."

At that her face turned a deep red and her eyes narrowed. "He can be a fool, but he is not that big a fool. Such a threat would serve only to bring his conviction more quickly and the axeman's stroke more efficiently."

"Of course," I agreed. "That is why he is holding back the letters."

She drew back from me as if struck. "You know about the letters?" But then the surprise on her face melted into understanding. "But of course, your friend Shakespeare told you. He was forever indiscreet. What else do you think got him killed?"

My heartbeat quickened. "You admit that you had him killed?"

"Ha! Have I not enough troubles as it is? No, I did not kill him, but I am sure that other of the king's friends did. They could not chance him being called to testify at our trial. He knew too much, too much of the truth of my husband's friendship with the king." She stopped, glancing fearfully at Malcolm.

I jerked my head towards the door. Malcolm looked uncomfortable. "'Twill be fine. The countess will not harm me."

He growled at her warningly, like a great mastiff, and then heeded my request.

With the door closed, 'twas just me and the countess within. "Let us be frank. When your husband decided to marry you, the king was, shall we say, upset. He was desperately seeking some way to keep the earl close. He turned to Shakespeare to write the sort of note that might persuade Carr to remain in the king's 'personal' service."

"You are not being frank; you couch your words. Of course, my husband and the king are two of the world's greatest sodomites. James is even now bedding George Villiers. And the king was most jealous of me when I took Robin's fancy. Yes, he did turn to Shakespeare to use his special talents to persuade Robin of the folly of this move. And the poet was paid handsomely."

"Was your marriage one of alliance more than romance?"

"Oh, no, Master Saddler. My husband is as skilled in pleasing a woman as he is in pleasing a man." The smile on her face was of such a nature as to ready my manhood for action. She was an entrancing woman, but I knew what lay beneath, the coldness of her heart. Still, I could see how Will had fallen to her charms.

"So Shakespeare crafted many of the notes that King James sent your husband?"

"I am not certain how many of them Shakespeare wrote, but I know simply from reading them that he penned a good number of those sent to Robert when he first showed them to me. Without the poet's touch, they would have simply been childish drivel, but he conveyed the king's message most convincingly, and in a most detailed manner."

"But not convincingly enough to bring Somerset back to the king's bedchamber," I concluded for her.

"My talents in that regard," she said, slowly running her tongue across her upper lip, "are many, and much better than the king's."

The countess stood then at that. "But despite my husband's skills in such things, his abilities in other areas are woefully lacking. He believes that threatening the king with his testimony in court will cause the king to end this charade."

"The death of Thomas Overbury was a charade?"

She turned. "The death of Thomas Overbury was something that everyone at court desired. He was a most disagreeable man. No one liked him."

"But he was your husband's dearest friend," I protested.

"Who do you think introduced Robert to sodomy? Robert has no head for state affairs. Overbury was his brain. Robert passed all state papers to Sir Thomas, who decided what action, if any, needed to be taken. But then Thomas made a drastic error. He opposed Robert's intimacy with the king, but more fatally, he opposed our marriage. That set him on a deadly path with the Howards. For if the king could not have Robert, he saw value in strengthening his ties with the Howards."

"Your family."

"My family. I admit nothing. But Thomas Overbury's horrid personality brought about his death as surely as if he had stabbed himself with a dagger. It really matters little who wielded the weapon."

"On the contrary, Countess, the law cares both who wields the weapon and who directs the killer's aim. If it did not, you and your husband would not be imprisoned here in the Tower."

"Granted." She paused and looked at me. "So you think that I had a hand in Overbury's death?"

"Quite frankly, my lady, I believe that you had both hands in Overbury's murder. I believe that it was most likely your idea. And I believe that Sir Francis and Sir Edward will not hesitate to hang the entire affair around your neck. I admit that it is a pretty neck, but it will soon be broken. There are but two weeks, a little more, left until your trial. Were I you, I would be seeking some advantage, some leverage, to avoid the axeman's stroke."

At that, she narrowed her eyes. "What sort of leverage?"

And now I was shooting my arrow blind, or, at the very least, with only a glimmer of light. "What else, the letters."

She huffed and turned away. "That would have been very foolish of my husband, to have kept those letters." But she could have fooled no one.

"You have already admitted that in most matters your husband is inordinately foolish. And you have already admitted that he held back the letters. Enough of this silliness. Here is what I believe. The reason the king is so worried about your husband's testimony is how affairs stood between them. What may be common knowledge at court plays out differently when sworn to at trial. And the reason that *someone* had Shakespeare killed was because he could verify at least some of Somerset's testimony. And, if the letters were still available, he could testify that he wrote them for the king at the king's direction.

"No matter what James's true role in the death of Overbury, he would be in danger of losing his crown at a public accusation of sodomy. The entire nation would be thrown into turmoil. Aye, it could even mean civil war." My words might sound extreme, but they were true. The king and Parliament were always at odds. Parliament thought the king spent far too lavishly and did not approve of his behaviour. The king thought Parliament was inconsequential.

"The man who controls those letters can control your fate and that of your husband."

"If that were true, I have plenty of friends who could retrieve them for me," she said, narrowing her eyes further.

"Ahh, but you are imprisoned. And stand accused of murder. None of your friends are likely to involve themselves in this. And if the king dreamt for one moment that they were here, he would have seized them already. I think that you need a third party, someone to negotiate a reasonable outcome."

"And you would be that man?"

I stood then and turned my back to her.

She leapt to her feet and advanced on me as if she intended to strike me. "What would you gain from this? No one does anything without gain."

I pivoted and looked at her. A thought crossed my mind, a sinful thought, but I put voice to it anyway. "Perhaps I wanted to taste the nectar that Shakespeare found so seductive."

In truth, I did not mean it. Why should I go where hundreds had been before me? I wanted only Peg; I could not have Peg again, not in the same manner as before. And I did not want any other woman either, noble or common.

"But I had rather know who ordered Will Shakespeare's

death. With those letters in my possession, I can use them to force an admission, at the same time as I negotiate an arrangement for you and your husband."

She grimaced at me. "You are a fool. If it were so simple, I would not be sitting here in the Tower. As soon as you have those letters your life will not be worth a penny."

"You underestimate me, my lady. I have a certain amount of protection from Coke and Bacon. Besides, what choice do you really have?"

"You truly are a fool. Do you not realize that Bacon and Coke will throw you to the wolves if you become a liability to them? And there will be no comfortable chamber in the Tower for you. No, for you there will only be a nasty cell for a night or two before you go to Tower Hill. No matter how debauched he is, James is still the king, and you are a nobody."

I smiled at her, and I think that enraged her even more. "Yes, my lady, I am a nobody. But James is happy now with George Villiers. Your own family, particularly your very powerful father, has come under the cloud of suspicion. The earl of Suffolk is believed in some circles to be making illegal use of the treasury."

"That is a lie!"

"Perhaps it is. But under the present circumstances, James is not inclined to be supportive of the Howards. Before Overbury's death, yes, he sought to build an alliance. But now, with you in the Tower, and Suffolk reeling from accusations, the king probably wishes he never heard of the lot of you. The page is beginning to turn on your family's fortunes."

"How would you know aught of these matters?" Her words were a challenge, but a challenge without the force of her earlier words.

"Everyone in London speaks of it. I heard talk of it two days ago at a tavern near Gray's Inn."

Her pretty eyes flitted about nervously.

"My husband is reckless about many things. He will not accept any sort of arrangement that requires him to admit guilt."

"Is he guilty?"

The countess did not respond, merely smiled in her beguiling way.

"Will Lord Somerset give testimony against James if he knows that he does not have the letters any longer?"

She shook her head quickly. "He is not that big a fool. What sort of arrangement do you have in mind?"

Quickly, I explained my scheme. She listened, intently. This was a formidable lady, of that there was no doubt. As I finished, she nodded curtly. "That is acceptable. With the added bonus of saving my husband from himself. Very well. The letters are secreted in three locations—my father's house at Audley End, the manor house at Chesterford Park, and Greys Court near Henley."

Perhaps this would be easier than I thought, at least obtaining the letters. "You will give me specific directions to where they are hidden." A statement, not a question.

The countess turned from me. "For Audley End and Chesterford, yes. For Greys Court, I cannot."

"Why?"

"My friend Anne Turner secreted them there. And she was hanged at Tyburn in November past." Lady Frances walked away from me then, and I sensed that she had more to say. "They crowded the gallows as if it were the king himself being hanged, you know," she said, almost in a whisper. "She was the finest friend a woman could have. And she faced her death with great bravery."

"But she never told you where in the house that she hid them?"

"There was not a chance. We were all arrested just after. I barely got them out of our Whitehall apartments before the king's men descended on us."

"Was that your principal residence? Whitehall?"

"In the city, yes. And the king's men ripped our belongings to pieces looking for the letters. Then your precious Coke and Bacon sent their minions and they did their worst." She turned back to me then and straightened herself. "The house at Audley

End is my father's. He will give you no trouble. At Chesterford Park, we still hold the lease, so you should have no trouble there either."

And then she told me where I could find the letters in the two houses. "At Greys Court I would suggest that you look in Anne's chamber first. If they are not there, I do not know what to tell you."

"Who else knows where they are?"

She shook her head sharply. "Many know that they exist; no one but me knows where they are hidden."

"Not even your husband?"

The countess smiled knowingly at me. "He would be the last one that I would tell. Robert is horribly indiscreet...." She paused for a moment as if searching for the right words. "He is prone to overreaction and such is deadly when dealing with a king. The game cannot be played that way, not when the stakes are so high."

"But the letters were his, not yours."

"Constable Saddler, just as Sir Thomas made Robert's decisions in regard to state papers, I must make his decisions in almost all others. Robert would have burnt the letters. He had no understanding of the leverage they gave us."

"Pardon me, my lady, but if this is all true, why would the king find him of the least interest?"

"Oh, Simon," she said, her eyes twinkling, "he's a pretty man."

Chapter Eleven

L ADY SOMERSET TOLD US OF A STABLE WHERE WE COULD
procure horses free for our journey, including extra
mounts, with the use of her name. I was hesitant; using her name anywhere in London seemed sure to provide us
with extra attention. But Malcolm was unconcerned. "We need
the horses. Unless you wish to buy them yourself, we could hire
them. But, the lady is discreet if nothing else. She would not send
us to someone who would talk."

The horses were fast and in good health. By midafternoon,
we passed the Church of St. Mary in Sawbridgeworth, Hertford-
shire. Just under a half hour later, we stopped at a stable near
the old castle in Bishop's Stortford to water the horses. Standing
there, I pointed to the ruins. "My father once told me that that
was a fine castle in its day. The first William gave this land to one
of his men, who built the castle."

"Hmmph!" Malcolm grunted. "Look at it now, the boards
rotting, the stones slowly being covered by dirt. It couldn't protect a herd of sheep. A lot of good all of that power did them."

"Don't worry, Malcolm. Money lasts even less time than
power."

"But it is pleasant while you have it."

I chuckled. On that, at least, he was right. But power, I knew,
had its value as well, while one held it.

NIGHT FELL as we passed Newport, just a few miles north of Bishop's Stortford. I had hoped to arrive at Audley End before all was dark, but I should have known when we left that that was a forlorn hope. Malcolm, as well, preferred a bit slower pace than I would have desired, but when he didn't pick up on my hint of riding out a little faster, I gave up and fell back with him.

We were no more than a mile past Newport when it happened.

The road sat a few feet higher than the surrounding fields. A rustle sounded first to the right and a few seconds later to the left.

At nearly the same moment, Malcolm and I pulled up and stopped. I noticed that he quickly reached into a bag tied behind him on the saddle. And I was amazed when I saw that he had one of the new French pistols, fired by a flintlock method. They were ever so rare, and this one looked as being heavily decorated with engraved metal.

Six highwaymen appeared, three to each side. One on the right rode two or three paces ahead of the rest.

As much as I could tell in the moonlight, the leader was a tall man, or rather boy, wearing but a shirt, hose, and shoes. No hat. Young, perhaps, twenty. He seemed a handsome boy with a thin moustache and smiled as he waved his sword.

"Gentlemen," he said with a distinct French accent. I hated the French. I glanced quickly over at Malcolm; the grimace on his face told me what he thought of the French.

"We have no money, if that's what you want," I said. My mind was working fast. Could Southampton have heard of our mission and attempted to stop it? Did Lady Somerset send them?

He jumped down from his mount effortlessly, his eyes sweeping over us and seeing the pistol in Malcolm's hand. "What is this? We mean no harm to you. Simply give us your money and be on your way."

"What?" Malcolm asked. "You don't take enough from your countrymen so you have to come over here?"

"We are more prosperous," I answered him, feeling a bit more comfortable now. By the time Southampton could have heard, his men would have been far to our rear. Only the countess could have moved so quickly, and I saw nothing she had to gain by having us killed.

Our French bandit laughed. "I love the British. Please, men who dress as beautifully as you, and who have such weapons, must have a great deal of money." He brought his sword up. "Your toy does not scare me. You can kill one of us, maybe. These things are far from certain. But one of us, perhaps. That will leave five swords to your two."

Before I knew what was happening, Malcolm said, "Then, let us not waste time."

The pistol blasted with a flash and a boom.

One of the bandits fell from his saddle.

I was on the ground, sword out.

So was Malcolm.

And then...

Two more bandits were bleeding, crawling away. The other three, including their leader, the young moustachioed man, fled, unmarked.

It all happened so quickly and effortlessly, though I was breathing heavily.

And we were alone.

"Where did you get that?" I motioned at the pistol, still a little confused and out of breath.

"An old employer," he answered, without further comment, turning and climbing into the saddle.

I followed suit, and we returned to our journey to Saffron Walden, never speaking the rest of the way.

WE ACTUALLY did not go into the village. Audley End, once an old monastery and granted to Lord Suffolk's grandfather by Henry VIII, lay a bit west of the town, and we approached from the southwest. It had been reworked into a magnificent home, I had been told.

But if I had thought Southampton House seemed like a royal palace, I had not seen enough such estates. Even though we had only the moonlight to mark our way, what Suffolk's architect had built reminded me of a poem, or part of a poem, that Will had made me read. 'Twas Edmund Spenser's *Faerie Queene*, and I couldn't tell why. I couldn't point to the specific part, but something about the way that the incredible place looked with hundreds of large torches to light the entrance and the eight visible towers. Somehow, the moonlight was reflecting off the roof in a way that made it seem that the entire house was framed by a silver, shimmering mist. I just immediately thought of Spenser's epic poem.

"Master Saddler," Malcolm said as we slowed our mounts to a walk, "you know that this is the Lord High Treasurer's home?"

"I do."

I had not chosen to explain everything to Malcolm. At least not before we set out. "We are here to retrieve certain documents which belong to his daughter."

"Can we not simply send in for them?"

"They are not widely known to be here, and I suspect that if the Lord Treasurer knew that they were here, we would never get them."

Malcolm looked down at me from his great height atop his horse. "I do not wish to be at cross purposes with the law. I have worked very hard to stay out of gaol."

"Did not Sir Edward Coke himself task you to my service?"

"He did, Constable, but only to keep you alive, not to aid you in breaking the law."

"If we are successful, I think that Sir Edward will reward you."

"It is in his interest?"

"It absolutely is."

"If we survive," Malcolm noted wryly. "Have you a plan?"

And I did.

In a manner.

As we rode along the broad drive to the great manor, I noticed that the formal gardens were still a bit unfinished. And workers, even at that hour, were replacing the translucent horn panes in the windows with glass. Apparently, Suffolk had been away from his newly remodeled home; glass was considered too fragile and too expensive to leave in the windows permanently. There was a work yard on the left of the front portion, still busy even at this hour.

Sir Edward's name was not greeted with as much cooperation as I hoped, but it did gain us entry and an audience with the earl.

The Lord High Treasurer of England was an imposing figure. He yet held the rank of admiral in the Royal Navy, and I could easily see him striding the quarterdeck of one of the great warships. Shed of his cloaks and accoutrements, he still wore his hose and shirt. His brown hair was carefully coifed and he raised a hand and puffed up his beard while considering us.

"I do not know you," he said to me finally. "This one I have seen with Sir Edward Coke, so I assume your claim to be his agent is accurate. What is it you want?"

This would not be simple. If Suffolk knew what we wanted, he would be more than loath to let items so valuable slip from his grasp. Granted, they were to be used for his daughter's benefit, but if I had learned anything it was that nobles rarely worried about saving anyone's hide but their own.

"You are aware of the enquiries into the death of Sir Thomas Overbury," I began.

"How could I not be, you fool? My son-in-law and my daughter are in the Tower."

"Of course. I am Simon Saddler, a constable of Stratford, where the poet William Shakespeare was recently murdered by poison. I am investigating any connection between his death and Overbury's." To that point, the truth had worked well for me.

The grimace that had been painted across Suffolk's face disappeared. "Sit, Master Saddler," he proffered. "I fear that you came a long way for naught. I barely knew Shakespeare. Oh, I attended a few of his plays at court, but I did not know him, not really. Dead, you say? By poison?"

"Yes, my lord. I have been—"

Before I could finish, Malcolm interrupted. "My Lord Suffolk, I have been unwell. If I could—"

"Yes, yes, yes," Suffolk said hastily. He motioned for one of the liveried servants hovering around, who scurried forward and led Malcolm from the room and into the inner sanctum of Audley End.

"Please forgive him, my lord. We encountered some bandits on the way here."

"French?" he asked.

"Aye, my lord."

He nodded. "A young rascal named Armand Duvall. He is quite a nuisance. You and your friend were lucky."

"We accounted for three of them."

"Then, well done!"

"Thank you, my lord. As I was saying, I have been authorized to pursue my enquiry into Shakespeare's death and since it has similarities to Sir Thomas's death, I have also been deputized by Sir Francis and Sir Edward to glean any information that might help their case."

Suffolk did not respond at first. When he did, it was as if his very breath came from the frigid north. The brief glimpse of co-operation he had proffered had been swept away.

"And you came here in hopes that I would give you evidence against my daughter?"

"My lord, I am simply gathering information about Overbury's death. How that information is disposed of is not my concern. I am worried only about William Shakespeare's murder."

"And I have told you that I barely knew the man and I know nothing of any involvement he had with Overbury. Before you ask, I did not poison Thomas Overbury, neither my daughter nor her husband poisoned Overbury. But I am not saddened by his death. The world is better without him."

It seemed to me that it was a miracle that Overbury had lived as long as he had. I had yet to find anyone who liked him. "Why did you seek this marriage between your daughter and Somerset so ardently?"

Suffolk cast a disappointed look my way. "You have no idea how affairs at court are conducted. Attempting to explain such as this to you would be time wasted. I have no reason or requirement to answer your questions. And I will not."

"My lord, I mean no offense," I hurried on. I needed a bit more time. "You are correct; I am but a country constable, and I am seeking to understand how matters stand. If I offend it is from my own ignorance. And, quite honestly, I care little for how Overbury died or who had a hand in it." And, in truth, I did not. "William Shakespeare was my friend, and I seek only to find him justice."

This seemed to mollify the Lord High Treasurer. "I may know something of Shakespeare, though I do not think it could advance your cause."

"Please, my lord. Anything you remember."

"I recall a day at court, Lord Somerset had just petitioned the king for permission to marry Frances. We all wondered how His Majesty would react, but to our surprise he began shouting for Shakespeare."

"In truth?"

"Aye. It was most puzzling. The king's favourite was marrying and His Majesty screams for a player."

Though I was playing a game, my next words had to be chosen carefully. My habit of speaking truly would not serve me well here, but I realized that it was a question that I needed to ask.

"Was Shakespeare..." I started over. "Did the king..."

Suffolk grinned at my discomfiture as I groped for words that would not get me a cell in the Tower.

"No, Constable. I do not believe that that sort of relationship existed. From what little I knew of Master Shakespeare, he preferred his companions to be more...traditional, let us say."

A thought occurred to me. "My lord, His Majesty has a reputation for bestowing monetary gifts on his friends."

Suffolk nodded.

"Over the last few years, Shakespeare's fortunes improved considerably. I wondered if that, perhaps, had been due to the king's largesse."

The Lord High Treasurer cocked his head. "Indeed, rumours had circulated at court that the king had given the player a sum of money." He paused. "And now you say he has been poisoned? In like manner as Overbury?"

"Aye."

For the first time since I had entered his house, I felt that he was truly looking at me. "Master Saddler, I am going to speak to you plainly. As man to man, not noble to commoner. Go back to Coke and Bacon and tell them that you found nothing to further their enquiry nor your own. Pray that this news circulates quickly. I will do you the favour of ensuring that it is widely known at Whitehall. Perhaps then you will be able to return to your life in Stratford and die peacefully and happily in your own bed."

I had tired of being told to abandon my quest. It was as if the court and, indeed, London itself, were a world apart from the rest of the country, a world where murder was common and dealt with by ignoring it. Speaking of such was the real crime. Such a state of affairs made a mockery of my work as constable.

"My lord, I have been given that advice so often in recent days, I have it memorised. But, alas, I cannot do that. I have a duty to investigate Shakespeare's death and an obligation, as his best friend, to find his killer."

Suffolk shrugged. "I commend your sense of duty; I will mourn your passing. I fear I have little else to tell you."

But before I could respond to that, Malcolm stumbled into the room, clutching his stomach.

"Master Saddler, we should leave. I am not well."

Suffolk stepped back. Illness was not to be trifled with.

From the back of the house, a shout arose. And Malcolm shot a swift wink at me.

"We have taken up too much of your time, my lord. I will

certainly take your guidance to heart. Come, Malcolm. We should find you a physician."

But by that time, Suffolk had nearly backed out of the room, anything to keep his distance from Malcolm. He seemed not to hear the growing clamour in a distant part of the house.

With Suffolk's hastily given leave, we left hurriedly, but not frantically.

Once outside, beyond the earshot of Suffolk's servants, I turned to Malcolm.

"Did you find them?"

"Aye," he answered, patting his stomach. "Just where the lady said they would be."

We had continued walking swiftly through the gardens.

Until…

Until a shouted curse erupted from the main house behind us.

Then we ran.

For a large man, Malcolm Gray moved swiftly. For an aging man, I did well to keep up.

The liveried guards at the main gate had moved into the graveled lane, trying to discover what was causing the commotion without abandoning their post.

Even in the dark we could see their eyes widen as we emerged into the torchlight. They raised their pikes in response.

But Malcolm was upon them before they could do anything. Grabbing the shaft of each pike in a hand, he shoved the guards backwards, sending them tumbling to the ground.

I did not stop to admire his handiwork. I untied my horse and Malcolm's, leaping upon my own as my companion caught up with me.

"Here!" I tossed the reins to him and we were off down the road, leaving chaos behind us.

A mile down the road, Malcolm pulled his horse to a halt and spun her around to face me. He reached into his shirt and pulled out a stack of parchments, bundled with a ribbon.

"I have just committed a theft at the Lord High Treasurer's

home. You strike me as a sincere, decent man. But now I need to know what is in here."

"Did you read them?"

"I cannot read."

I considered how much to tell him. Indeed, until I actually had the chance to read these notes, I was not certain that I had anything to tell him. This had been but a grand gamble. For our land, the night was unusually warm, and I smelt the scent of baking bread from a nearby house as I thought.

"You have trusted me, so I shall trust you. Those documents in your hand are notes written by my friend Shakespeare for His Majesty, to Lord Somerset. I believe that they may hold evidence of the king's complicity in the murder of Sir Thomas Overbury, and I am nearly certain that they contain evidence of the true nature of Somerset's relations with the king."

At that, without a moment's hesitation, Malcolm tossed me the bundle.

He saw the puzzlement in my expression. "I have no interest in seeing those letters, Master Saddler. My life would not be worth a penny if it were thought that I knew their contents. You are a walking dead man."

THE RIDE to Chesterford Park did not take long, perhaps an hour. And at any moment, I expected to turn and find that Malcolm had abandoned me. But each time I looked, he was there, riding by my side.

His loyalty surprised me. We had known each other but a day, and yet he followed me.

THE MANOR at Chesterford Park required no such subterfuge as Audley End. It was still under lease to Somerset and, in his absence, was dark. A pair of drowsy guards gave us only a cursory glance, and a servant at the door did not bar our entry. I simply said that we had been sent by the countess to retrieve some of her belongings that she needed at the Tower.

A chambermaid took me to the countess's rooms, and while

Malcolm occupied her with idle chatter, I easily found the letters and secured them inside my shirt. Snatching a pair of books from a shelf to cover my theft, I followed the maid as she led us out. I think she regretted having to part ways with giant Malcolm. Alas, we had little time for love.

ONCE BEYOND the village, I reined my horse to the side of the road.

"Malcolm," I began, uncertain of exactly what to say, "I believe we should part ways here. The next leg of this journey will take nearly two days and one hundred miles. I cannot ask you to continue on."

Though both of us were on horseback, he yet towered over me. When he spoke, it was in a soft voice that belied his size. "You are an odd man, Simon Saddler. You are far more intelligent than I, yet you persevere down a path that can only end in your death.

"I have seen men take their own lives, through shame or disgrace or failure. But you do not wield the weapon yourself; you force others to wield it against you. What sort of man are you?"

'Twas a good question, and one that troubled me considerably. Common sense dictated that I should have run back to Stratford at Southampton's first warning. And after the second attempt on my life, I should have stolen the fastest horse in London and galloped back home. Yet, I had not. 'Twas as if some maddening obsession ruled me. Perhaps this was what it was like to be consumed by a devil. Those considerations, those thoughts did not stop me from uttering the next words.

"I am simply a man who wishes to see justice done." I paused. "You have done more than Sir Edward asked. And if I live long enough to see him yet again, I will tell him so."

Malcolm, his face darkened with a need to be shaved, shook his shaggy head. "You are a most irksome man. And a liar, if I judge you correctly. Sir Edward charged me to keep you alive. So whither you go, so shall I. Where is the next stop on this outrageous journey?"

"Greys Court at Henley."

"Seat of the Knollys family?"

"Aye, and this will not be so easy."

"And Audley End was? You have already turned me back to the thief that I was. What could be worse?"

I looked away, embarrassed at the words I was about to speak. "We do not know exactly where the letters are."

"Master Saddler, do you have any idea how many rooms there are at Greys Court?"

"No, and neither do you. Enough of this. If you are coming, let us go. We have a very long ride."

Malcolm grumbled, but when I kicked my horse in the flanks, I heard the comforting sound of his horse's hooves in the lane behind me.

BY THE time that we reached Greys Court, nearly two days and two changes of horses had occurred. And we had not exchanged five words beyond those necessary.

As the afternoon sun stood low in the sky, we sat atop our horses outside the grounds of Greys Court. Malcolm turned to me. "Do you have a plan?"

"I do." A simple one had occurred to me on our journey, though it had no guarantee of success. "Sir William Knollys is the brother-in-law of Lady Somerset. I will simply tell him that her friend Anne Turner left some of the countess's documents in the chamber Anne recently occupied, before her, um, untimely death."

"And you believe that will gain you entry?"

"It may. Have you a better idea?"

"I do."

After he explained it, I saw then the absolute beauty of it. Malcolm Gray was a man of no mean intelligence. What he advised did not make my ultimate plan any less dangerous, but it provided a better chance for success.

AT THE front door of the imposing three-storey house, we were met by a manservant with a sour expression. "Sir William is not in residence." He took a look at Malcolm. "And traders are greeted at the rear."

I drew myself up. "We are here at the command of the Lord Chief Justice Edward Coke. I am Constable Simon Saddler, and this is Malcolm Gray. We seek certain papers that may have been secreted in Mistress Turner's chamber that pertain to the coming trial of Lord Somerset and the countess."

Suddenly, the manservant was unsure of himself. "The chief justice? Mistress Turner?" He repeated the names as if they were new to him.

Malcolm reached past me and shoved the manservant out of the way. "It is an offense against the Crown to hinder his servants in the performance of their duties."

The poor man stumbled backwards into the house and we filled the breach, leaving him nearly gasping at the force of our entry.

"Quickly, man! What chamber was allotted to Mistress Turner when she lived here?" Malcolm had become the leader of our expedition, and I was deeply impressed.

A handful of liveried servants appeared in the entrance hall, expressions of both surprise and fear marking each face. They fell away as our greeter, now bereft of the power assigned him, led us uncertainly up the staircase to the rooms allocated on an upper storey for lesser visitors. In truth, even in those days, maids and manservants often slept on the floor in the rooms of their masters.

We came to a small chamber, and the manservant held open the door.

"I do not know what you could find. This room was thoroughly turned out after Mistress Turner, umm, departed."

"You may be gone," I ordered. He seemed indignant, but left rather than face Malcolm's bulk. I shut the door behind him.

"Where should we look?" my giant companion asked.

"Anywhere that is not obvious."

I proved more adept at searching than Malcolm; his gigantic hands and powerful fingers were more attuned to destruction than the sometimes delicate task of finding that which was hidden.

The room was small and sparsely furnished in comparison to the bedchamber of a noble woman. But the bed was modestly large, and there was a single table, covered with a Turkish rug. The table was a piece of about waist height. And the rug was affixed to the table about the circumference with some sort of paste or glue.

A casket sat on top, and I opened it, knowing that the late Mistress Turner would not have been so careless as to leave the letters there. And she had not.

I went to the bed and looked beneath.

Nothing.

After some minutes of searching the chamber, we had found nothing resembling the letters. I nodded to the door, and Malcolm jerked it open to find the manservant and half the staff crowded in the hall outside.

"Take us to the chamber that Lady Somerset used during her residence."

One storey below, our guide let us into what was in reality a suite of chambers, a suite that was far more impressive than the simple room that Anne Turner had occupied.

It took us nearly an hour to search the apartments. Nothing. I stood next to one of several tables, yet another covered with a small Turkish rug, and considered our course.

"Perhaps we should simply use what we have and not worry about these," Malcolm said. "I am certain that Sir Edward will be pleased."

I had lied to Malcolm, as much to protect him as to gain his assistance in my quest. "We do not know how much he knows about these letters. He may know, if not exactly how many, then a general sense."

My new friend nodded reluctantly. "Then where else can we look?"

My lips pursed, I did not answer immediately. "I am not certain." Clenching my fingers together absently, several seconds passed before I realized that the Turkish rug draped over the table next to me was coming up with my fingers.

Without telling Malcolm what I was doing, I rushed to the other two such tables in the chamber. Those rugs were not affixed either.

I burst through the door and took the stairs two at a time as I rushed back to Mistress Turner's former chamber. Lifting the edge of the Turkish rug, I found that it was affixed to the wood around the edge. Quickly, I picked up the beautiful wooden casket centered on the table. And there they were!

Not simply lying on top of the rug, but forming a thin, rectangular bulge under it. Turner had been quick and clever. A chambermaid, cleaning, would not have picked up the casket, and if she had, probably would not have noticed the faint outline.

I pulled my dagger out and, holding up the rug, separated it from the table. Once I had created an opening large enough for my hand, I slid it in and felt the satisfying texture of folded paper.

A few seconds later and I had retrieved the small bundle.

"You are charmed," Malcolm said. "We have invaded three country houses in three days and only encountered obstacles at one."

"Aye, I am blessed," I said with a hint of a laugh. But the sarcasm was too heavy to hide. "Let us return to London and put an end to all of this."

"You will find no argument from me."

I WAS so tired, so supremely tired. If I were to survive the days ahead, I had already decided what I must do. I would negotiate a bargain to get everyone what they wanted—King James, Lord and Lady Somerset, Coke and Bacon, and, most especially, myself.

We rode away from Greys Court, headed along the road to London. Neither of us spoke much.

A half hour, perhaps three-quarters of an hour into our journey, we stopped at a simple farmstead on the southern edge of Henley-on-Thames to water our horses and ourselves.

Malcolm lithely climbed down from his horse and led him to the trough. I would never understand how a man of his bulk could move so effortlessly. I had been fortunate that Sir Edward had favored me with such a useful partner.

Which made my next action all the more difficult. I reached under my cloak and retrieved the wooden truncheon I kept there.

"These folk will see to you," I said, nearly in a whisper.

And at that I swung the truncheon hard enough to render him unconscious but soft enough not to kill him. It was a blow that I had practiced many times in Stratford to subdue some recalcitrant sot.

Malcolm collapsed to the ground.

Chapter Twelve

I WAS NOT TRULY BETRAYING MALCOLM, I TOLD MYSELF. BUT he served Coke, not me. And no matter how much I liked him and trusted him, he would serve his master, not me. Still, I did not relish my next encounter with Malcolm.

The palace at Whitehall lay some forty miles distant from the farmstead, but I took a more roundabout path. I could not chance the straighter path. Malcolm might find a fast horse; I had taken his. With luck, I would arrive at Whitehall before Malcolm and could avoid Coke and Bacon.

I chose my route carefully, backtracking to Henley for the ferry. Once across, I made my way to Wargrave, a small village with an ancient parish church.

These last days riding throughout the regions north of London made me homesick for Stratford. I loved our small towns and villages. The odours, the sights, the people. On market days in the summer and fall, you could get any vegetable you wanted, fresh from the garden. In the winter and early spring, foreign traders would bring exotic spices for cooking, cloth for making our clothes. I relished all of that; even our garbage and the smoke from our chimneys spoke to me of home.

The problem with London and other big cities was that every day was a market day. You could not mark the season by walking down the High Street. And the smoke and the waste smelled more bitter, perhaps even more evil. I savoured the taste of home and turned to my present task.

St. Mary's lay on the western edge of Wargrave. Midnight had nearly come by then, and I stopped in front of the church. After our encounter on the road to Saffron Walden, I was flinching at every shadow. And the stones in the graveyard of St. Mary's cast strange shadows indeed in the half light.

Tying my horse to a yew tree, I slipped into the yard and found a tall stone next to an effigy near the centre of the yard. I took my dagger and quickly cut a square of turf away, digging even deeper in the earth. Soon I had hollowed out a neat little grave.

Pulling three of the letters from a bundle, I slid them into a waterproof pouch. With a prayer, I buried the letters, replaced the dirt and sod on top, and stepped back to consider my work. Someone would have to look very closely to see. 'Twould do.

I thought about staying at an inn. I had passed one on the way to the church. But as tired as I was, I could not chance it. It was not inconceivable that Gray would stop here. I did not need a chance meeting, though the idea of a soft bed in a friendly inn certainly sounded appealing.

Retrieving the horse, I set off on the road to London, secure in the thought that I had bought myself a bit more life. Perhaps, I mused, enough life to see this affair through to the end.

THE LONDON I reentered was just as dark and gloomy as the one that I had left. I still could not fathom how a child born of the country, where the air was fresh and clean and the sun shone as it should, could ever find happiness in such a hideous place. It stank of rot and decay, even more so now that I had visited its royal underbelly. With luck, I had not been permanently stained by its stench.

If I lived beyond the day.

And that possibility seemed as remote as snow in July when I approached Ludgate. The contingent of the king's men was not there to joyously celebrate my return. The lines marking their faces were those of men with a difficult, even unpleasant, job to do.

My stomach roiled when I saw a shadowy figure on the edge of the group. George Wilkins. That he was there boded nothing but ill for me.

Three of the king's men stepped in front of me, blocking my entrance to the city. One took my horse by its bridle; another relieved me of my sword and dagger.

"In the name of the king, I arrest you!" he intoned loudly.

Before I could dismount and surrender, one of the men yanked me from the saddle and hurled me to the ground, waves of pain shooting through my shoulder.

As I rolled over, another of the guards jerked me to my feet. Weaving from pain, I caught a glimpse of Wilkins among the onlookers, looking very satisfied at my dilemma. I saw too, with no surprise, the familiar figure of Ben Jonson lurking in the shadows.

Suddenly, I was simply very tired, very ready for this affair to end, no matter how. Whether from exhaustion or pain or some other cause, everything turned black and I knew no more.

I BLINKED. Even in the darkness, I recognized the dank odour of the Bloody Tower. This was not one of the fine chambers occupied by Somerset and his wife. No, I had been placed in one of the lower rooms, stones covered with human dung, an oaken bucket of fetid water in one corner.

All of my possessions had been taken save the clothes on my back. It was cold, and I soon found myself huddling in a corner searching for warmth. I wanted to dream of home fires, a cup of Peg's hot spiced wine, any memory that could bring warmth, no matter how false, to my bones.

"Seems that you need a friend?"

A voice sounded from a dark corner.

"I do, but it seems that I have none. Have you come to repay me for my unkindness?"

Malcolm Gray laughed. "I have just completed my last official act as a servant of Sir Edward. I have delivered the letters we took to him, so that he might use them as best he sees fit. I come now as your friend."

"Indeed? You are not angry with me?"

He rubbed the back of his head tenderly. "I should be, but I am not. I would have done the same thing in your place. Besides, I think the northern climes are better suited for my health. Perhaps somewhere in Warwickshire."

I smiled. "Have you ever been to Stratford?"

Malcolm shook his head. "My duties have never chanced to take me there."

"Well, you will be welcome there. Though, I do not think I will be able to enjoy your company." Looking about, I added, "I think this may be my last abode."

"Do not be hasty, Simon. Your gamble may yet yield rewards. A word of caution. When you deal with His Majesty, cajole, yes, but do not threaten. He does not take well to threats."

"Why does he need to deal with me at all? He has all of the letters."

"Simon, Simon. I am no fool and neither are you. The first thing I would have done is hide some away after you had rid yourself of me." He held up a hand. "Say nothing of it to anyone else. Coke and Bacon will assume you did, but they will not speak of it. The king would not imagine that you would defy him thus, and you may need it as a bargaining tool."

"Then why am I here?"

"To teach you a lesson, about your place in life. Be patient. The king is most anxious to see you, but he worries about Somerset and what he might say at trial."

Malcolm stood then and slapped his knees. "I must leave you now, but I will be about when all is settled. Remember, pay His Majesty proper obeisance, but stand your ground."

And with those enigmatic words, Malcolm was gone, and I fell asleep.

WHEN I next awoke, it was to the jarring thud of a boot in my side. It took me but a second to straighten myself. Coke and Bacon.

"You are a most disagreeable man," Sir Francis said. "You do not follow orders. You choose the most dangerous of all paths."

"With all respect, Sir Francis, I did not come to London to assist you in your prosecution of Somerset and his wife. I came to London to enquire into the death of William Shakespeare. I came to believe that the king might have knowledge of interest to me. But one cannot simply question a king. I needed something to 'encourage' him to speak with me. When I realized that His Majesty had paid Shakespeare to write those notes to Somerset, to dissuade him from marrying, I knew that I had found what I needed. In the process, I have also arranged for the countess to confess and plead guilty to Overbury's murder, which should make your jobs all that much easier." Under other circumstances, I would not have dared lecture Coke and Bacon. But I was already in the Tower, and I was exhausted, both physically and in patience.

Sir Edward Coke threw his head back and laughed from deep within his belly. "He is his own man, Francis. And in this day and time, that is of note."

"He should have his head parted from his shoulders," Bacon grumbled.

"Come, Francis. He is right. He is making our jobs much easier. And, thanks to Malcolm, we will have the pleasure of delivering the offending letters to the king, thus solidifying our positions in his favor." Coke was certainly pleased, but Bacon yet frowned.

"Yes, and he could have just as easily brought this all down about our ears. You are too accepting, Edward."

"No, Francis, I care only about the results. You care more about how the results are achieved. That will forever separate us."

"As you like."

"Master Saddler, I assume that you held some letters back, as insurance."

"You assume correctly, sir." Malcolm had erred in his prediction. But I saw no reason to lie.

"The king will want to deal with you personally. We will hand over the letters that we have as, truly, they have no bearing on the case against Somerset. He will go through them and realize that some are missing. We will find it necessary to tell him that we suspect that you retained some of the letters."

"He will know who I am?"

This time, both Coke and Bacon laughed. "The king knows your entire history, Saddler. He leaves little to chance. Do not fear, Constable. I believe that he will deal fairly with you. He has been afraid of two things for several months now. First, that these letters would somehow become public. Second, that Somerset would say something in court that would either implicate him in Overbury's death or embarrass him. You have now, cleverly, eliminated the first concern. The king is, if anything, an appreciative man."

"Come, Edward. We have work before us."

And again, I was alone.

THEY CAME for me sometime past the midnight. I was trussed up like a pig, blindfolded and tossed in the back of a wagon, a wagon that had recently carried horse manure. We rumbled and bumped through the streets of London for what seemed like hours. When we came to a stop, I heard my guards dismount and the sound of their feet sloshing in mud.

"Look, Alec, he's still awake."

"I'll fix that."

And then a dizzying pain burst in my head and all was black.

WHEN I awoke this time, it was in an apartment of a palace. That much I could tell from looking about me. Which palace, I had no idea. But the arras were fine and the rushes on the floor fresh, and the smell of rosewater hung heavy in the air. And such was only the case in palaces and the homes of the most wealthy. Even I had been cleansed and perfumed. Since I had been arrested on the king's orders, it seemed likely that I was in one of the palaces, though why I had been taken from the Tower was a mystery to me.

"Och, man! You air a difficult one to deal with." The Scottish accent left no doubt about my companion's identity.

I rolled off the couch and took a knee. "Your Majesty."

"If I had a sword handy, I would cleave your head, you rascal."

He circled about in front of me, a parchment in his hand, and bade me arise.

James was a good-looking man, bearded. His Scottish brogue lay heavily in the air. "Let us deal as men; I dinna wish to tarry long with this matter." He had broad shoulders atop a slim frame. "Here, you may sit."

"As you command, Your Grace."

My head throbbed as I found a seat near him. "So Shakespeare was your friend?"

"From childhood."

King James nodded. "He was a likable sort."

"Aye, Your Majesty."

James was silent for a moment. Then he waved the parchments at me. "These are not all of them."

"No, Your Majesty, they are not."

"You chance a meeting with the axe, Constable."

I nodded. "I do, Your Majesty."

"Coke and Bacon tell me that you think someone murdered Shakespeare."

"His son-in-law, Doctor John Hall, says it is so. I came to London seeking his killer. I did not come to involve myself in this matter."

"Yet you have."

"It seemed unavoidable."

"You have done all of this to find justice for your friend?"

"Every man deserves justice, Your Majesty."

"Be careful, Constable. You are a man of morals, and men of morals usually have short lives." The king paused. "But I do owe you my appreciation for bringing me at least this many of these notes. They were a worry."

"Your Majesty, I think that I have a solution to this problem."

James raised his eyebrows. "Indeed? Tell me."

"Lady Somerset will confess her guilt in the death of Overbury, if you promise to commute her sentence, which is bound to be death. Lord Somerset refuses to confess, but will make no 'damaging' statements in court. One year from today, assuming that we are all still alive, I will bring you the remaining letters."

"You would blackmail the throne?" Fire shot from his eyes.

"No, Your Majesty, I am bargaining with the throne."

"Six months from today, you will present the letters to me."

"Agreed." Though James could not see it, I breathed a sigh of relief. But I had one more issue to deal with. "I would also like to know what information you might have of Shakespeare's death."

He calmed at that. "None. It did not profit me to have him killed. He was a good and true servant, and I am sorry that he is gone." The king paused. "Somerset and his wife have agreed to this?"

"I could not have found the letters without their guidance." To tell him that 'twas Lady Somerset who took command for her husband served no one and probably would not have surprised him.

The king nodded. "You have read the letters?"

"Only enough to ensure that they were what I sought. I have no desire to pry into Your Majesty's private life."

"You are a wise man, Master Saddler. A weaker man would not have been able to resist."

"A weaker man, Your Majesty, would be more the fool."

The king threw his head back and laughed. "You have something of Shakespeare in you, Saddler. Do you have this agreement with Somerset in writing?"

"Your Majesty, you know full well that such a document would be as damning as those letters."

"Coke said that you were clever. Very well. I could have you tortured to reveal the location of the other letters, but not all men break under torture. I understand that you served in the Low Countries."

I nodded. "I did."

"Battle-tested men are all the harder to break. I will honor your service by not testing your resolve." He paused. "I will have to tarry a bit before commuting their sentences. But I set the time and date for executions, and they should not be concerned. I will honour my word."

"Your Majesty, a question if I might."

He nodded curtly.

"If you had no involvement in Shakespeare's death, why did you have Southampton dispatch men to Stratford to go through John Hall's notebooks?"

King James laughed again. "You are bold. Yes, I am responsible for that visit. When I learned that Shakespeare had been poisoned, I had Southampton send them there to find Hall's notebooks to see if they could shed any light." He looked away for an instant. "When you are king, sometimes acts are committed in your name or for your benefit that you do not sanction."

"You were afraid someone killed Shakespeare for you?"

He nodded.

"Did you learn anything?"

At that, the king stood. "I learned more than I wanted to know, but nothing I will tell you. Your bargain is satisfactory. I will have my men take you back to the Tower. You will want to advise Somerset that the bargain has been struck. After that, you will be free to return home."

Disappointment did not begin to measure my feelings at that moment. "You will tell me nothing?" My entire reason for coming to London had been dashed upon the rocks like a ship on an angry sea.

"William Shakespeare is dead, Constable Saddler. Leave it at that. I do not mind telling you that I have been impressed with your abilities in this matter."

I wanted nothing more than to strangle the man, but I was no fool. "Your Majesty is too kind."

"And you are a cheeky fellow," he answered with a wink. And he was gone.

MOMENTS LATER, his guards fetched me and returned me to the Tower. But this time I was allowed to enter under my own power, and the warders treated me with a deference prisoners rarely saw.

The countess joined me in the front room of her small suite. Her eyes brightened when she saw me there. "You have made the bargain?"

"I have, my lady. As long as you can keep your husband from saying anything embarrassing, then His Majesty will respect the agreement."

She narrowed her eyes. "Have you this in writing?"

"As I told the king, only a fool would put something like this in writing. But I held back a handful of letters as security against anyone reneging on the bargain."

"Very wise of you. And my sentence will be commuted?"

"It will, but the king said he would have to wait a bit before doing so. To prevent any talk of impropriety, I am sure."

Frances nodded. "Of course. I trust the king's word. It is too bad, Master Saddler, that you and I did not meet under other circumstances. I would have enjoyed knowing you better, and more intimately."

Despite the burning under my collar, I turned my most withering glare on her.

"I am not of this city, my lady. I am of a town where people have secrets, but the only lives that those secrets would destroy are their own. Here, it seems, everyone has secrets and each of those secrets could hurt hundreds or thousands. William Shakespeare was my friend nearly from birth. He had a wife and children, but more than that he was in love with words and how he could use them to make people happy.

"Then he came to London to pursue that dream. And your lot seduced him with your gifts and patronage and scarlet clothing. And you twisted him to your ways of debauchery. And you ruined him for decent people. I do not mourn the man he became. But I mourn greatly for the boy he once was."

I spun about and left, without seeking her permission.

She said nothing.

THE DAY was almost come, but I knew that I was far too exhausted to begin my journey home. I would go to the George and spend the day and night resting, then start for Stratford on the morrow. At that moment, I yearned for nothing more than home, and I realized with a start, Peg. Though I had not discovered who killed Will, something had broken his hold on me. I was ready to love my wife again.

Without a horse, I trudged wearily across London Bridge, dodging the occasional dumping of water and garbage from above, the din of hawkers selling their wares and tinsmiths at their craft lost to me.

The innkeeper did not seem surprised at my appearance.

"Do I still have my room?"

He smiled. "Of course, Master Saddler. Your credit has always been good here."

"Then I will pay you double for uninterrupted rest. Can you assure me of that?"

"As long as you stay within the George. Out there," and he indicated the frenetically active street, "I can offer no guarantees."

"Good enough." I had been gone for more than a week now, over a week since I had seen my girls, and my Peg. I was anxious now to see them all. I had tired of London and the court.

After a cup of strong beer, I went to the room he had let to me. It was at the opposite end of the inn from my original room, but the stench of burning wood and a sweeter, more sickly odor still stung my nostrils.

I was exhausted, and I stripped off my clothes and lay down, luxuriating in the simple pleasure of lying still on a soft bed.

But I could not sleep.

I twisted and I turned.

Yet that blissful state would not come.

I sat up. Too much sun streamed through the window. Too many thoughts still rattled through my mind.

After an hour of fruitless search for sleep, I arose and dressed again. I knew full well that leaving now for Stratford was a mistake. The events of the days had taken a heavy toll on me. I would be careless, and our roads were not a place to be anything but extra-vigilant.

The innkeeper gave me a puzzled look but said nothing as I wandered out of the George, my feet moving me aimlessly into the frantic noise and constant movement of the Liberty-of-the-Clink.

I found myself before Bishop Andrewes's home. To this day, I do not know why. Though it was yet before noon, I knocked at the door. The same servant who had appeared on my first visit answered the door this time also, but upon seeing me, cocked his head as if he had a question but then thought better of it, and he bade me enter.

When the bishop came down the stairs, he raised his own eyebrows at me. "Master Saddler! I had heard that you were dead. But I see that you have not yet entered the heavenly gates."

A smile leapt onto my face. There was something soothing in the old man, with his pointed white beard and flat hat peculiar to clerics. He took me by the arm and directed me into his sitting room before the great fireplace.

"Now, sit, and tell this old priest what brings you to my door again."

I stared at my hands, scarred from years of working in the wool and from years of fighting in the Low Countries. "Your Grace, do you know His Majesty well?"

"As well as any of us do, I suspect. Who truly knows the mind of a king?" He paused, sensing that I wished no light tones or jovial comments. "My experience with him indicates that he is a man of his word."

"Is he a good man?"

Andrewes steepled his fingers together in front of his mouth, almost as if saying a prayer. "That is a difficult question to answer. What makes a normal man good is not the same thing that makes a king a good man. They are measured with different rulers."

"Let me be frank. I have entered into a bargain with His Majesty."

A smile lit the old priest's face. "And you wish to know if he will be faithful to his promise?"

"Aye."

"King James is many things, but I believe that when he makes an agreement he remains faithful to it."

"Truly?"

Andrewes nodded so vigorously that his beard brushed his chest. "It is in his nature."

"There are other, less holy, things in his nature, I am told."

At that the bishop smiled again softly. "Different rulers, my friend." He stopped smiling and leaned forward. "This bargain you have entered into, does it have aught to do with our friend Shakespeare's death?"

"No, I was pursuing that when I was swept up by other events. I hoped to use my involvement in that affair to force out information about Will's murder, but the king would not tell me what I wished to know. He said that what he knew of it, I would not want to know."

"Master Saddler, I know something of that other affair that James mentioned, aye, and your involvement."

My eyebrows then raised.

"I have many 'friends' at court. A bishop must have if he wishes to remain a bishop. You have worked against forces far greater than you. And you have shown great courage and daring in pursuit of your quest. Were Will Shakespeare to speak to you one last time, he would praise what you have done to fulfill his last request. If the whispers I hear are true, you have done far more than almost any other man would have. Sometimes you cannot succeed, but that does nothing to devalue your effort. I suspect that your fervour in seeking Will's killer, whether you know it or not, sprang from guilt."

"Guilt?"

"Aye, guilt that you never forgave him for the wrong he did you."

At that, I drew back as if struck. "You know of this?"

Bishop Lancelot Andrewes nodded. "He sat where you sit now and confessed to me his sin. He hated himself for being so weak. He tortured himself for betraying his one, true friend."

I hung my head. "I came to London to find Will's killer, yes. But I wanted to learn also how my friend could change so much that he would risk losing his oldest friend for a moment's pleasure."

"And have you?"

"Forgive me for saying this, Your Grace, but customs and behaviour at court do not always conform to the edicts of the Church. There is a freedom, a liberty to do what one pleases. I think that Will was seduced by that."

"But surely you knew that many nobles respect only power and money? You are far from an innocent. I see in your hands that you have been no stranger to hard work, perhaps even war. The scar on your face looks as if you were marked by a spear point."

"Under Sir Francis Vere in the Low Countries," I confirmed.

"Then the liberties taken by the nobility should not surprise you. Ask me if this pleases me, and I will tell you that no, it does not. Ask me if I can change it, and I will tell you no, I cannot. Will Shakespeare wanted one thing above all others—acceptance. Acceptance as a poet, as a playwright. He never understood that he had achieved that. And that he did not need the court to confirm it."

The old bishop was right. I thought about how hard Will had strived to become a respected citizen in Stratford, to repair his family's reputation after his father's misfortunes and bad judgement brought disdain to them. Even in his birthplace, he wanted badly to be accepted. For, nearly from birth, he was different, and people saw that.

I still suspected, as did the king, that someone had killed Will to prevent him from embarrassing James over the notes to Carr. I believed that either Wilkins or Ben Jonson had administered the poison. Both were connected to Southampton, and both were in a position to commit this horrible deed. Southampton needed to further secure himself in the king's favour. But I would never be able to prove it. I rose.

"But I failed him. I did not find his killer."

"My lad, the William Shakespeare that I knew would forgive you this failing, if only because you risked so much in pursuit of his charge to you."

"Thank you, Bishop Andrewes, for helping me to settle my mind on these questions. I think that now I can return to Stratford and take up my life once again. I have been away from it too long."

The bishop stood, more slowly than I, and clasped my hand in both of his. "You are a good man, Simon Saddler. No one, including William Shakespeare, would deny that. I suspect that whilst you follow the law on church attendance, you do so only because you must. But if you would listen to the lessons that the Church would teach you, you might find more solace."

"Perhaps," I replied, with little conviction.

"Occasionally, my path takes me to Stratford. Someday I might chance to visit you, and we can discuss this further."

Lancelot Andrewes had a way of speaking, a soft, yet firm tone, that was pleasant and agreeable.

"I would welcome that, Your Grace. Thank you for listening to me."

The old man spread his hands out and gave me a simple bow. "That is what an aging bishop is for."

It took little imagination to see why Will found comfort talking to Andrewes. A weight had been lifted from me, and I felt suddenly weary, and sleepy.

I do not remember going back to the George. But I remember waking up in the late afternoon from a dream of Peg. A good dream.

Chapter Thirteen

I SENT ONE OF THE STABLE BOYS TO THE GLOBE TO FETCH Burbage. This would be my last night in London for a long while, and I would spend it with friends. Night was beginning to fall, and the players would be finished for the day. I found a table in the tavern and drank a mug of ale while I waited. God help me, but I was feeling very satisfied, not smug, but satisfied.

Though Will's murderer still walked at liberty, I had done my best. But be it Jonson or Wilkins, both had the patronage of Southampton, and they would be difficult, if not impossible, to bring to justice. If I admitted the truth to myself, Will had given many men reason to kill him. Since coming to London, I had given John Davenant no thought. Nor Thomas Quiney for that matter. I could not rule either out, but at the same time I did not feel their guilt strongly. Too many pieces of this puzzle seemed to have their genesis in London and the royal court.

Returning to thoughts of Jonson and Wilkins, I considered simply killing them both. No one would miss Wilkins; he was a despicable creature. But with the king about to settle a pension on Jonson, he would have many powerful friends looking to avenge his death. And, after recent days, no doubt suspicion would fall on me immediately. I had no desire to be imprisoned or hanged for killing the likes of Jonson. He too had been seduced by the court, and he, like Will, had learned to hold friendship cheap.

"Simon!" It was the increasingly frail Richard Burbage, answering my summons.

"Richard. Sit with me. I'll treat you with an ale."

The old actor shook his head in amazement and sat. "In a short week, you have arrived in London and set the town on its head. Will had nothing on you. Then, you are said to be dead. Then, you are not. And now, after I hear tales of you being thrown in the Tower, I find you drinking at the George, appearing for all the world carefree."

I could not help but grin at his recitation. "It has been an eventful few days, Richard. But for the grace of God, I would be dead now, aye, several times over."

"Tell me, please."

And though it was horribly indiscreet of me, I told him most of it, saving but the nature of the notes that Will wrote for the king. No one else needed to know that. I cast them only as notes aimed to discourage Carr from marrying Frances Howard. But Richard had been to court innumerable times, and he could hear what I was not saying. After all, it had been Burbage who had first explained Carr's relationship with the king.

"What of Ben Jonson?"

"What of him?" I answered, a bit more sharply than I intended, and I quickly softened my tone. "I have been unable to discover in whose service he has acted." I paused. Burbage must deal with Jonson regularly, and it did no one any good for me to muddy the waters between them. The Thames was quite muddy enough. "Ben is beholden to both Southampton and the king for his pension. Like Will, he will act on their orders when forced to, even if it might go against his better nature. Perhaps, one day, he and I will reconcile our differences, but that day has not yet come." No purpose was served by telling Burbage of my suspicions that Jonson may have had a hand in Will's death.

But Burbage simply nodded and accepted my words. "We are all servants of some master, though our apprenticeships ended many years ago. That is the way of it."

He looked at me then, his eyes old and watery. "I remember when we first met, Simon, in Stratford. You will pardon me for saying this as I mean no insult. After I had read that bit of Will's work, and realized that he truly was a writer of no small talent, I looked you over and wondered how a man of that intelligence and wit could cling to you as his friend. You seemed but a simple lad. I understand now. You have great depths, depths that Will must have sensed from the beginning. I see you in many of the characters he created. His best characters. There's even a touch of Lear in you; madness seems a trait you both share."

And that would have angered me, but for a moment, the briefest of seconds, I saw those watery eyes become bright and alive again, much as they had been that long-ago day in Stratford. To see that flashing glimpse of the actor that Burbage had been was worth a minor slight.

Moments later we were joined by his brother Cuthbert, John Heminges and Henry Condell. John's beard reached down nearly to his chest. Henry was a taciturn man, his face unadorned with a beard. These four men were Will's oldest and best friends in the theatre world. They had trusted him enough to make him a partner in the Globe. They had loved his plays well enough to make him their lead playwright.

"Simon returns to Stratford on the morrow," Richard told them.

"Did you find who killed Will?" Cuthbert asked. He was not a player; he was saltier and more common than his famous brother. But he managed the Globe as if it were a child that needed extra attention.

"No," I said. "I did not. I can guess whom his death profited, but I could never prove it. And unless you can bring the guilty to account, what good is knowing? That way lies only disappointment and frustration. Will is gone. I am not sure that the how and why are important any longer."

Heminges and Condell nodded their agreement, but I saw doubt in Cuthbert's eyes. He was more a man of the streets than a player at court. He sensed that I was leaving much out, but said not a word. Richard would keep my confidence, of that I had little doubt.

My words put us in a dark humour, and we sat silent for several minutes, drinking ale and contemplating our tankards.

Finally, Condell broke the silence. "I suspect that you will not be returning to London for a while, Simon. We will miss your antics. The stories that have been told about you over the last week have been entertaining indeed. Aye, neither Will Kemp or Richard Armin could hold a candle to you in playing clowns."

His voice was soft and joking.

I tipped my mug to him. "I am glad that I supplied you with some laughs, Henry."

"Tell me, Simon. I have heard rumours that you struck Ben Jonson. Did you truly?" asked Heminges.

With a chuckle and dropping my head in feigned embarrassment, I nodded. "I did. But 'twas not the first time."

At that, all jaws dropped.

"I do not believe it," crowed Cuthbert. "I have heard naught of this. Unless you did it in Stratford, for Ben is not one to announce when he has been bested."

"Neither here nor there," I answered, feeling the warm glow of the beer in my stomach. "'Twas in the Low Countries, with Vere."

"You served with Ben?" Heminges asked.

"Aye, I did." And for the next two hours, I passed the time pleasantly, telling stories of Vere and Jonson and the Low Countries. I rarely even spoke of those times, but after what I had endured in recent days, it seemed a quite peaceful time. But I still did not talk of the fighting, the dying. I told only those tales guaranteed to make my audience laugh.

And laugh they did. They obliged by telling tales of Will Shakespeare. Of "William the Conqueror," who bested Burbage in the pursuit of an admirer. Even that old story did not dampen my humour.

I retired to my chamber late that night, genuinely tired

from laughing. As my eyes closed, I realized with a smile that it had been years since I had truly enjoyed myself. The world was a better place that night than it had been for a long, long time.

On the morrow, with my head still ringing a bit from drink, I rose and dressed early, intent on returning to Stratford swiftly. I had much to set right, and I wished to waste no more time doing so.

But when I opened my door, I saw that it was not going to be that simple.

Ben Jonson was standing there.

I dropped my bag, in case he should attack. But he just raised both hands, open.

"I did not come to fight you, Simon. I came to make my peace with you."

Something in his eyes told me that he was sincere, so I stepped back and bade him enter.

"You should know," he began, "that I refused to take part in Southampton's plans." We were sitting on opposite sides of the chamber. "When he suggested that Wilkins cause you to cease being any trouble, I walked out. I have never been your enemy in this, Simon."

"You have said that many times over the last fortnight. But if that is so, you have hardly been my ally."

Jonson shrugged. "I have simply attempted to keep you from getting yourself killed. If that is reason for your anger, then so be it."

My face flashed red. I felt the heat rise. "You have been kissing Southampton's arse, attempting to ensure that you get your precious pension. Do not class your meddling as something innocent. It is not."

"Am I trying to protect myself? Certainly. But that does not mean that I am your enemy. What Southampton wanted to do was wrong, but he is obsessed with securing preferment with the king. You speak of me meddling, but it is Southampton who meddles in matters that he should stay out of."

"That's a pretty speech, Ben. But you did nothing to stop Wilkins from trying to burn me within my room."

"I assumed that you could handle scum like Wilkins and would not need my help."

"Such is a facile answer." But then something occurred to me, something that I had not stopped to wonder about in the hurry and panic of recent days. "Who was the man burned in my place?"

Again, Jonson shrugged, but this time his movements played him false. He knew something of it. "That is unimportant."

And then I understood. "Where did you find him, Ben? A drunk in the streets? Or did you steal a body from somewhere?"

"Your life was in danger! I did what I did to protect you."

"And yet here I am. It would seem that your protection wasn't required."

Jonson laughed uneasily. "Your life was not worth a penny. Though I hoped to hurry you out of the city before it was discovered that you yet lived, you played it to even greater advantage. You have more than a little of the dramatist in you."

"Perhaps," I answered, suddenly weary of all of this. "And now I will take my leave of you. I have a long ride ahead."

"So you will not be seeking Will's killer anymore?" He seemed relieved, and I thought once again that he might very well be the man that I sought. But there was no proof, nothing with which to arrest him.

"No, I will not. My friend is dead before his time, and the only one that can be held to account is him. If he had stayed with us in Stratford and never come to this cesspit, he might have lived a much longer life."

At that, Ben Jonson scowled. "You never really knew him. He could never have remained in Stratford. It was too small to hold a man of his dimensions. It would have choked the life out of him."

"Hmmph! Seems to me that 'twas his life in London that choked his breath from him. Ben, we have known each other too long to lie. I am not interested in your evil deeds. I suspect that whoever you threw into a burning room deserved it. But that doesn't make you less guilty. If I could prove it, I would move heaven and earth to bring you to justice. But, I cannot. So now I will go home. But occasionally, just occasionally, I will think of you and of Will's death. And I will wonder just what hand you had in that affair."

Jonson rose. "Well, at the very least, this time we did not strike each other. I am sure, however, that our paths will cross again. And I repeat, I am not your enemy."

He could repeat that until the heavens broke open and spilled souls out like raindrops, and I would not believe him. And if it weren't him, if it was Wilkins, they were both scum, skimmed from the same pond. Someday, yes, someday when I had repaired the fabric of my family, I might return to the chase, to see if I could catch Ben Jonson in my snare.

"Prosper, Ben Jonson. That is the least I can do, wish you prosperity."

And Ben was gone.

As I went down to the tavern to settle my account, I noticed yet another acquaintance, seated with his back against the wall and smoking a pipe of this tobacco from the New World. Southampton, dressed more common than usual. He took the long pipestem from his mouth and used it to motion me over.

Sighing, I paid my bill and then joined the earl.

"How may I be of service to you, my lord?"

Southampton frowned at me. "You are an annoying man, Saddler. I try to warn you away; you ignore me. I send men to kill you; you escape with your life. What is the source of this confidence and your incredible luck?"

"My lord, I am simply a common man trying to fulfill the oath I took as constable. Whatever good fortune Providence has given me must be from God himself."

Southampton shook his head at me. "Please, Master Saddler, do not assault my ears with such phrases as you learned at Bishop Andrewes's knee. Don't speak!" He said with a raised hand, stopping my words in midflight from my mouth. "You are a fool if you don't think that I have you followed. I know that you made a bargain with the Somersets, and I know that the king has agreed to it. The king holds tightly to his word, but others are not so trustworthy. You have made a number of powerful men very angry. Your safety is not yet ensured."

"My lord," I began, the frustration growing heavy within me. "What do you hope to accomplish with this diatribe? You cannot frighten me. You cannot intimidate me. I am going home to Stratford and do not intend to trouble you or your city any longer."

At that Southampton leapt to his feet, and for a moment I thought I would have to defend myself. But he stopped short. "At first you were merely a meddlesome country constable, poking his nose about where it did not belong. But now, you know things, things that others wish to keep hidden. That is what killed your friend Shakespeare. And it will kill you too."

He blocked my path, but I had heard enough of his blustering. I lowered my shoulder and bowled him out of the way, just as if I were opening a recalcitrant door.

Southampton went flying, his long-stemmed pipe spinning across the room leaving sparks in its wake, and he slammed against the wall with an *oomph!* I just shook my head at him as the other patrons looked on astonished.

Stopping at the bar, I flipped a coin on the counter. "Buy my Lord Southampton something to ease the sting."

And I left the George behind me.

FOR SOME reason, I did not hear the noise and din of the city. My mind was one hundred miles away, in the quiet lanes of Stratford. Though I had not succeeded in my quest, I was at peace with myself. I believed that I knew what had occurred.

At first, King James was strongly opposed to Carr's marriage. He did not want to lose his favourite to Lady Frances. A wife might very well spell the end of the king's "special" relationship with Robert Carr. With either a sense of urgency or a sense of desperation, James turned to Shakespeare to help him woo Carr back, for which he paid Will handsomely.

Oddly, in this matter, Overbury was the king's ally. He wanted Somerset and Lady Frances together even less than the king.

But no matter how hard Will had worked on the king's letters to Carr, the efforts failed, and James reluctantly agreed to the marriage, or perhaps George Villiers had already caught his eye and he had lost interest in Somerset. Certainly the king began to see wisdom in an alliance with the Howards.

But when the king's mind changed, Overbury's did not. And he continued his objections to the marriage privately and publicly, leading the Howards to concoct the scheme to send Overbury to Russia as ambassador. In his inimitable way, Overbury destroyed that opportunity, giving James reason to confine him to the Tower. Even there, however, Overbury continued to be an obstacle to the marriage. Enter the Howards in the person of the former Lady Frances. Events move swiftly. Overbury dies on 15 September 1613. By September 25th, the king has arranged the annulment of Frances's marriage to Essex. In December, Carr and Frances are married.

Then all is quiet for a spell. Until rumours begin floating throughout the city that King James himself is complicit in Overbury's death. Coke is forced to launch an investigation to finally sort out the affair.

The most likely scenario from this point was simple: the Somersets are imprisoned. James worries aloud about what Carr might say; perhaps he even expresses concerns about what Shakespeare might say. Some noble, like Southampton, who was not completely secure in James's circle, sees an opportunity to better secure his position in the King's favour. He dispatches Ben Jonson to Stratford, and there begins the poisoning, though King James is oblivious to it.

But the poison acts too slowly, so Wilkins is dispatched with various documents and to finish off the job. Which succeeds. Then word spreads in London that a Stratford constable is asking uncomfortable questions. Of the attempts on my life in London, I suspected that Southampton had a hand in those, but I could not be certain of any but the fire at the George. Unfortunately, striking Ben Jonson and bowling over Southampton were the only acts of revenge I could commit for Shakespeare's murder.

The one most important thing that I had learned in London was that both Will and I were its victims. It was London that made Will what he ultimately became, and it was that new Will Shakespeare that had violated the trust of our friendship. London was power and fame and money, and those were the most seductive mistresses in the world. Will had slept with each of them, and he found them good.

Now, at last, with this knowledge to comfort me, I could mourn for my friend properly. And I could love my wife again, and bring happiness to my house.

I STOPPED once more at John Davenant's inn. Such was my good humour that I spent an hour outside playing with young Will Davenant. The more I looked at him, the more I realized that he was indeed Shakespeare's son. But I would say nothing to anyone, neither furthering the rumour nor stopping it. Let people think as they would.

Jane Davenant wanted to know all about London, what the women were wearing and did I see the queen. John was more the businessman, wishing to know about prices and what London inns were charging for a chamber. Did their wine seem watered? How much did the hostlers charge for seeing to horses? Such things as I would never think to question. But it reminded me that I needed to see Matthew, who ran my business. He was a good strong, solid man. Once I had seen him as a proper match for my daughter Margaret, but it had been some time since I had let my mind wander afield in that vein. Now, with this behind me, I could once again be a proper father to my children.

But the next morning, as I went down to the tavern to break my fast and prepare to leave for Stratford, I was startled to see a new customer, seated with his back against the wall. Malcolm Gray.

He smiled at my entry, but it was a sad sort of smile.

"Simon! Please join me." I saw nothing threatening in his posture, and so I did as he asked.

John Davenant brought me some eggs and crusty bread with a bit of pork. Malcolm had the same.

"What brings you to Oxford, Malcolm? I thought I had seen the last of you, at least for a while."

Malcolm paused in his eating, wiped a crumb of bread from his beard, and leaned down into a satchel at his side. Rising up, he put a bound book in front of me. I recognized it immediately, one of John Hall's casebooks where he recorded the treatment of his patients.

"Where did you get this? Was it you who attacked John and stole the book?"

"No, one of George Wilkins's scum did that. The king ordered me to bring this to you."

"The king? I thought you served Edward Coke."

Malcolm grinned. "One man may have many masters, but I lied to you earlier. Coke recognized my abilities, but he brought me to the attention of His Majesty, who saw something in me that he could use. It was King James who kept the noose from about my neck. I was on loan, shall we say, to Coke."

"So he sent you to return John Hall's property to me?" I was truly confused.

"Open it to the week before Shakespeare's death. Read the entries." He paused and motioned for John Davenant, who hurried over with a tall mug of ale.

"'Tis too early in the morning for drink, Malcolm."

"Read the passages."

And I did, slowly. They were written in a sort of Latin abbreviation, but I had had reason before to read passages in John's books, and he had taught me something of how he wrote them. At first, my reading was desultory, uninterested, but then with widening eyes and fear chilling my bones.

I slammed it shut.

"No! I will not believe it!"

"Did the king not tell you that he learned more of the poet's death than he wanted to know?"

"Aye."

"This is why."

My gaze swung to and fro about the room. I could not focus,

not at first, and when I did it was as if my mind was shutting down. I could not think to speak or even grunt.

Malcolm pushed the mug over, and I snatched it up and emptied it. But all that did was enrage me further. Suddenly, I felt limp, the room spun, and all turned black.

When I awakened, I found myself back in my chamber at Davenant's. Jane sat next to me, applying a cold cloth to my head. "You had a mighty fall, Simon. Good for you that the big man was there to keep you from hitting the floor."

I jerked my head from the pillow, and it immediately exploded in pain. "Where is he?"

"Right here, Simon," came a voice from the corner of the chamber.

"Why?"

Jane, glancing back and forth between us, gathered her things and left us alone.

"Why did I bring this to you? The king felt sorry about not giving you what you sought. At first, he thought he had done you a boon, but as he considered it further, he decided that you did him the honour of returning his property and he could do no less for you. He sent me after you with that."

"Did you read it?"

Malcolm nodded. "I did."

"Then you know what it means?"

Again, he merely nodded. "Some truths should remain hidden but others must be faced. This is one of those times, Simon. You sought the truth of the matter. It is in those pages."

I felt that I was in a dream, a nightmare, and that it must all return to normal. But this was no dream. Malcolm was real. The inn was real. I was real.

Jane Davenant hurried in with a mug. "Here, drink this. It is an extract of valerian root and will calm you."

I took a sip of the bitter fluid. But after the heat struck my stomach, I did feel calmer. I read the passage again and again. Finally, I looked at Malcolm. "You know that there's only one way to interpret this."

"I would wish for others, but you are right. John Hall, and others, have much to answer for," Malcolm added ominously.

"What will I do? What can I do?"

Malcolm crossed the room and laid a friendly hand on my shoulder. "We will go to Stratford together, and together we will seek the best way to resolve this."

I waited wordless as he paid my bill. He said he had four horses outside, a remount for each of us. Malcolm Gray was a man of many parts. He had known what my reaction would be, and he had prepared everything for that event.

"Not a word to anyone, Malcolm. I must deal with this directly. I do not need gossipmongers blocking my path."

"In this," my giant friend said, "I am your servant. I have never been a member of such a close community. So, I will watch and learn, and lend my counsel when it seems needed."

"You sound as if you have planned all this?"

"No, not planned. I am just skilled at stage managing."

I found it difficult to stand, but Malcolm gave me his arm and navigated me out of the room into the bright morning sunshine. On any other day, I would have reveled in it. Not this day.

"If it helps, the king knew that this would be a shock to you, but he thought it better that you knew. He told me that perhaps you could have the strength to bring this to a conclusion."

"How kind!" I muttered bitterly, as Malcolm held a beaker to my lips. The beer burned going down, but it could not help the burning in my soul. "Are you prepared to leave for Stratford?"

"Shouldn't you rest a bit more?"

"I have rested too long as it is. It is time for me to go home."

With that, my big friend helped me upon my horse, then he mounted his. I felt comfort at his presence. In the short while that I had known him, I had found him to be an honest man, no matter his earlier life.

Malcolm led the way, as I simply remained blank, clutching John Hall's notebook fiercely. "John, John," I thought. "How could you let this come to pass?" For that matter, how had I let it come to pass? I wondered then if the blame could be laid at the feet of all Stratford, and London. But I was seeking scapegoats, others to blame than my own transgressions.

"You should approach this directly, and rid yourself of this burden once and for all," Malcolm counseled. "The sooner you put this behind, the sooner you may live again."

"Aye," I answered simply. But I knew my life would never be the same.

It was the longest journey of my life, and I fear I was poor company for my companion. But Malcolm Gray was not an ordinary man. I saw that from the first. He was content to keep his own counsel, and happy to refrain from offering his counsel to others.

Usually, on such a trip in the spring, I would enjoy the budding flowers and new growth. But on this trip, I did not even notice them. 'Twas as if I lived in a world without smell or sound, a world without colour.

An hour or two beyond Oxford, I turned to Malcolm and broke the silence. "I have been town constable for many years, Malcolm, and yet I have never faced a situation like this."

"Every situation is different, Simon. But you are a man born to survive. There are not many like that in this world," he said. He pointed towards a grove of yew trees off the trail. "It is late. Try and resolve this now and you will make a mess of it. Sleep, and face the world rested. The world will look less dangerous tomorrow."

So I did as advised, but my dreams were filled with images of Will and Peg entwined, of George Wilkins laughing at me, of Jane Davenant laughing at all of us.

Chapter Fourteen

THE SIGHT OF SEVEN RIVERS ROAD WAS A WELCOME ONE. How oft had I traveled this road with Will at my side, going to or returning from the fleshpots of London? We had not a care in the world then. As we passed Holy Trinity Church, I realized with a start that my old friend lay there, already decaying. I remembered something he had written once about sullied flesh resolving into a dew, and the memory sparked a shiver down my back.

The bridge into Stratford was just as I remembered it. With a start, I realized that it had been but ten days since I left. It seemed so much longer. On the morrow, Will's killer would either be revealed or I would be dead. I should have seen it from the first; I could have saved all of us much pain and sorrow.

"Malcolm, I would have you stop at my house as my guest."

He shook his head. "No, I will stay at Perrott's and gauge the mood of the town. I can learn more by listening to gossip if considered an outsider than a friend of yours. People will be guarded if they believe that I am allied with you. If I am a foreigner, they will be more willing to talk amongst themselves."

With that, Malcolm went his way to Perrott's and I turned towards Henley Street and my family. I opened the door, and all was quiet within. Mary was not chattering away. Margaret was not scolding her. I heard no sounds at all. I wandered through each room, but all were empty.

"Peg! I am home!"

The words echoed through the empty house.

"Simon."

I turned and there, standing alone in the doorway, was my cousin Hamnet, the corners of his mouth turned down in sadness. "Hamnet, where is my family?"

"They are at my house, Simon. Mary has taken ill, and we brought her there so she could be better cared for. As soon as I heard you had returned, I came straightaway."

NOT FIVE minutes later, I rushed into Hamnet's house to find my darling baby lying listless, nearly lifeless it seemed, in Hamnet's best bed, the one reserved for guests. Peg, Margaret and John Hall hovered over her still form.

"What has happened here?" I cried.

Peg turned to see me enter, and I gathered her up in my arms and held her tightly to my chest. The act sparked a cry of surprise from her, and she pushed me away, but just a bit. "Simon?"

I looked down at her. "We have no time for explanations now. Tell me what has happened here, John." Later would come the time to hear his story of how Will had died; now, I cared only for Mary's life.

John, looking pale and shaky, shrugged his shoulders in a gesture of defeat. "I do not understand it, Simon. She was fine yesterday, and today she is near death. It makes no sense, but she exhibits the same symptoms as Will Shakespeare did."

A perplexed innocence coloured his words, something that I noted but had no time to pursue. All that mattered to me at that moment was my baby girl.

"Father," I heard Margaret say. "You have changed!" The wonderment in her voice was pleasing to hear, but did nothing to dispel my panic over Mary.

I released Peg and went to little Mary's side. I took her hand in mine, her tiny, tiny hand, and squeezed it gently. Mary's eyes fluttered open and she attempted a smile. "My stomach hurts, Papa."

"I know, child," I said to comfort her but with no conviction in my voice. "Cousin John will help you."

Releasing her hand, I gestured with my head for John to follow me into the next chamber. I took a moment to study him. Wilkins or whoever had been sent to steal the book had done a pretty piece of work on him. Both eyes were still blackened, though the bruises were beginning to lighten. He still wore a bandage about his forehead.

"John," I began. "I have your casebook, the one that detailed Will's treatment, the one stolen from you when you were assaulted."

Shock and disbelief spread across his face. "Simon! If you were involved in this…"

But I stopped him with a raised hand. "I was not, John. But I know who was and I cannot tell you. Let me simply say that there was a reason behind it. Perhaps not a good one, and certainly not one that demanded that you be so savagely beaten. I can tell you that I have exacted at least a measure of revenge for your treatment. But the words you wrote in your casebook have caused me to reach some conclusions on the death of Will Shakespeare."

John narrowed his eyes. "Speak plainly, Simon. You have never hedged your words before. Do not start at this late hour."

I waited an extra second. "Very well. Just before Will's final decline, you gave him a purgative to cleanse his system. Immediately after, he fell into a coma and never awakened."

The physician nodded. "If my notes say so. I hoped that it might serve to flush his body of the illness, a forlorn hope, but a method that has worked in the past."

"Were you aware that Sir Thomas Overbury died in a very similar way to Will, and that it is now proven that the purge used on him was poisoned? The Somersets, husband and wife, go on trial in a few days to answer for this crime."

"I had heard such, aye. What is this about, Simon?"

"I believe that you poisoned the solution in the purgative to kill Will."

The surprise could hardly have been written more clearly on John's face. "But why would I wish him dead? What possible reason would I have to do such a thing?"

"You and Susanna inherited New Place, did you not?"

John Hall stepped back and straightened his shoulders with indignation. "I am a man of medicine, Simon. Life is sacred to me. Besides, I liked Will. We got along well. I repeat: I had no reason to kill him."

Malcolm Gray joined us. I did not ask whence he came; I was merely grateful to have him with me.

Turning back to John, I gave voice to my accusation. "I have the casebook, John. I know that you gave Will a purgative immediately before his final decline. I know that Sir Thomas Overbury was murdered in the same way. The earl and countess of Somerset will be tried in the next days for that murder." A thought struck me. "Perhaps you were coerced into helping when the initial attempt to poison Will did not succeed quickly. Will knew things, John, that were a danger to certain powerful men. They were frantic to kill anyone that could endanger them. Perhaps that is the reason that you were so passionately trying to warn me away. Perhaps that is even the reason you were so horribly attacked. You became yet another man who knew things that he should not. I arrest you, John Hall, for the murder of William Shakespeare."

My old friend stepped back, again aghast. "You cannot be serious, Simon! You have no proof."

"I have enough to hold you as I gather more."

"But what of your daughter?"

I struggled with my answer, torn between duty and Mary. But if I left John free, he might well flee the town, and then Mary would be in just as bad a condition. My daughter won. "You have always been an honourable man, John, though recent events would argue otherwise. I will trust you not to attempt to flee. I will set Malcolm upon you if you do."

John glanced up and down at my giant friend. "Have we met before?" he asked.

"Not that I am aware of, Master Hall."

Malcolm turned toward the door. "I will wait out here, Simon, if you should need me."

I returned to Mary's bedside. Peg grasped my hand as I sat down.

"What has caused this sudden change in you?" she asked.

I hesitated before answering. Something deep within was troubling me, but I could not fathom exactly what it was. "I saw many things in London, Peg, many things that caused me to look at life differently." I paused. "Let me just say that I peeked beyond the curtain at the world that made Will what he became. And I understand it better now."

"I am glad," she answered, but there was still much scepticism in her eyes. Only time could dispel those clouds.

But, at that moment, my mind was still wrapped around the matter of Will's death. I could not see how I could be wrong. The coincidence was just too much to ignore. Just as with Overbury, Will was given a purgative and then began his fatal decline. And, after Will died, John was the next man to fall victim to a horrible assault. And, as I had pointed out, it was John who first and most insistently tried to persuade me to abandon the enquiry. Everything pointed towards John. I did not like it, but I could not avoid it.

Poor Susanna, I thought. She would be devastated that her husband had a hand in her father's death. Anne Shakespeare would not care. Her passion for Will had cooled many years ago. She might even think that John had done her a boon.

Yet when I looked at him, caring so fervently for Mary, I could not reconcile the man to the deed. "Peg, will you fetch some water?"

She narrowed her eyes, suspicious as to my purpose, but she went to the door, only to be nearly bowled over by a panic-stricken Henry Smythe, Stratford bailiff.

"Simon! What have you done?" he exclaimed, pausing long enough to bend over and prop his hands on his knees, so out of breath was he.

"What do you mean, Henry?" But I knew what he meant.

"You...and that...behemoth...from London. Arresting... John Hall! How dare you?"

Peg, who had crossed the room to my side, now drew back, shock writing a frown across her face. "Simon? Why would you arrest John?"

"Why indeed?" John echoed.

No matter how much I would have wished another time and place for this, I had to answer her, and Henry Smythe too. "The evidence indicates that John participated in Will's death. While I believe that he was not the only one involved, he is the one that I have the most evidence against. Given enough time, I believe he will lead us to his fellow conspirators."

"What evidence?" But it was not Henry who challenged me; rather it was Peg.

"It is best that I not talk about it now. There will be time enough when he appears before the justice of the peace."

"Which is me," Henry reminded me. "So, stop this nonsense and tell me."

I certainly did not want to explain my actions in Susanna's presence. I took Henry by the elbow and led, or rather dragged him from the room.

"Simon, I have sent for Sir Walter. If you are going to continue this nonsense, he will have to be involved. Now, tell me why you think John Hall killed his father-in-law."

I began to outline the basic elements that I had drawn together. I could not tell him all. But I was willing to tell him as much as possible.

But then the door burst open and Susanna Hall strode into the room, sparks flashing from her eyes. She walked right up to me and struck me with her open hand.

"How dare you!" she screamed as I reeled back, the sting of her hand radiating throughout my face. "John Hall is your friend, and he loved my father. Your bitterness has finally stolen your common sense. No wonder Peg took up with my father," she spat at me. "You are a madman."

I took a step towards her, for what purpose I do not know. I do not think that I would have struck her.

Whatever my purpose, what happened next surprised all of us. Peg moved like lightning and planted herself between Susanna and me.

"Do not speak about what you do not know," Peg retorted. "Simon Saddler is a good man. Even you, Susanna Hall, should know that Simon has excellent reason to suspect John or he would not make such an accusation." She stopped and swallowed hard. "I cannot see that John would have done this thing, but I know my husband."

For a moment, it seemed that Peg was going to strike Susanna, but then an even more amazing thing happened.

Henry Smythe bounded into our midst. "Stop this right now!" Our bailiff was finally taking charge. "Susanna, you will desist. Simon was duly approved in this investigation. He even sought the approval of Sir Walter Devereux, which was given. While his enquiry has been somewhat unorthodox, he has been successful in these matters far more often than he has failed. If he believes that he has reason to suspect John, then I have no choice but to bow to his wishes." I smiled at his reversal.

"But Master Smythe," Susanna began.

"No, Susanna," John ventured. "Henry is correct. The only way that my name can be truly cleared is through an official hearing." He turned to me. "You realize, Simon, that having my name connected to such a deed could end my work as a physician."

I nodded. "I do not do this lightly, John." Every word he spoke went to the logic of his position. But the casebook told the tale. Still, if John did not kill Shakespeare, I truly had failed.

Henry stopped Susanna's coming protest with a raised hand. "I am sorry, Susanna. Coming so soon after your father's death, I know that this is difficult for you. But Simon brings with him a man, Malcolm Gray, in the service of Sir Edward Coke, the Lord Chief Justice. I just asked Master Gray if he concurred with Simon's actions. He said that he had seen the evidence and that he did, in fact, concur. I cannot overrule Simon, despite the fact that I believe he is completely wrong. As much as I regret it, we must wait until Sir Walter arrives to resolve this."

Susanna's mouth flattened into a straight, angry line. "He had best resolve this. My husband is a good man, who would never participate in such a plot." And with that, she stormed from Hamnet's house.

Henry left as well, and John returned to caring for Mary.

My cousin stood, stunned, in the middle of his own house. "Simon, if you are wrong, you will have done great damage to our families."

"Hamnet, if I am wrong, I will be all the happier. The roots to Will's death are underneath a tree far greater than any we have in Warwickshire. Much of it can never be told, but the evidence against John is persuasive. I was astonished, but when I considered all that I knew, the way pointed clearly. I care not about my reputation, only justice for Will."

Hamnet opened his mouth to speak, closed it, then spoke. "A fortnight ago, you would have been the obvious suspect in Will's murder. And now you cry of justice for him? What did you learn in London, Simon?"

I did not answer right away. I walked to a window and looked out into Henley Street. "I learned how the laws that I have spent most of my life enforcing are but words on parchment, how they only apply to those without money, preferment, or titles. I learned how Will became who he was. I learned finally that he was not totally to blame for his actions. The court, dear cousin, operates with its own set of rules, rules that bear little resemblance to those that we commoners must follow."

Hamnet shook his head. "And this surprises you? Come, Simon, you are no freshling just out of the nest. You fought in the Low Countries. You have dealt with nobles throughout your life."

"We harbour within each of us a need to believe that those who lead our country do so with the best motives," I said. "I can tell you this, without hesitation, the one nobleman who treated me with respect and honesty was King James. The rest lied at every turn."

My cousin's eyes grew wide. "You dealt with the king?"

"It was a necessity, and at his request."

And those same eyes narrowed with doubt. "At his request? Please, Simon. This is too much. Why should the king wish to speak with a simple constable from Stratford?"

"It is true," came a booming voice from the chamber door. "And I will deal with any man that disputes it." Malcolm Gray.

"And who is this, Simon?" Hamnet asked.

"This is Malcolm Gray, and he answers to only one man in England."

"So, tell me, Malcolm Gray, what services do you provide the king?" A taunting tone colored Hamnet's voice, unusual for him, but this entire affair was unusual.

But Malcolm just smiled. "The sort of services that he does not advertise. But be at ease, Master Saddler. I have been privy to the same information as Simon, and I agree with him that John Hall must have done this thing. The evidence only allows for one conclusion."

I nodded, though doubt still rang in my head like a church bell.

Hamnet just shook his head. "I am not learned in these things. Simon has a good record of sorting out such affairs. But I would have wagered my house that John Hall does not have murder in him."

Malcolm turned to me then. "Come, I will see you home. You will not be very popular in Stratford once word of this spreads."

"No, I will stay here with my daughter. I could not sleep if I tried."

"Then I will stay with you."

Before I could protest, Malcolm snatched a chair and set it outside the chamber where Mary lay.

Hamnet grimaced, but made no comment.

I went back in and joined Peg, Margaret and John. Peg and

I did not speak, but we held hands and watched our youngest daughter. Margaret sat on the floor before us, and occasionally would look up at us with a brief smile.

At one point she took the time to pat us on our shoulders. "She will be fine, Father. Just wait and see." She squeezed my hand and Peg's, still enmeshed. "You do not know how I have hoped for you to settle your differences."

I wanted to be as certain as Margaret, but little Mary lay there, so pale, so ill, I could scarce give her sister credence.

We talked again, Peg and I, and Margaret, as we once had, as a family. There were yet things bothering me in this affair. Something nagged at me that I could not name. I reached into my leather bag and removed John's casebook, that which had been stolen from him.

I heard a laugh behind me. Turning, I saw a bemused smile on John's face.

"You have a good memory, Simon," he said. "I am surprised that you remembered how to read my notes."

And that was all it took. John's words snatched me from a half-slumber and jerked me upright. I considered it from all perspectives. Suddenly, it all made sense. "Listen," I said to Peg, Margaret and John. "There are things that I must tell you."

They listened and I spoke, far into the night.

LATER, AFTER the midnight, I wondered idly if Malcolm had found sleep. But once I heard a booming laugh that could only have been him. Perhaps he and Hamnet had struck up a friendship. And before I realized it, dawn appeared.

"Simon?"

My cousin Hamnet.

I stretched, hoping to rid my bones of the stiffness gained from sleepless nights and long rides. "Yes?"

"A word with you."

I cocked my head and looked at him with a question in my eye, but I squeezed Peg's hand and went to see what Hamnet needed.

He wasted no time in telling me. "Your man, Matthew, just sent word. Some rogues from London are trying to enter your wool shop. He has held them off so far, and Malcolm went immediately to his aid. You should go. I will keep vigil with Peg, and if there is any change, we will send for you straightaway."

Rogues from London? Only one name sprang to mind.

AND I was correct. The gang of four men was headed by George Wilkins. Matthew stood before the door to our shop, his sword drawn, daring them to move against him. I glanced around quickly, and just as quickly found what I was seeking. Malcolm's great bulk was in a doorway, in the shadows. I had no doubt that were Wilkins to charge at Matthew, Malcolm would make short work of them.

"George Wilkins!" I shouted as I appeared in the street. "What business have you here?"

Wilkins turned, saw me, and sneered. "The earl of Southampton sends his regards. He sent us to collect damages for the harm you did him."

"He should have come himself. I would have added yet more to my account."

"Get this hired boy out of our way. We have no quarrel with him."

Matthew bristled at the description. "Any quarrel you have with Simon includes me as well."

"And me," came a surprising voice.

Ben Jonson.

I could not be certain, but I suspected that Ben had ridden in with Wilkins. To this day, I do not know why I immediately thought the worst of Ben. But he cured me of that with his next action.

"George Wilkins, leave this town and take your scum with you. Southampton deserved what Simon gave him."

Wilkins backed up a step, uncertain suddenly of the odds. I was fairly sure that he had not yet detected Malcolm in the shadows. With the sun nearly up, people were beginning to venture into the streets. We were attracting an audience, and I was confident that that was not to Wilkins's liking.

Ben moved to join me. "I stand with you, Simon. In this and in everything." He faced Wilkins, now with a dagger in his hand.

"You are a fool, Jonson. Southampton will withdraw his support of your pension."

"Let Southampton do what he wishes, George. If he was so brave, he would be here himself instead of sending a scoundrel like you. Come, it is four to three now. When we finish with your companions, we will draw and quarter you. Simon and I know exactly how to do it."

I winced. We did indeed, in the Low Countries, and it was not a memory that I wished revived.

"Step aside," came a voice I was coming to know well. "I will deal with them by myself." Malcolm Gray emerged from the shadows onto Henley Street.

Malcolm dwarfed even Ben Jonson. Wilkins's companions looked to each other, then threw down their swords and ran.

"Cowards!" Wilkins spat after them. He turned back to Malcolm. "Another time," he said. "Keep looking over your shoulder, Saddler. If not me, then someone else will be on your trail. Nobles have long memories." With that, he was gone.

Ben turned to me then. "He's right, Simon. Southampton will not forget."

"Am I to be arrested when I am next in London?"

"No. I am told that the king laughed heartily when he heard how you had dealt with Southampton. Of all of his courtiers, Wriothesley is one that fawns perhaps too much. Even the king's patience has limits."

"Why did you come to Stratford?"

Ben shrugged. "Wilkins, who thinks that I'm merely one of Southampton's minions, told me that he had been instructed to settle scores with you. I decided that I needed some fresh country air."

"Ben, I still believe that you played a role in Will's death."

He brushed my comment aside. "You should look elsewhere for Will's murderer."

"I have," I answered. "But I hesitate to speak of it yet. Sir Walter Devereux, sheriff of Warwickshire, is on his way here to assist our justice of the peace in sorting through this affair."

Ben's eyebrows nearly jumped from his face. "You have discovered the murderer? Who? Who is it?"

Firmly, I shook my head. "I will say nothing more until Sir Walter arrives."

"Still as stubborn as always," Ben said, sardonically.

"But not for much longer." I knew that if Ben stayed in Stratford, he would hear about John Hall virtually within minutes. I just chose not to be the man to enlighten him.

Matthew appeared at my elbow. "Should you ever need me, Simon, I will be there."

"Of that," I replied, "I have no doubt. Now go see to our shop. Hopefully, we have seen all the trouble we are going to on this day."

But such was a forlorn thought.

Chapter Fifteen

SIR WALTER DEVEREUX WAS NOT A HAPPY MAN. IT TOOK BUT one look to see that. We were alone in the Guild Hall, and I had sent Jack Addenbrooke to fetch John.

"Simon, I told you not to involve the nobles," he chastised me, as we met in private.

"They involved me. I did not have any choice."

"Hmmph. I am told that you brokered a deal between the king and Somerset. And Suffolk has complained that you invaded his house and stole some property."

"What property?" I was curious as to how much Suffolk knew.

Devereux turned away, with a half smile growing on his face. "He did not say. Indeed, I doubt that he even knows. 'Twas but a guess." He looked back to me again. "Look, Simon. I do not care for Suffolk, and I have never cared for Somerset or his wife. Whatever role you played in their affairs, I do not wish to know about. But, quite frankly, the only thing that has kept me from slapping you into the gaol is a note that I received from the king."

So that was how he knew of my dealings with Somerset. His Majesty was a complex man, but it would seem that he was, in most ways, an honourable one as well.

"Now, tell me of this evidence against John Hall. I would hear it from you before we bring him in here."

"Gladly, Sir Walter. I think, since there are yet some questions to be answered, that we should not make a public spectacle of this."

And Sir Walter did flash a smile at that. "It is already a public spectacle, Simon. But I agree that nothing official should be done until I have both heard from you and questioned Hall. If he proves innocent, then we can concoct some story to explain all of this. If your evidence proves out, there will be a trial."

With that, I explained everything to him, the examination of Will's body, the casebooks, the assault on John, all of it. Sir Walter did not speak, just nodded his head as he listened.

"You have been constable long enough to understand these things, Simon. I trust you, but I think you are risking much."

Devereux was right.

"Then let us find out what John has to say."

TEN MINUTES later, our little group had convened in Henry Smythe's chamber. John's face held a sad smile. Beyond myself and Sir Walter, we were joined only by Malcolm Gray and Henry himself. 'Twas a fitting council. Both Sir Walter and Malcolm represented the Crown's interest. Henry was the justice of the peace. I was the constable.

"John, this is unofficial," Sir Walter began. "We hope that your answers to a few questions will remove the cloud of suspicion hanging over you. So, I urge you to feel free to answer our questions honestly."

I thought he was going a little far, but he and John knew each other well.

For the benefit of all present, I repeated what I had said to John the night before, the possibility that the murder had been committed to ensure Susanna's inheritance earlier rather than later. And I mentioned also my suspicion that he had been added to the conspiracy after initial efforts to poison Will failed.

John shook his head and chuckled. "Simon, please settle on one theory. Either I killed Will for my own profit, or I did it at the behest of some unnamed schemers who then tried to kill me as well. But both of your theories are sadly lacking in proof. Let me also assure you that your story is also sadly lacking. While it was my finding that Will had died of poison, I do not think it was the purgative."

"Well, of course you would say that," I answered, hesitantly.

"Why do you not think it was the purgative?" Sir Walter queried.

"Because I would never have done that."

Sir Walter shook his head. "John, that is not much of a defence." He looked to me and then back again at John. "I see no other recourse but that you be held. I am sorry. But until this is properly investigated, that is all that I can do."

John hung his head. "As you order, but I did not do this thing, no matter what Simon says."

And Malcolm led him back to the chamber where he would be kept.

AFTER TAKING my leather bag to my house, I had returned to Hamnet's and sat throughout the day. Malcolm and Ben Jonson (much to my surprise) stayed with us. Mary was feeling better; John's efforts had succeeded for her where they had failed Will. Jack Addenbrooke stopped by and told me that George Wilkins was yet in Stratford.

HOURS LATER, after darkness had fallen, I found myself alone in our house, sitting in the same chair where I had determined to pursue Will's killer. Just a few embers burned orange in my hearth, not enough to provide any light.

A PART of me hoped against hope that I was wrong yet again. But I knew that I was not. So, I waited.

The first sound was faint, like that of a mouse searching the house for a bit of food. But then it grew louder, and I rose and faded into the darkest part of the house.

The door opened, slowly, carefully, and a shadow slipped inside.

I reached out in the dark to make certain that all was prepared.

The shadow, illuminated by a passing lantern, made for the stairs.

And just as it began its ascent, I leaned forward, touched a bit of paper to an ember and lit my lantern, casting a yellow circle of light around the room.

"How long have you known?" said a familiar voice.

"Not for certain until last night, but I began to wonder much earlier. In truth, I am not sure why it took me so long to realise it. Tell me, were you seeking the letters for Southampton or so you could blackmail the king?"

"What do I care for Southampton?"

"You poisoned Shakespeare on his orders."

"Perhaps, perhaps not. I was well paid. How did you learn the truth? Or did you guess it?"

"Two things pointed me in your direction. When we first met, you told me that you could not read. So, that left me wondering why you would lie about what was contained in the letters. As I cast about for an answer, I realised that it could be a ruse to remain close to me. You might not be able to read the letters, but you had seen them and would recognize them again. And you knew that they would be worth a great deal to the king."

"Perhaps I lied about my ability to read," Malcolm said.

"Perhaps, but then, last night, John expressed surprise that I could still read his notes, as they are written in an abbreviated Latin. Hence, even if you could read, you would not have been able to read the casebook.

"Finally, as we entered Stratford yesterday, I invited you to stay here, at my house. You said that you would stop at Perrott's. But we had not passed the inn. And you claimed never to have been to Stratford before. Yet you navigated quite easily around the town without once asking for directions. Tell me, Malcolm, does the king know that you killed Shakespeare?"

No answer.

"You came to Stratford in search of the book."

"Aye, I preferred not to cause more of a commotion than necessary, but Hall resisted. Let me guess, you began to wonder when we were assaulted by the bandits?"

"It just seemed too easy."

"Duvall was angry that we shed so much blood. I should have killed you when we had all the letters," Malcolm Gray said. "I think I will kill you now. It will be better that way."

I moved nearer the shadows. "I could always cry for help."

"You could," he said, producing a dagger from his waist. "At least the player had the courtesy to die quietly."

"Did you really think that I came here alone?"

Malcolm's smile slipped a little. "Who else could be with you? Now, tell me where the letters are, and I will make certain you die swiftly, without much pain."

'Twas my turn to smile. "Many miles away from here."

His eyes grew wide. "No! He said you would have them close by."

"Who said that, Malcolm? Who is guiding your hand now?"

But rather than answer, he bellowed and lunged for me, dagger first.

I sidestepped his thrust, though it caught in my shirt and ripped it.

Grabbing his arm as it moved past, I yanked him towards me, using his momentum against him. His head cracked with a sickening thud, and he collapsed in a heap on the hearth.

"Quickly, John, Hamnet!" I shouted for my friends and they rushed into the room with lamps. "Tie his hands!"

And they set to work, but John placed a hand over Hamnet's. "Hold." He reached down and felt of Malcolm's throat. "He is dead, Simon."

"Do not worry, Constable. His guilt is beyond question," Sir Walter Devereux said, coming down the stairs. "John, you were masterful as the accused innocent."

John Hall chuckled. "I learned something after all from Will Shakespeare. But was it necessary, Simon?"

"Oh, yes," I said with a nod. "With suspicion falling on you, he felt comfortable enough to try for the letters. He had to know that the longer he stayed in Stratford, the more likely that Anne or Susanna or Judith would recognize him as Will's mysterious London visitor. So, the sooner he could find his treasure and leave, the better it was for him."

"He was taking a great chance nonetheless," John pointed out.

"He was, but the reward might have been great as well. King James was most anxious to acquire all of them."

"What are these letters you keep talking about?" Sir Walter was perplexed, and I could not blame him. How much to tell? That was my worry.

"Will did some writing for the king. It was most sensitive, and the king feared that they would fall into the wrong hands. I was engaged to recover them for the king." My answer held some truth and some falsehood, but it was enough. "I was forced to secrete a small number of the documents along the way. Those were the ones that Malcolm wanted. He intended to ransom them back to the king, for a princely sum, I imagine."

"Who was this Malcolm Gray?" Hamnet asked.

Such was a good question, and one that I could not immediately answer. "I do not know, not really," I admitted. "He was the kind of man that men of wealth and power turn to when they have distasteful jobs to be performed."

"For whom did he work?"

I shrugged. "For whoever paid him the most, I suspect." I considered my audience—John, Hamnet and Sir Walter. "I believe, though I cannot prove it, that Malcolm was hired by Southampton to kill Shakespeare. Will was 'involved' in the Overbury Affair, and there has been concern that he might have been forced to give testimony at the trial of Somerset and his wife, testimony that could be…embarrassing to the king."

"But Southampton was Will's patron," John protested.

"Aye," I agreed. "He was. But that was when both of them were young. Remember that when James came to the throne, Southampton was still in the Tower over the Essex Affair. James freed him, but I doubt that Southampton has felt secure at court. Anything that he could do to curry favor with the Crown must have seemed like a good idea to him.

"But now, it is all past. Malcolm admitted to poisoning Will. On whose orders he did such is not provable, not now at any rate. We will have to be satisfied with a small bit of justice."

"But if there are others who bear responsibility for Will's death, should they not be pursued?" Hamnet argued.

"Simon is right," Sir Walter interjected. "Will Shakespeare was not Sir Thomas Overbury. There would be no enthusiasm for prosecuting Southampton; indeed, considering all that we now know, I doubt that the king would sanction such a course of action."

THAT EVENING, I sent a message to London by Matthew. He was instructed to wait for an answer. In the meantime, Mary had recovered enough to be taken home. While relations were better between myself and Peg, I was still distant. But now I was not angry with her or with Will. Now, I was angry with myself, for missing the obvious for far too long, and for losing so much time with Peg by my self-pity. Thankfully, Peg seemed to understand without my speaking it aloud.

Within the week, Matthew had returned. The response was what I expected.

AND SO, six months later, I rode the short distance to Kenilworth. I was expected, and though I was the object of many stares and whispered questions, I was swept into an inner chamber quickly.

"Och, man. You have given me several sleepless nights." There was no mistaking the Scottish brogue. King James stood, facing me, his hands on his hips, shaking his head in disapproval.

Taking a knee, I lowered my head. "My apologies, Your Majesty."

"Stand up, man. Let us speak frankly to one another."

I rose. "Yes, Your Majesty."

"Gray is dead."

"Yes, Your Majesty."

"'Tis a pity. He had his uses." James paused. "Indeed, I am learning that many people used his services. I did not order him to kill Shakespeare. Had I questioned, even for a moment, the poet's discretion, I would never have used him."

"I never thought otherwise, Your Majesty. Both of us know who commissioned Gray for that."

The king nodded. "You understand that I cannot move against him."

"I do."

"We have just ended Somerset's trial. The trial of another noble would be…inconvenient."

Neither of us spoke during the moment that followed.

"The other letters?"

I had known this was coming. Slipping my hand inside my shirt, I withdrew a slip of paper and handed it to him.

He unfolded it and read it in silence. "Wargrave? Very clever, Constable Saddler. We shall speak no more about this matter."

"As you wish, Your Majesty."

"Tell me, Master Saddler, did you accomplish anything in your unusual investigation? Was all of your bashing about worth the trouble?"

"Yes. It was. I understand my friend much better now."

"And that was worth nearly losing your life, several times over?"

"Aye. It was."

James nodded. "You have proven yourself a good and true servant, Master Saddler. With Gray dead, I will occasionally need someone of your talents."

Knowing that I might regret it later, I bowed and said, "I serve at your command, Your Majesty."

And thus ended the Overbury Affair and the case of the murder of William Shakespeare.

Chapter Sixteen

I AM STILL A CONSTABLE IN STRATFORD, THOUGH I SEEM TO have little time for that. The king was true to his word. He has called me to his service a number of times over the years since Will's death. I have served him honourably, I hope. Perhaps if time and health allow, I will be able to record something of those adventures as well.

Margaret did marry Matthew, and I will someday give them the wool business. Mary has also grown into a beautiful young woman.

Peg and I are in love once more, the kind of love that only a lifetime can breed. Mary will marry soon, and we will have the house on Henley Street to ourselves again. I take great comfort in Peg's love, and visions of her with Will no longer haunt my dreams.

SUSANNA AND John Hall moved into New Place with Anne Shakespeare. Susanna had a plaque placed at her father's grave with a curse for anyone who would attempt to intrude on his eternal sleep. She put word about that Will had feared that his bones would be unearthed and placed in a charnel house. I have always believed that she did that to keep anyone from ever discovering the truth of her father's death. In truth, Will had never worried about such things as charnel houses.

"Simon," he told me once, "life is but an unweeded garden that grows rank and gross. The only thing we know for certain is that someday our bones will lie in cold obstrution and rot as is the natural order. The rest is nothing."

Author's Note

THE POSSIBILITY that Shakespeare was murdered was first floated back in the 1970s by handwriting expert Charles Hamilton. The academic community condemned him because he was not one of them. But he did read secretary hand (that form of writing prevalent in the Elizabethan/Jacobean Age). And he was an acknowledged expert on handwriting. Hamilton was a key figure in exposing the purported Hitler diaries as forgeries. I would be inclined to listen to him, but the academic world is so territorial that they refused even to countenance Hamilton.

A few years ago, the theory popped back up, brought to the forefront again by...an academic. However, this time it was a university pathologist who had been involved in the exhumation of famous post–Civil War outlaw Jesse James. He proposed exhuming Shakespeare to test the poisoning theory. But he indicated that the family's permission would have to be obtained. As anyone even remotely familiar with Shakespeare would know, the famous poet and playwright has no direct descendants. As I write this, yet another attempt is being made to exhume Shakespeare, this time to see if he smoked marijuana and also to try and answer questions about his death.

At any rate, this is a novel built around the idea that Shakespeare may have been murdered. The only cause of death over the centuries has been the old story about him, Ben Jonson, and Michael Drayton drinking, after which Shakespeare contracted a fever and died.

Of other matters, some are true, some are not. Shakespeare did suffer financial reversals in the first years after he returned to

Stratford, and he came into a good deal of money in the months surrounding Sir Thomas Overbury's murder. I have linked the two, though there may be no connection.

Charles Hamilton's favorite suspect in the supposed murder of William Shakespeare was Thomas Quiney. And Quiney was much the way that I have portrayed him. He came from a respected Stratford family, but apparently none of that respectability rubbed off on him. The changes in Shakespeare's will did indeed keep Quiney from profiting from his father-in-law's estate while preserving Judith's inheritance.

Sir Thomas Overbury was murdered. Frances, countess of Somerset, admitted her guilt. Robert Carr, earl of Somerset, proclaimed his innocence but was convicted at trial in late April 1616. According to contemporary records, Sir Edward Coke and Sir Francis Bacon did indeed find letters from the king to Carr in the earl's rooms at Whitehall Palace. And Coke did turn them over to the king without revealing their contents.

For the record, I am not an Oxfordian or a Baconian. I believe that William Shakespeare of Stratford-upon-Avon wrote the poetry and plays historically attributed to him. I find that those who refuse to believe that a simple boy from Warwickshire could write such masterpieces as *King Lear*, *Macbeth*, and *Othello* are embarrassingly narrow-minded. Genius is not restricted to the nobility or wealthier classes. Genius comes from every walk of life.

The last paragraph of the book contains quotations from *Hamlet* and *Measure for Measure*, and "obstrution" is not a typographical error. As I am certain that there are errors elsewhere, they are mine and mine alone.

About the Author

In addition to writing fiction, Tony Hays was a working journalist who covered topics as varied as political corruption, Civil War history, the war on terror, and narcotics trafficking. The latter earned his newspaper a state award for public service.

His novels include an award-nominated four-book Arthurian mystery series. He resided in Tennessee.

Tony Hays died suddenly in Egypt in January 2015 at the age of 58.

More Traditional Mysteries from Perseverance Press
For the New Golden Age

The Color of Light
ISBN 978-1-56474-542-2

Disturbing the Dark *(forthcoming)*
ISBN 978-1-56474-576-7

Janet LaPierre
PORT SILVA SERIES
Baby Mine
ISBN 978-1-880284-32-2

Keepers
Shamus Award nominee, Best Paperback Original
ISBN 978-1-880284-44-5

Death Duties
ISBN 978-1-880284-74-2

Family Business
ISBN 978-1-880284-85-8

Run a Crooked Mile
ISBN 978-1-880284-88-9

Hailey Lind
ART LOVER'S SERIES
Arsenic and Old Paint
ISBN 978-1-56474-490-6

Lev Raphael
NICK HOFFMAN SERIES
Tropic of Murder
ISBN 978-1-880284-68-1

Hot Rocks
ISBN 978-1-880284-83-4

Lora Roberts
BRIDGET MONTROSE SERIES
Another Fine Mess
ISBN 978-1-880284-54-4

SHERLOCK HOLMES SERIES
The Affair of the Incognito Tenant
ISBN 978-1-880284-67-4

Rebecca Rothenberg
BOTANICAL SERIES
The Tumbleweed Murders
(completed by Taffy Cannon)
ISBN 978-1-880284-43-8

Sheila Simonson
LATOUCHE COUNTY SERIES
Buffalo Bill's Defunct
WILLA Award, Best Softcover Fiction
ISBN 978-1-880284-96-4

An Old Chaos
ISBN 978-1-880284-99-5

Beyond Confusion
ISBN 978-1-56474-519-4

Lea Wait
SHADOWS ANTIQUES SERIES
Shadows of a Down East Summer
ISBN 978-1-56474-497-5

Shadows on a Cape Cod Wedding
ISBN 1-978-56474-531-6

Shadows on a Maine Christmas
ISBN 978-1-56474-531-6

Shadows on a Morning in Maine
(forthcoming)
ISBN 978-1-56474-577-4

Eric Wright
JOE BARLEY SERIES
The Kidnapping of Rosie Dawn
Barry Award, Best Paperback Original. Edgar,
Ellis, and Anthony awards nominee
ISBN 978-1-880284-40-7

Nancy Means Wright
MARY WOLLSTONECRAFT SERIES
Midnight Fires
ISBN 978-1-56474-488-3

The Nightmare
ISBN 978-1-56474-509-5

REFERENCE/MYSTERY WRITING

Kathy Lynn Emerson
How To Write Killer Historical Myster
The Art and Adventure of Sleuthing
Through the Past
Agatha Award, Best Nonfiction. Anthony and
Macavity awards nominee
ISBN 978-1-880284-92-6

Carolyn Wheat
How To Write Killer Fiction:
The Funhouse of Mystery & the Roller
Coaster of Suspense
ISBN 978-1-880284-62-9

Available from your local books
or from Perseverance Press/John Daniel & Com
(800) 662–8351 or www.danielpublishing.com/persever